FREEDOM'S FIGHT

by
Gary Phillips

Zora is an imprint of Parker Publishing LLC.

Copyright © 2009 by Gary Phillips
Published by Parker Publishing LLC
12523 Limonite Avenue, Suite #440-438
Mira Loma, California 91752
www.parker-publishing.com

ISBN: 978-1-60043-031-2
First Edition

Manufactured in the United States of America
Printed by Bang Printing, Brainard MN
Distributed by BookMasters, Inc. 1-800-537-6727
Cover Design by Jaxadora Designs

Parker Publishing, llc
www.Parker-Publishing.com

DEDICATION:

To my father Dikes, sometimes called Joe, his brother Norman nicknamed Son, and the youngest brother, Sammy, referred to as Sipsy, World War II vets -- and most especially to Lt. Oscar D. Hutton, Jr., my mother Leonelle's brother, a Tuskegee airman killed in action on an escort mission over Memmington, Germany, July 18, 1944.

CHAPTER ONE

August 1944 – Belgium

The left side of Corporal Schiller's face disappeared in red mist. Part of his nose landed on Private Gil Giabretto's grimy shirt. Schiller's folded in the foxhole, as if it were a target dummy tossed from the back of a supply truck. Giabretto was hunkered down opposite, not more than a foot away. Giabretto choked down bile as he stared at the malignancy of exploded flesh that had once been the tow-headed man's handsome face. Somehow the left eye had remained intact and was fixed on the open ground before it. The same ground he'd been discussing how best to cross with Giabretto when his face was torn apart by a bullet from a German Mauser.

Giabretto heard a voice as if calling him from a great distance and it was several moments before he could understand.

"Schiller, was Schiller hit?" Sergeant Robeson was yelling.

"He's dead," Giabretto said softly.

"Is Schiller all right?" Robeson repeated.

Giabretto cleared his throat and shouted, "Gone." He couldn't take his gaze off that goddamn eye.

"Are you hit?"

"No."

"Then what do you see?"

Giabretto was being sucked down into the pulpy mass. It seemed to fill his entire vision.

"Private," Robeson hollered. "I need a reconnaissance. Now."

The mass loomed bright and festering and threatened to swallow the enlisted man.

"Giabretto, goddammit, did you hear me?" Robeson railed.

"Yes sir," he snapped, swallowing the saliva that coated his throat and stomach with fear. Gunfire from the German karabiners erupted again from the orchard about a hundred yards across the open ground. Giabretto sunk down, one of his hands gripping the top of his helmet even though it was buckled under his chin.

He waited for the white-hot sting of bullets to penetrate his muscles but felt nothing but the tight ball of air trapped in him. The shooting halted, and Giabretto moved over to the dead man. Blood and flesh decorated the Schiller's uniform. Giabretto pulled on the Corporal's shoulder to raise his body to free the strap attached to his binoculars. He was startled as the man's helmet fell off, rattling in the dirt.

"Careful," Robeson warned. He and the four other squad members were about seventy yards behind Giabretto. They were sheltered behind what remained of a farmhouse in the Metz countryside. Artillery bombardments had decimated the main structure and the barn, and left holes in the earth in a haphazard pattern.

Giabretto latched onto the field glasses. Their surface was slick with gore and another bout of nausea assaulted him. He breathed rapidly and wiped the lenses off against his pant leg. In the dirt near his knee was the piece of the corporal's nose that had landed on him. He set his mouth in a line and swung the binoculars into position. He scanned ahead, the sunlight filtering through the canopy of foliage and branches.

"Anything?" Robeson demanded.

"Not yet. The Krauts are probably using camouflage."

"We have to shake them loose, Giabretto. They must be a light detachment. They're can't be too many of them and they must be traveling light."

Fat lot of good that did Schiller Giabretto reflected. "So far all we've heard is the whine of their Mausers."

"That don't mean they ain't got a Bren or MG-34 tucked away, y'all," a new voice cracked. It belonged to Grady Langford, a thick-eared Texan from San Marcos. He was the squad's Browning Automatic Rifle man. "They could be trying to get us in the open, then light us up with machine gun fire."

"We go by what we see, not what we guess, at least for now," Robeson declared.

Giabretto had his chin jammed into the soft rim of the foxhole, his head tucked as far down as he could between his shoulder blades. The binoculars had been coated with black Kiwi shoe polish to cut the casing's glare. But that had been partially removed when he'd rubbed off the dead man's blood. He imagined a German sniper breathing as he sighted through his scope as his finger caressed the trigger of his rifle. He could feel the bullet entering the front of the binoculars and the back of his head disappearing like Schiller's face.

There.

"Giabretto."

Shut up, Sarge. He refocused and noted a disturbance of greenery to his right. The shifting of the leaves stopped. "Anything?" The sergeant anxiously asked.

"Yes."

"What?"

"How do we know one of these Jerries doesn't sprechen English?" Giabretto wondered aloud.

"We don't. But we have no choice. We have to move forward, private."

Giabretto also wondered, and not for the first time, how the hell it was that Robeson had made sergeant. As far as he could tell after five months with the man he wasn't what his granddad would call "quick on his feet." It wasn't as if Robeson was a gold bricker or company man, looking to ass kiss his way up to being a lieutenant.

He was concerned about the welfare of his men, and was always intent on carrying out his orders. But he was sorely lacking in a hunter's sense of things from what Giabretto could tell. Robeson understood what the objective was, but he could only figure out how to get to it by going in a straight line.

Giabretto lowered the glasses and turned around in the foxhole. He chanced a wave of his hand to get his squad's attention. What he got was a round nearly taking his hand off. "Sarge," he yelled, giving in to the only way to communicate. He prayed there wasn't an English speaker among their ambushers.

"Yeah?"

"I'm guessin' there are three snugger n' bugs in a rug in there. Four tops."

"Schiller had a grenade, didn't he?"

"Yeah, but what's good tossing a pineapple in there blind?"

Giabretto searched the body but didn't find a grenade.

"Flush 'em out then we charge those goose-steppers shooting."

"I think we have to out-flank 'em. Get them to either retreat or push them into the open."

There was a pause. Then Robeson said, "I've already lost one man on this patrol, Giabretto."

The sergeant wasn't that slow. "What's our other choice?" Giabretto shouted back. The enemy must have just been getting into position when he and the corporal had zigzagged their way toward the glade. Otherwise, they would have cut them down as they crossed what was left of the farmer's bombed out field.

Initially it was a voice in the brush that had alerted them. In a quiet panic they had been heading toward a burned out hulk of a tree limb.

The foxhole was like God had suddenly reached down and scooped it out for them, it had appeared so suddenly in their path. The duo gladly tumbled into it as gunfire blazed around them. Their squad returned fire.

But God had a sick sense of humor, Giabretto observed. The Schiller hadn't lived more than two minutes after they'd fallen into their shelter. He took the glasses down again and yelled back toward the farmhouse. "Krauts seem to be standing pat, Sarge. You must be right; it doesn't seem like they understand what we're saying. So why didn't you try to circle around?"

"That leaves you exposed."

"What else is new?"

There was more silence as Robeson conferred with his men. Giabretto realized how much the sergeant had relied on Schiller for quick decisions. He'd better wise up or more men would be dying under his command. It wasn't like command had more experienced or savvy men to put in the field as it was. He'd read in a recent Stars and Stripes that there was a push on for more women to join the working ranks in war industries back home to free up more men for duty.

"Hull's gonna try to work his way west of you and the rest of us go toward the east then circle around."

That was good, Grady Langford had a steady hand and was a good shot. "Okay, I'll sit tight." Unless the Krauts charged. That made him look for the grenade. Giabretto's hands explored the corpse. Flies were already buzzing around the oozing face. Gingerly, he rolled the body toward him, the man's blue eye even more intense in death.

Grimacing, his hand probed Schiller's body and he got queasy again. It wasn't like he was stealing the man's boots. Not like those Germans prisoners he'd seen being marched into camp, some of them stomping around in GI gear. He finished, but hadn't turned up the grenade. Robeson was probably wrong. It was just going to be him and his M-1. The rifle had more kick than what he'd grown up shooting, but to his way of thinking, you couldn't beat a Sharpe's for accuracy and distance.

Though the carbine was better for power, and its shorter range matched the kind of warfare the dogfaces were ground up in over here. But Giabretto fancied himself more of a, well, what did he fancy himself? A tracker he supposed.

The particular retort of a German rifle brought Giabretto back to the present. He turned in the foxhole and could see Langford darting from the farmhouse toward a broke down tractor. Giabretto put the binoculars up to his eyes to sight the flashes of gunfire, then quickly tossed them aside to heft his carbine. He fired instinctively. There was a yelp and elation stretched a taut smile across his face.

Langford propped himself against the tractor, taking in ragged breaths. There was nothing else but a ruined tomato field between him and the foxhole. Fortunately he was at an angle to Giabretto, and could also get a bead on the enemy. He figured if he had hit one of them, the Krauts would be fanning out now. They might have seen Robeson and the other members of the squad moving out. He didn't know if the German's had radioed for reinforcements. And even if they had, that didn't mean they'd be forthcoming anytime soon. The Germans, like the Americans were thin on replacements. Metz was one of those places where various battles had seen the town seesaw from Nazi to Allied control. This latest excursion part of command's plan to see to what depth the Germans were bivouacked in the area.

The war was happening on many fronts, grinding up a lot of foot soldiers. And too goddamn often for Giabretto's liking, the lives of some he'd shared a smoke with or heard about from another buddy were reduced to weekly battle casualty reports. And the big wigs at HQ would take those reports and do up their charts and graphs, and move more pieces around on their large maps. This way they could come up with what town or hill next the poor slobs who were losing legs and arms and hemorrhaging from all openings had to take next. And lucky them, they got to be more statistics in one more useless goddamn report and their dog tags were sent home to their mothers or girlfriends.

There was a disturbance in the brush and Giabretto and Langford opened up with their weapons. The cracks of the Mausers responded and for several seconds, the air was filled with metal mosquitoes seeking flesh and blood.

"Two rifles were firing," Langford announced as another lull descended.

"Yeah," Giabretto responded, "the others must have gone off to catch the sarge."

"I feel funny just holding my dick, Giabretto."

"You'd be surprised what will come to you when you wait." Then gunfire erupted again. Robeson and the men with him had encountered the remaining Germans.

Giabretto snaked his rifle out in front of him, along the parched ground, as he simultaneously pushed his body more into the side of the foxhole. He stared through the gun's rectangular sight, getting ready. There was yelling in German and a flash of gray streaked in the green topiary. Giabretto fired, tracking ahead of where he assumed the soldier was running. He tasted grime as he bit his bottom lip, the carbine's recoil reassuring an urge buried within him.

Langford's M-1 also barked, and Giabretto could hear its crack getting closer. That crazy country boy was shooting as he ran across open ground.

"Whowee," Lankford hollered. "We got 'em, son, we got them crooked cross fucks but good."

Giabretto didn't dare look behind him as he too rose and found his feet carrying him forward. This was nuts. He could get his head blown off at any second and he'd deserve it. But he too found that a hot breath of elation had gripped him, telling him like some alluring woman that the battle was theirs to win. But some other part of Giabretto knew the same whore whispered to the German dogfaces too. Didn't they believe they were destined to rule the goddamn world, the Thousand Year Reich their Fuhrer promised them?

Giabretto stumbled on some loose rocks at the same moment a German came crashing out of the orchard's brush. The enemy's Mauser roared, the sound the only sensation the frightened soldier could hear as he tried to keep his balance. His cheek was seared and he fell to one knee, shooting his rifle as he did so. The German had continued hurtling forward, and suddenly his eyes went wide with peace, his shirtfront wet from blood.

The German's body did a half-turn, his weapon discharging into the air. He dropped to the ground, his eyes fixed on a point beyond this world. Giabretto was already past him aa he and Langford plunged into the thick area of apple trees.

"Get down, get down," Robeson hollered. The rest of the patrol swarmed in from the left.

One of the Germans was planted behind a stone well and had aimed his gun at the new arrivals.

"Shit," Langford cursed as blood spurted from his thigh. He sagged against a knotted tree.

Giabretto grabbed him and leaped sideways. There was no cover and the two fell into a carpet of dead leaves. More bullets flared and Robeson fired his Thompson and the man at the well duck for cover.

His lungs aching from exertion and panic, Giabretto got to his feet, and dragged the wounded Texan with him. They ran and stumbled across what at first he assumed were logs. But once they were flat on the earth, he recoiled at the sight of a dark socket glaring out at him. It was two dead German soldiers, one clumped partially on the other. The face with the hole in was unlined and unblemished – not more than twenty.

"Knew these fuckin' Krauts were good for somethin'," Langford joked. He groaned as he scooted his body away from the corpses, trying to make sure he was lower than their height. His right leg was wet. "Come on you silver-throated guinea, heat that rifle up."

Giabretto shook his head. "Cracker." He crawled forward, resting the barrel on the leg of one of the dead men. It was soft and yielding and Giabretto had to control his stomach. But the leg had enough bulk that it did the job. Robeson and the others were back in the overgrowth, pinned by the man at the well. Apparently they'd been able to take the remaining landsers. But now the last one was in a good position to hold them off.

Robeson's Thompson raked the ground and ate into of the stone of the well to no avail. A lot of dust and the frenzied flight of birds accompanied the rapid fire but didn't touch the German.

From where he was, Giabretto could only see part of the man's steel helmet. He was smart, saving his ammunition. He didn't return fire, content to either have his attackers try to get him and maybe pick them off one-by-one. Or maybe he had a hole card, maybe reinforcements were on their way.

"Did they have a radio man?" Giabretto said.

"No," the sergeant answered. "Looks like they were sent out here as an advance patrol but without communications."

"That doesn't make sense," Giabretto responded.

"The last bombing raid disrupted the supply line from Lyon," Robeson said. "Could be the radio was out and they were waiting on a replacement.

"Yeah, I can see that." After all, their patrol hadn't been given a radio either. Command felt men were more expendable than precious equipment. The German didn't flinch. He must have nerves as hard as the stone he was hiding behind.

Giabretto cupped a hand to the side of his mouth. "Hey, Frtizy, you understand what I'm saying?"

"What are you up to?" Langford said. He'd ripped part of the shirt of one of the dead men and used it as a tourniquet around his wound.

Giabretto yelled again. "If you know what I'm saying, you know you're not getting out of this. You know we're going to plug you sooner or later." Nothing. No words or gunfire to acknowledge he had any idea what the hell Giabretto was saying. What difference did it make anyway? It was kill or be killed in this man's war and that was the objective Giabretto had to keep forefront in his mind. If you worried that the guy you were shooting at had a mother like you, had a girlfriend that was sweet as yours, maybe even had kids, that was just going to mess with you when it came time to pull the trigger.

You damn well could be sure the clear-eyed bastard on the other end of the rifle wasn't letting those sentiments slow him down. He was going to put one through your heart and go back to base to have his knackwurst and sauerbraten or whatever the hell the German K-rations consisted of in their field packs.

It was if the M-1were an extension of his arm. Time became irrelevant, and the thud of his heart ticked off the rise and fall of the sun and stars. His universe was the carbine and its intended target, the man beneath the dull sheen of what little part of the helmet he could see. Giabretto blew shallow breaths through pursed lips and slowly teased the trigger of his rifle. He moved the mechanism a hair's breadth, just enough to feel the resistance of the rifle's inner spring.

The helmet shifted, and Giabretto didn't move, didn't squeeze any further. His chance would come. His grandfather was there and that was all he needed.

"Can you get him," Langford rasped.

Giabretto didn't move nor said anything to break the spell.

The helmet moved again, and the air from his mouth was cold across his parted lips. A shot rang out from one of the men on the squad and the German soldier stopped. He'd seen something that wasn't in Giabretto's line of sight but he couldn't let his mind wander. He had to have his shot and the only way to accomplish that was absolute concentration. The helmet shifted but didn't lift up. The German let off two more shots from his rifle and Giabretto's squad shot back. Neither exchange of gunfire hit anything.

It got quiet again and behind him Langford coughed. "Sorry," he said.

Giabretto let a brief smile flit across his strained face. Then there was another sound, a moan and it wasn't from the Texan.

"Shit, one of these birds is alive," Langford exclaimed.

There was another moan and Giabretto listened for the rustle of cloth or a vibration in the leg his rifle rested on as to which one of the men was breathing. There was no movement, and for several seconds no other indication of life. The helmet then changed position. The opposing soldier had heard too. But he was cagey and wasn't going to expose himself to danger.

"Hey, Adolph," one of the squad members said from the brush. "You better see about your buddy."

"Yeah," another piped in, "stand up so you can get a good look."

The helmet might as well have been on top of a statue. Long moments dragged on. Then the groan sounded again and this time they were sure where it was coming from.

"It's the guy on the bottom," Langford whispered. "Shake him, Gil. Maybe you'll draw the other one out.

"All right," came his hoarse reply. Slowly he took his left hand away from supporting his rifle and brought it down without looking. He felt moist fabric and tugged on the material. There was an anguished cry and reflexively, Giabretto took his hand away.

The German crouching behind the well raised up for an instance but the infantryman only had one hand on his rifle. "Grady, can you belly crawl over here? I need you to pull on this egg while I take a bead on the Kraut."

"Yeah," the other man replied. Weirdly, several birds had begun chirping again as Giabretto listened to the labored effort of the wounded Boche inching his way forward through the bed of leaves. The German said something in his language but his comrade didn't respond.

"Get ready," the BAR man said. Just as he said it, there was a sharp cry of terror and Giabretto looked down to see Langford poking the Landser with his bayonet. "Come on, Fritzy, let 'em hear you back in Paree." Langford was smiling. The wounded German sputtered some words and the one at the well answered back.

"That's enough," Giabretto hissed.

"It's never enough with these mugs," Langford said.

"If you kill him, the plan won't work."

"All right," the Texan reluctantly replied.

The wounded German began to talk again and the helmet at the well twisted up. Concern for his fellow at the hands of the enemy was getting to the soldier. Giabretto found himself empathizing with the man. But this was not the time for him to see the opposition other than what he'd been taught at basic at Fort Huachuca – find the enemy and kill the enemy before he kills you.

He told Langford. "Do it once more." The harsh voice that came from him sounded like it belonged to someone else.

"With pleasure." He sunk the tip of the 10-inch blade into the wounded man's shoulder and he wailed with intensity.

Like the two were hooked by invisible wire, the German hidden by the well poked his head up just enough, a blistering torrent of words pouring out from him. As he cursed the Americans, Giabretto took his shot. It rang clean and true like those days back home. The body beneath the helmet collapsed like an unstrung puppet.

Robeson and Bassettt crashed out of part of the orchard as Giabretto reached the man he'd just shot. The hole in the helmet was jagged, but smaller than he imagined it would be. The man was crumpled on his side. Bassettt kicked the helmet and as it came off, brains and bone spilled out across the ground.

"Good shooting," Bassettt remarked, tapping his helmet with his fingertip. In civilian life he'd been a high school math teacher and basketball coach. He had a quiet, contained way about him.

"We got some recon to finish, boys. We'll back slap later," Robeson looked back at Langford who was now struggling to his feet. "How you doing?"

"I'll hold on till we get back to base."

Robeson took a few steps toward him, and threw him a packet of powdered sulfur. "The medic gave me a couple of these just in case. Sprinkle that over the wound and we'll be back soon."

"Thanks. Next time see if you can throw in some of that Old Fitzgerald the officers are always soaking their tonsils in." Langford sat down next to the well, impervious to the still form near him.

"What about this goof?" Sutter, a lanky soldier from Detroit pointed at the wounded German Langford had been pig-sticking. His shirt was dotted with red blossoms. His eyes were open, and he anxiously glared at the Americans.

"Leave him," Robeson declared. "If he's alive when we get back, we'll get brownie points from HQ for bringing back a prisoner they can interrogate."

"He might have an accident 'fore y'all get back." Grady remarked casually, as he shook the sulfa powder on his wound. It had stopped bleeding.

"Leave him be," Robeson ordered. "I don't have any love lost for these buzzards either, but we're not resorting to outright murder just yet."

Bassett snorted. "This is war time, sarge. The Army might court-martial you for VD, but they'll pin a goddamn medal on your chest for one less Jerry."

"That may be," Robeson said, draping the strap of the Thompson around his shoulder. "But on my watch, we do as I say." He looked at his men. "Is that clear?"

"Yes sir," Giabretto answered. He too didn't have a taste for this kind of killing by committee as if it were sport. Sure he knew the Germans weren't square shooters. He'd heard the stories of Krauts who'd be waving a white cloth. Then when some dogfaces went to collect them

14

suddenly a hidden machine gunner would open up on the Americans. Or their soldiers who'd ride in an ambulance to get closer to the other side then jump out and start blasting away.

As they got ready to finish their recon, he couldn't help but look over at the German lying on the ground, his dead compatriot stacked across him. He put a hand to his chest, maybe it was the knife wounds or maybe there was a problem inside his body, a collapsed lung or blood filling the sacs. The man, kid really, younger than Giabretto's twenty-six years, looked to each face for a sign of empathy.

Giabretto averted his gaze when those baby browns came to him. He couldn't do anything for him, nothing.

When he was thirteen, the man now calling himself Giabretto had seen a lynching. This black man, Jonsey, had been a handyman in town. He'd been accused of beating, raping and strangling a white widow to death. Everyone in the colored section had heard the truth from the lady who was the white woman's house cleaner. She knew this woman kept company with several men in town and a few who passed through. The house cleaner, Clara, saw a big fleshy white man lying in the woman's bed the morning she'd come to do her work.

The man threw back the sheet to expose his throbbing erection to her, laughing that she should take a ride. She could also see a jar of corn liquor and a glass half empty on the nightstand. The sobs of the woman could also be heard by Clara coming from the closed bathroom. The stranger took a swig of his hooch and got out of bed. Naked, he began banging on the bathroom door.

"Get out here, you spoiled frail. I've got more I need to show you how to do." He laughed joyfully, and resumed pounding on the door, rattling it on its hinges. "We gonna have your nigra join us too." He laughed again and winked at Clara, fondling himself. The cleaning woman bolted from the house. When the news of the woman's murder spread through town that evening, she tried to tell the sheriff what she'd seen. But the incensed peckerwoods who'd gathered around his office didn't want to hear anything about the facts. This had been the excuse they'd been waiting for, and weren't going to be denied the opportunity.

Jonsey was an independent sort. Independent by a white man's standard for how a colored man should act anyway. He didn't call them Mister Mike or Mister Bob, didn't cross the street when a white woman passed, and it was rumored he'd had some learnin' at Wilberforce, a black college. He also made enough in the odd jobs he picked up in and around Five Points to have a little shop opened in the colored section as well. An enterprising black man who simply tried to make it the best way he could, who didn't brook no guff from black nor white, well that was a man who had it coming.

Jonesy had the misfortune of having done work for the widow. The way lestGiabretto heard it, the woman wasn't averse to bedding a black man either. So this and the jealousy of the whites led to a rowdy bunch that jumped the handyman two days after the murder occurred. They didn't wear hoods and didn't strike in the dead of night.

It was a pleasant day, the sunset a rusty orange haloing across the nearby hills. Jonesy had been out on a job fixing some shutters in the town next door and was returning to his home. He knew about the rumblings but he was going to be damned if he ran. Jonsey had served in World War I, seen death first hand with the 369th on the front lines with Marshal Foch. He was going to be damned if he was going to run away as the minister Abraham Theonus Hargrove had warned him.

He was driving back through the glade just out of town in his Hispano-Suiza. He was blind-sided by a group in a Ford Model A panel truck. One of the men bounded from the truck. He was the first angry white man to assault Jonsey, and he leveled his 20 gauge packed with double-ought on the self-reliant black man. "I'm'a rip you down to your backbone, boy," the white man promised.

Jonsey put a hole in the man's gut with his Automatic Colt Pistol, 1911 model. "Who's next?" he calmly asked, turning in a semi-circle to take in the men ringing him. The man who'd been brandishing the shotgun writhed at his feet.

Several stunned seconds elapsed, the whites not sure what to do with a victim not willing to play the part. Then a revolver echoed and Jonsey was hit in the upper body. But as the bastards rushed him, two more retorts from the automatic boomed and another attacker went down. They stripped him of his gun and beat him with fists and ax handles. Even then, he put up a fight and got his hands around the sheriff's neck, squeezing with all that remained in him.

In the end, winch cable was tightened around Joneys' neck. Half dead, the man was suspended from an oak said to date back to the times of Stonewall Jackson. The mob whooped with pleasure and flailed at his body with whatever they could hold. By this time several women had been let in on the festivities and several jugs were passed around also. A fire was stoked under him and the too sweet smell of roasting flesh mixed with the lavender in the air.

Watching from hiding, that thirteen-year-old and his two friends' nostrils were assailed by the peculiar aroma. One of his friends, Willie Adams, peed on himself he was so scared. He and the other boy were just as scared, but their fear seemed to make every sensation, every organ cease to function in their bodies. From where they were, buried in the sticky undergrowth of a thatch of creosote bushes, they didn't dare move lest the murderers find them.

The boys had been hunting bats in Lawson's Cave -- named for a confederate soldier from the town said to have single-handedly killed five blue bellies in the War Between the States -- with their slingshots and lost track of time. On their way back home, natural curiosity made them see what the commotion was all about. Now they'd seen more than they ever wanted to, and couldn't wait for the mob to be done with its murderous revelry. And from that time on, the man referring to himself now as Giabretto made certain decisions about the course his life would take.

"What do you think, Sarge?" Bassett took the field glasses away from the outcropping of his helmet.

Robeson was making a diagram of the town square the GIs were overlooking. The quartet were sequestered atop a hill behind a church with massive spires. Radiating around the area below them were shot up storefronts, a large edifice that had a governmental look to it, and an open space where sandbags had been stacked. Normally that meant a mortar launcher or tripod for a machine gun was to be put in place, but there was none present. There were several German soldiers moving about or some knotted together, laughing and talking.

The sergeant looked up, tapping the end of the pencil against his teeth. "I figure they're re-establishing a base here, but this time I bet it's some kind of advance force."

"You mean like a look-out squad?" Sutter broke in.

"Yeah," Robeson allowed. Trois-Points has gone back and forth in control. When the 1st Infantry had to be pulled off because of the push at Omaha Beach, the town was up for grabs again."

"I heard when the Krauts came back they took it out on the villagers because they'd been good to our boys," Bassett said, the anger rose incrementally in his voice and flushed his face.

"This is not a revenge mission, Bassett," Robeson reminded him. "We've got a job to do. We don't have to like it, but it's what we're supposed to do, private"

"I get it."

Giabretto pointed at a soldier carrying a large toolbox. "They got a motor pool going?"

Robeson looked through the binoculars again and watched the man disappear around a corner of a building. "Or he's a tank jockey. The

German had some Panzers cooling here before."

"We got to find out, huh?" Sutter said, a note of weariness in his tone.

"I'll go," Giabretto volunteered.

Bassett snorted. "You learn to speak German? And what makes you think them Victor Mature looks of yours are gonna let you slip around down there?"

"I'm not that fool hardy," he answered. "But I figure one man can walk around quick in one of the kraut's uniform."

"That's a hell of a risk," Robeson said.

Giabretto noted, "Like you said, we got a job to do."

Robeson made a sound with his tongue. "We can only cover you from here. Once you turn that corner, you're on your own.

"When you hear the first shot, you better fall back. Better the Germans just nab me than all of you," Giabretto said.

Robeson studied the man intently. "You don't have to do this, Giabretto. We can report what we suspect, no one will say we should have gone down there in the lion's den and chanced suicide."

"I know."

Robeson stepped close to the soldier. "You don't have anything to prove, you understand me?"

"What are you sayin'?" Giabretto couldn't help it; he let the country in his voice slip out.

"You know." And a slow sly smile parted the top kick's lean face. "There's nothing to prove here."

He began to stammer then got his words in order. "I, ah, all I gotta do is walk in a straight line, Sarge. I see what's behind that building and then I'm out of there."

"Now that you've said it, Gil, that is nuts." Sutter made a derisive slice of his hand through the air. "The only way out is probably back this way. One of those buzzards is bound to stop and ask you for a smoke or notice you aren't Hans."

"Yeah, they're right," Bassett added. "What do you say, sarge?"

"We go back and make our report and get some R&R 'cause we fucking earned it." He nodded at Giabretto. "Even if you did spot some tanks, you'd for sure get spotted too. Then what good would it be? You'd be captured and we still wouldn't know anything?" He chuckled quietly. Then he slapped Giabretto on the back and winked at him.

Back at the well, Langford was awake. The moaning German had expired. Nobody was sure if there were a few more knife holes in him. Out of some stuff they found inside the farmhouse, they made a litter and took turns carrying Langford back to base. From his expression, the Texan could have been dwelling on the life he just hastened from this world or what Rita Hayworth would be wearing on the USO tour. No one asked him for an answer.

Giabretto could barely contain himself. He wanted to grab Robeson and shake him. He'd been so careful to construct his illusion. The man had been living as Gil Giabretto since leaving home at sixteen, already then over six feet tall and his deep-set dark eyes making older women take notice. He snuck glances at Robeson, particularly when he was helping to carry Langford and he walked near him. If the sergeant knew, he was playing his cards very close to his vest.

So what did he want? Or maybe, Giabretto supposed, he would let him be, let him continue the masquerade. At this late date, what would it matter, he hoped? What would Robeson gain from exposing him? Really, what did any of them gain by tormenting men like him? But such larger concerns were not his to wrestle with at the moment. For now, he was too much consumed on maintaining the history he'd constructed for himself and the future he imagined -- a careful construction that might be coming down around him.

CHAPTER TWO

May 1943 – Harlem

"Is not the Negro's blood the same as the white man's?" The stentorian voiced man asked rhetorically from his seat in the spare conference room. "Hasn't Dr. Charles Drew already proven that it's all the same with his plasma and transfusion breakthroughs?" The speaker, the barrel-chested, silver-maned Reverend Carter Jervis Hardune of the Second Ethological African Methodist Church on Amsterdam Avenue -- and 38th Degree Prince Hall Freemason -- underscored his point with the slap of his palm on the table. The windows were open, a light breeze blew through.

"Don't get too heated, Hardy, you better save something for Sunday," Virgil Crimpshaw, a big man in a big suit said jocularly. "We got a long way to go before we lie down."

Hardune lifted a graying eyebrow at his compatriot. "I know, Brother Crimpshaw, I know."

Alma Yates moved her hand in front of her mouth to hide her smile. Was it small wonder the Negro movement for betterment was in the state it was in? Not if the men, and save for her, all the other occupants of the room were male, didn't mean well. Their past and current efforts were fine examples of their sincerity. It's just too bad the very tenacity and courage that made them so valuable to the cause, also contributed to them having heads too big for their hats.

"All right gentleman, and lady," Ferguson Mylo, cut in, nodding his head at Yates. "Let's keep on track, if we can. This has been a productive meeting so far, and I believe we all agree the joint letter we'll deliver to Mrs. Roosevelt will be the decisive blow to break to dismantle the racial barricade."

Crimpshaw laughed hollowly. "The light of your optimism touches us all, Fergie."

The crisply attired Mylo cleared his throat and poured himself some water from one of the decanters on the long table. "I'm simply trying to present the whole picture, Virgil. It's not as bleak as you always make it to be." He sipped soundlessly, the product of proper upbringing at Mrs. Stamphill's School of Etiquette and Manners still on 111th Street.

"Nor as cheery as you would have it," Crimpshaw retorted. He pivoted to look at Yates. "And you can quote me, if you like, miss."

Yates nodded briefly. These men surely loved to hear themselves pontificate.

"Don't you get your name in the paper enough?" Jerome Lindsay of the Double V Committee sniped.

Crimpshaw's fingers brushed at his pencil mustache. Just like the one he'd seen Billy Eckstein sporting in a story about the singer in Phylon magazine. "It's not about me, it's about advancing the interests of the Brotherhood."

"Which of course is synonymous with the interests of A. Philip," Reverend Hardune intoned. It was unclear to Yates whether he was being sarcastic, insightful or both.

Mylo went on. "What we have to do in this letter, is logically and irrefutably poke holes in the War Department's arguments for not activating the colored soldier. Latrine duty and smoke detail has its place, but that is a place we can't allow ourselves to occupy as our one contribution."

"Tell that to guts and glory General Patton," Lindsay chimed in. "He's been quoted in the white and black press stating the Negro does not have the intellectual capacity to handle the complicated machinery of a tank."

"But some huskie from Iowa who's only shoveled shit is over-qualified, huh?" Crimpshaw bellowed contemptuously.

"Your language." The reverend inclined his head at Yates. "This is not a meeting of your sYork Times
leeping car porters playing tonk in the back of the freight car."

"My apologies, but I'm sure Miss Yates has heard a lot worse."

"Don't worry, I have," she said, and didn't offer she'd been known to swear as well.

Crimpshaw touched a finger to his brow slick with lotion. "But these are not times for polite letters and petitions, gentlemen. This Administration may have brought in the New Deal, but we're still getting the discards."

For the first time since the meeting had been underway, Yates detected irritation behind the calm facade of Mylo. She resumed taking notes.

"No one respects Phil Randolph more than I do," Mylo began. "And while there were many factors leading to the President signing into effect Executive Order 8802 last year, all of us around this table acknowledge that his threatening to pull off a March on Washington added the needed push to get the order signed."

Crimpshaw leaned forward. "You didn't ask me here as a representative of the Chief to laud our praises. We'll take care of that," he added testily. His blunt index finger tamped on the table for emphasis. "I'm here because like it or not, you in this room can't ignore us, though some of you disapprove of our methods of agitation and confrontation. Well gentlemen, and I exclude Miss Yates because she's here in her capacity as a reporter, the fact remains the order was signed and it was directly because following a meeting Roosevelt had with Mr. Randolph, he understood he wasn't dealing with go slow Walter White."

Yates let her smile show this time. This was getting good. "Nonetheless," Lindsay interjected, seeking to stave off an escalation of the rhetoric. "The order is only that in name only. It is supposed to be about no discrimination in defense industries or government employment. Sure we have workers swelling the lines in Detroit, California and the like, but we still have mess boys and stewards overseas who only see action when a plate falls in the kitchen. Even though the Tuskegee 99th Pursuit Squadron was finally sent overseas this month."

"And that's why we need to press the point home," Mylo said. "Mr. White does not fly off the handle as Mr. Randolph has a tendency to do, then scramble to back up his bluff."

"The March on Washington was no bluff." Crimpshaw speared his finger through the air.

The reverend held up his hand out as if signaling for a cab. The nails, Yates noted, were neatly clipped and buffed. "But we are agreed that we must do something, correct? As it stands now, too many in the federal government think we are content with this half measure."

"Then the letter has to be matched with a demonstration," Lindsay opined. "Not on the scale of what Phil proposed, but a homegrown effort, a mass effort." He winked theatrically at Crimpshaw.

"We hold it here," Lindsay beamed, tapping the table with the flat of his hand.

Mylo looked at the reverend who fluttered his eyebrows. "Are we talking about the fall?"

"I think the summer, August," Lindsay said. "That way we build for when the Cabinet and Congress are back after vacations. Coupled with the letter, a demand really, we will put public pressure on the President to respond." He smiled, the plan forming in his head. "And we must make sure to publish the letter in the New York Times and Washington

Post. We can't do it like always and just be happy with coverage in our papers. This is the time to put this square in the laps of the white establishment."

"That doesn't give us much time to pull it off." Reverend Hardune massaged his chin between thumb and forefinger. "Though one supposes waiting longer will only cool our people's ardor and attention."

Yates finished transcribing Hardune's quote in her notes and used another sheet to write the names Marcus Garvey, C.L.R. James and Ranon Colin Bowlden. Each name had a question mark by it.

Marcus Aurelius Garvey, born in St. Ann's Bay in Jamaica, had been the proponent of a Back to Africa movement in the '20s and '30s. Garvey was at odds with others in the Negro betterment vanguard and constantly under attack by the white authorities. He'd had been jailed several times and finally ignominiously deported. He died disillusioned two years ago in London. But steadfast followers of Garvey's United Negro Improvement Association still carried the torch and had been vocal and persistent in denouncing any black life sacrificing itself for the paper democracy of America.

C.L.R. James and Bowlden were radical intellectuals. Neither had called for returning to Africa to solve the blacks in America problems. Bowlden's disagreements with Garvey were quite sharp and he'd denounced Garvey as a tool of the imperialists in a famous debate they'd had at the Harlem YMCA. And both men argued that black leaders should stop clamoring for overseas duty and call for an invasion of Georgia if they were serious about fighting for freedom.

Yates was forced out of her reverie by something that Ferguson Mylo was saying.

"That might work," he nodded spiritedly. "If we can get the congregations and social clubs behind the idea. We can get a turn out worth the expenditure of manpower and money."

"And let's not skip over the fact that Miss Yates' predecessor at the newspaper, Ted Poston, is part of Roosevelt's Black Cabinet." Lindsay waved a hand in her direction. "He will be a useful conduit to keep them appraised that we mean business."

"What do you think, Miss Yates?" Reverend Hardune clasped his hands across his rounding belly.

"I'm sure Mr. Poston will do what he can to convey this body's messages to the President." Inwardly, she felt that only Poston and a few others, including Frank Horne, singer and actress Lena Horne's uncle, judiciously used their access to the White House. From her observations, too many black folks were happy to mention they had coffee with the president, rather than press important matters.

And Poston had been kind to her when she'd come aboard the Pittsburgh Courier newspaper. The Courier had run Poston's column and reportage on black life for many years, and he was considered a trailblazer for the younger generation. He was now head of the Negro News desk of the Office of War Information in Washington, and a member of the cadre of blacks who unofficially advised and beseeched FDR -- his "Black Cabinet."

Poston, and earlier Ida B. Wells, a newspaper publisher who was a champion of civil rights, were the kind of people Yates wanted to become. Their examples of using words as tools to advocate for fairness and equity had spoken to a women like her who wanted more than just being a housewife in a walk up underneath the elevated.

The meeting continued and assignments were divvied up. It was agreed that providing their respective organizations signed on, the ad-hoc committee putting together the Harlem Patriot's Rally would meet again in two weeks. The event was planned for the second Saturday in August. The heat and humidity would be a factor, but that also assured more people would be out on their stoops than cooped inside hot apartments. Sure there'd be some at the air-conditioned picture shows, but the build-up to the rally was bound to capture the imagination of thousands.

Yates caught up with Crimpshaw as he finished chatting with Lindsay. "What do you think Mr. Randolph and his board will say about this proposal?"

The union organizer flashed big teeth. "The Chief has a lot of sway, Miss Yates, but he's a big believer in equality in his office as much as he thinks it ought to be practiced inside a Pullman car. Anyway, I can't see a problem in us endorsing and helping build the rally." He strode toward the door. "Can I buy you a cup of coffee? At least we don't need to use our ration stamps for that."

"Why not?" She smoothed her skirt and was glad she'd worn her only good pair of nylons. There was an inch run in the back of the left leg but the nail polish she'd applied blended in okay. She wasn't on the make, but knew these type of men expected a professional colored woman to present herself correctly. Whites and blacks were so judgmental.

The two left the building housing the Double V Committee offices. They then crossed 135th as a streetcar glided past on greased rails. Sitting inside, Yates could see two men in sailor's caps. She wondered which ship they were serving food on as stewards, having to do smiling and thanks yous all around but denied the chance to be real service men.

Reaching the other side, Crimpshaw hailed a slightly built man walking by in a boxy checked coat and tan slacks.

"Hey, Chet," Crimpshaw waved.

"Hey yourself, you dusky Joe Hill." The other man laughed and the two shook hands.

"Say, man, this good lookin' gal is a writer too." Crimpshaw briefly touched Yates on the upper arm. "Alma, you don't mind if I call you that do you?"

"That's fine, Mr. Crimpshaw."

"Hell, I ain't that used up, am I?"

Yates smiled. "I guess not, Virgil."

The one he'd called Chet scratched behind an ear.

"Anyway, This here is Chester Himes, a sho nuff book writer, Alma," Crimpshaw said.

"Great pleasure to meet you," Yates replied. "I can't say I agree with everything you wrote in the Lonely Crusade, but that was a fine book."

Himes let his eyes get wide. "Uh-oh, an educated woman, Virgil, you better be careful."

Crimpshaw's mustache twitched mischievously, and he said, "She's a reporter for the Pittsburgh Courier. Alma's being sent around the country to do articles about the colored war effort."

"The only effort I'm expending is in lifting whisky sours," Himes quipped.

Crimpshaw said, "Sure sorry to hear about what happened at Warner Brothers out there in California."

"What happened?" Yates asked.

"Jack Warner don't want no niggers writing his movies." Himes said it off-handedly, but Yates could see the disappointment briefly cloud his face. "Well, I ain't no fan of George Raft anyway."

"Where you staying?" Crimpshaw asked.

"At the McFadden on St. Nick." Himes patted a coat pocket as two big men in long topcoats and sweat mottled hats stalked along the street. One of them was on a par with Crimpshaw's size, and his wide feet clad in brogans slapped the pavement with ferocity. His companion was even taller, and on top of his head rode a black slouch brim of undetermined age. He kept his head down and Yates caught a glimpse of scarring on one side of his brooding Masai features.

The stouter one touched the crown of his fedora as he neared the woman. The two traipsed on with purpose. Himes had dug out a Lucky Strike pack and shook a cigarette loose for his friend. The union man declined and Himes lit one without duplicating the gesture to Yates.

"Look like a couple of hog farmers in their Sunday-go-to-meetins'," the book writer muttered. Himes watched the two ramblers stride down the street, Harlemites stepping around them as they passed.

Yates studied Chet's face, something going on behind his eyes as he noted the passage of the two distinctive men.

"I'll get you on the blower in a day or two and we'll go over to Sylvia's and swap lies about the old days, man."

"Lies are all we have, Vigil." Himes said, the cigarette tucked in the corner of his sardonic mouth. He also ambled away and the man and woman entered Byrd's Grill and Domino Emporium.

The melodic shuffling of the domino tiles on wood rubbed shiny greeted their ears as they crossed the threshold. Set parallel to the twin picture windows on either side of the door overlooking the avenue were domino players engrossed in their games. Mostly they were older men, their backs stooped from decades of chopping cotton and hauling slabs of ice way before they journeyed north.

A domino was slapped down, its companions on the table rattling from the impact. "Fit'een," a man with a front tooth missing hollered.

"Don't stop writing yet, sco' keeper," one of the other men holler. He whacked down a six-five tile and yelled, "Twenny, goddammit." Upon noticing Yates he cackled, "I'm sorry, little lady, I didn't see you standing there."

"But I guess it's okay to swear around me, with your dried up self." The speaker was an ample-proportioned waitress in a spotted apron.

"Aw, damn, Myrna, you the one that taught me how to cuss," the old timer roared, getting a chorus of chuckles from his peers.

Yates and Crimpshaw slid opposite one another in a booth. There was a discarded copy of the Communist Party's Daily Worker newspaper on the seat next to her. The front page article and accompanying photo was of a wildcat strike at a Ford plant outside Los Angeles at a place called Pico Rivera.

Patting his stomach, Crimpshaw said, "Guess I better get a hamburger to help me get my coffee down. What about you?"

"Coffee is fine by me."

"Yeah," he admired, "I can see you pay attention to what you eat all right."

She got her pad out of her purse. "You're not trying to get a rise out of me, are you, Virgil?"

"No ma'am," he managed with a straight face. "But you gotta understand, most of my time is wrapped up in visitin' my members when they sleep over at some flea bag hotel trying to catch a few winks in between their runs. A bunch of jokers in long johns stinking of cheap whiskey and watching slop boiling over on the hot plate is about all I get in the way of entertainment."

"Yes, I can imagine how hard it is for you."

Crimpshaw shook his head. "You just don't know." He looked up at her and they both laughed.

The waitress who'd cracked wise with the old man came over to take their orders. "Sorry," she said, after the Sleeping Car organizer made his request, "but we're out of beef till next Tuesday. Our soldier boys needs they iron. Ham and cheese okay?"

"Sure, anything for the effort," Crimpshaw flashed a 'V' with his two fingers. "Victory at home and victory overseas. Yes sir."

"You better be careful, Virg," the waitress warned. "You already skatin' on thin ice with them Hoover boys 'cause of y'all incitin' darkies to stand up for theyselves." She marched away, whistling.

"How do you find the time to work?" Yates kidded.

He settled his solid frame in the leatherette booth. "I'm just a ball of energy, Alma."

She asked him some questions she already knew the answers to about the Brotherhood of Sleeping Car Porters and he gave her ready-made answers. On the wall framed in Bakelite was a photo of Duke Ellington and Billy Strayhorn composing at the piano.

"Now what is it I can really do for you and that outstanding paper you work for now that we've danced around awhile?" Crimpshaw said.

"I wanted to talk with one of your porters, a man named Stanley Bascome. I know he's here in town, but he's been ducking me.

Crimpshaw's brow bunched in consternation. "That's why you agreed to sit with me. And just why is it you want to talk with brother Bascome?"

"The rumor."

"Huh?"

She lowered her voice. "About a handful of black soldiers murdered and buried n the Arizona desert."

He pushed on the inside of his mouth with his tongue. "I've had to deal with my share of nutty stories working for the union and knowing what the Pullman Company was capable and willing to do. And let me tell you, sister, old man Lincoln was willing to do a lot. But this tall tale, this is hogwash. And I've heard some crazy stuff."

"That's what I'm trying to find out. There's been lynching of Negro GIs near bases, shoot outs between black and white soldiers -- this might not be so fantastic."

Crimpshaw ran a rough hand over his broad face. "You know how that makes us look with that kind of talk, don't you?"

The waitress returned with their orders and they remained silent until she departed.

"I don't need to use his name, but I want to see if there's anything to it." Yates sipped her coffee. It was heavy with chicory to stretch the grounds. The boys overseas sure ate well, she reflected. At least the white boys did.

Crimpshaw leaned forward, "Look, not only do I not want my union in no way caught up in this foolishness, you of all people know this pushing and pulling we're doing with FDR is like dancing with a drunk. We got to hold up more than our end and sure ain't getting much in return. We're making some headway toward the decision of letting colored boys into the fight. Not that I'm eager to have our blood splashed all over France and the Pacific." He took a bite of his sandwich.

"Especially since it gets spilled enough here at home." Yates stirred her coffee.

"My uncle was one of the Black Rattlers, you know about them?"

"The 369th, sure. They fought the longest with the French on the front during World War I."

"Yeah," Crimpshaw talked around more of his food. "How you gonna keep 'em down on the farm once they seen Paree," the ofays sang once the Negro troops got home – the ones left alive at least. Plenty of them got chewed up in that goddamn slaughter ground of the Argonne Woods and what not."

"Including your uncle?" She held the cup half way to her mouth.

"He lost a leg and an eye," Crimpshaw confirmed. "But he and his pals, damn near 200 of them, got their medals. The frogs awarded them the Croix de Guerre, the Cross of War. That sure got the white boys riled up with jealousy."

"Yes," she concurred, "I've read accounts of the rioting by white against returning black soldiers. Men who came back home and assumed that their sacrifice overseas would mean something better for them here. That they would respect us for doing our share."

A silence extended between them. The raucous sound of the men playing dominoes came to them as if through a heavy fog. Then Crimpshaw spoke, "And that's the reason you can't be looking into this mess, Alma."

"This may not be some old wife's tale," she said. "This is about a persistent rumor that the United States Army willingly participated in, and covered up a secret fatal experiment of 20 Negro soldiers after a violent altercation at Fort Huachuca." She frowned at her cooling coffee as if it were wheat paste suitable for gluing.

"And you want to be the one to break the big story? The first colored reporter to earn herself a whatdoyoucallit, Pullzer?"

"Pulitzer."

"Yeah. Or maybe that nigger hatin' Jew Jack Warner will make a movie out of it, and you can be played by Lena Horne or that gal I saw in that Herb Jeffries cowboy movie."

"Are you scared I'll embarrass the Brotherhood by talking with Mr. Bascome, or what white folks will say if some part of this is true?"

"The union will survive because we've come through hell to get what's due us, Miss Yates. But we also understand when to confront and when to compromise when larger matters are at stake. And you stirring this up is bound to have repercussions among those we're trying to motivate. The Tuskegee airmen are itchin' to fight, Alma. We got fellas that have trained and re-trained for combat in all its forms. This dam is about to break."

"Then Bascome won't hold that back," she countered. "Have you talked with him about his brother? The one I understand was supposedly one of the murdered men?"

Crimpshaw blew out a loud gust of air. "Not directly. But I heard he tied one on one night and was going on about it. But it's not like Bascome's got the straight dope, he wasn't there you know. His mother got a letter from the War Department saying his brother died in the service of his country."

Yates asked, "Had his brother shipped out?"

"Don't know many more particulars than that."

"Then all the more reason I should talk to him."

"Other than that one time, I understand he ain't exactly chatty on the subject," Crimpshaw said.

"I'm not out to hurt our cause," Virgil," she soothed. "But there's been some bad incidents at several bases, Fort Dix, Fort Bragg, and I hear Camp Van Dorn in Mississippi is a powder keg waiting for the match to be struck." She gestured forcefully. "At Freeman Field in Indiana, 100 Negro officers were arrested for trying to enter an officer's club reserved for whites. They'd planned this to show just how hypocritical the Executive Order really is. That no matter what we do, Jim Crow is the order of the day no matter where we find ourselves. So I'm not saying I believe or don't believe this story. But it's persisted for months now on the Negro grapevine. The fact that the Department of the Army hasn't done more than say there's nothing there, has left a very unsatisfied taste in a lot of mouths."

Crimpshaw put up a hand as if trying to hold back gravity. "Good to see you get passionate about something."

"I don't consider myself a frivolous woman, Virgil. I know I got this assignment because a lot of able-bodied men at the paper have done their duty and volunteered for the Service. I started there as a secretary but quite frankly, I found it incredibly boring work. And I don't want, at least right now, some big shouldered, swivel hipped man to come along and be my black knight," her eyes sparkled when she said that.

"I see," was his subdued reply.

"I'm no man-hater, Virgil," she smiled. "I like to have fun too."

"That mean you'd consider accompanying me to see Prez at the Five Spot Thursday night? I haven't seen Lester Young wail on his sax since he and that singer, Gil Giabretto, played the Cotton Club a couple of years back."

"If I get to talk to Mr. Bascome."

"You drive a hard bargain, woman."

"I have no choice."

He sighed but he knew he was going to give in. He'd been in knockdowns with Pullman's goons and kept swinging until his arms were too heavy to lift. But the turn of an ankle and a pretty girl's face got through his defenses every time. When would he learn? "Okay, but don't let this get back to the Chief."

"It won't, at least not from my end." She finished her coffee, watching the man over the rim of her cup. He was a little too taken with himself, but there was a forcefulness to him she found appealing. As the steam warmed her face, she was glad her mother, Clara, wasn't witnessing this. What would she say about her properly raised daughter flirting with a known red labor agitator? What indeed?

CHAPTER THREE

"Look out, son, you're crowdin' me."

"Throw nigga."

"If I don't six, there ain't a Jesus. Ugh."

The dice were thrown against the scrubbed wainscoting, and bounced like the cubes were filled with grasshoppers.

"What am I talkin' about?" The thrower said. The dice had come up four and two.

"Youse one lucky so-and-so," a sweating balding man retorted. "But I guess you needs that chicken feed to pay for Randolph's ivory handled LaSalle."

"The Chief don't put on no airs," said the man who'd tossed the dice. He was a solidly built individual in an athletic T-shirt and dungarees. He was down on one knee, a semi-circle of players around him. The small group was crowded into the common bathroom of the Marquee Arms on 127th Street.

Alma Yates came to the door of the washroom. "Mr. Bascome, can I have a few words with you?"

"Damn," one of the men exclaimed, "you the prize I get to take home when I clean these jokers out, honey?"

"Shut up, Mosley, can't you see she's a lady?" Bascome got of his knee and wiped his hand on the side of his pants. "Yes, ma'am, that's me all right." He stuck out his hand before she could offer hers and shook vigorously. "Now what can I do for you I'd like to know?"

"I need to speak to you in private, if I could. I'm with the Pittsburgh Courier."

That got some curious looks.

"That's not a problem, no siree, not a problem at all." Bascome bent down and scooped up the bills lying on the hexagonal tile. "Sorry, suckers, I'm giving you a break from taking your money."

"Aw quit squawkin' and let a real gambler show these chumps how it's done." The man who'd complimented Yates put down a dollar and palmed the dice. He cupped his hands together and shook the dice vigorously. "Who's gonna fade me, come on, don't be shy."

Yates spotted a poster taped to the bathroom wall behind Bascome announcing the last performance of the crooner Gil Giabretto before he'd gone into the service a month ago. The Paul Whiteman Orchestra had backed him, and the engagement was at the Cobalt Room. This was the only downtown club that allowed black patrons to sit anywhere they wanted.

The other men got back into the rhythm of the game as Yates and Bascome stepped out into the hallway. "I sure hope you ain't a bill collector," the Pullman Porter said. "But if you is, I'm bettin' you can't catch me on a dead run." He grinned, displaying uneven teeth.

Yates explained again who she was and why she was there.

"You might as well try to find Santa Claus, lady." They had walked along the hall, the floorboards creaking underneath them. Now they stood near the stairwell.

"So your brother never mentioned any problems at Fort Huachuca?" she asked.

"What colored man in the white man's Army ain't been havin' the blues?" Bascome dug in a pants pocket and took out a rumpled pack of Chesterfield's. "Like one?"

"No thanks," Yates said.

He thumbed the wheel on his Ronson lighter and got his cigarette going. "So how'd you know I laid over here?"

"I asked around, I wanted to talk to you about the incident involving your brother, you know, what you'd heard had happened."

He plucked a fleck of tobacco from the tip of his tongue. "You mean how my brother Jordy was kilt on accident?"

She was caught short, but answered, "That's right." From the bathroom, someone whooped as the sound of the rolling dice echoed off the walls. "But you've heard the rumors going around haven't you?"

He looked at her blankly. "What's that?"

"That some colored service men died under questionable circumstances out there in the Arizona desert."

He jammed his hands in his pockets, twisting his shoulder blades. "You got me, Miss Yates. I ain't got no truck with that kind of talk."

She frowned. "So you never made mention of anything funny going on at the fort?"

"Nope." He blew smoke toward the ceiling.

"What is it your brother did at the fort to get him killed, Mr. Bascome?"

"What you think a boot get to do in the service, fly one of them B-25s? He got to dig latrines and learn to paint camouflage."

"He ever write you from Huachuca?"

Bascome sucked deep on his cigarette. "Jordy wasn't much on letter writin'."

"The reason I ask is because Huachuca has the all-Negro 93rd stationed there, infantry units. Now as far as I understand, they've yet to be activated for combat. So how did he die?"

The Chesterfield smoldered in his line of a mouth. "Like I said, he wasn't soldering, not really. But it was a mortar accident. Something went wrong with the launcher and he and another man got blow'd up."

She wasn't going to ask that other name, not yet. Yates wanted him to relax, feel comfortable with her. "So what was his actual attachment?"

"It was quartermaster, part of the 369th which is also there at the fort."

"I guess it was a closed casket?" The reporter had her note pad out, making the effort appear natural and unhurried.

Bascome bobbed his head up and down. "Yeah, they said they did what they could to put him back together but..." and he didn't finish. "Mama and me claimed his body and buried him back home. The pay that was coming to him helped take care of that. Plus the Army gave a little boost on account of feelin' bad about him getting done in like that."

"And where's that?" she asked nicely.

"Shreveport, you ever been there?"

"No, but I've been through New Orleans once." She made sure she made eye contact with him. "So your brother never kept in touch, huh?"

"Well," he drew out, "not exactly. Mama did get a few letters about camp and what they ate, stuff like that." Bascome ground out his cigarette on the landing. "Listen, I got to get back in there 'fore my hand cools down." He whistled air across his fingers.

"Sure, sure, she said absently, making her notations. "Say, do you remember the name of the other man who was killed along with your brother?"

"Jones, Johnson, sumptin' like that," Bascome replied. "Hey," he quickly added, "it was swell meeting ya." He smiled, gave a half-salute and walked back to his dice game. Inside the makeshift game parlor, he leaned against the wall, his face suddenly locked in a gloomy cast.

The loud mouth, the one who'd made the crack about Yates looked over at Bascome. He just won ten dollars on the fade line. "Hey, gate, what's with the long face? She turn you down for a date?"

Bascome managed a smile with some effort. "Aw, man, that chick was all wet. She's just writin' about how we all got to be for the war effort, colored and white."

"Shit," his buddy said, "we catch enough hell bowing and scraping fo' them white folks on the rail cars. I'm sure glad my prison record kept me from getting my black ass drafted."

"Yeah." Bascome agreed. But as his friend turned his attention back to the game, he watched the woman recede along the hallway out of the corner of his eye. His hand was shaking, but not in anticipation of throwing his lucky number.

Yates walked slowly down the stairs trying to make sense of what Bascome had told her or rather hadn't told her. It could very well be that Crimpshaw had heard wrong, certainly that was possible. He wasn't there when allegedly the Pullman porter was drunk and railing against whomever about what had befallen his brother? Or it could be just like how these stories go; whoever else was there at the bar was drunk too and had simply misunderstood what Bascome had been going on about?

Yet, she reminded herself as she stepped outside to sunlight; Crimpshaw was not the only one who'd acknowledged hearing the rumor. She'd been doing an article on women riveters in Detroit when she'd first heard the story some five months ago. This had been from an imposing woman named Regina Lawson who worked swing at the Ford Willow Run plant.

Lawson had a boyfriend at Fort Huachuca and he'd written her that one morning he'd expected a friend of his who'd been drafted to show and he didn't. He was told his pal and nine others had been shipped to other camps. That wasn't unusual as the segregation polices practiced by the armed services led to breaking up black detachments at a given fort while white ones were left intact. Separate and hardly equal dictated that there had to be facilities for the colored men apart from those for the Caucasian troops and officers.

When space was at a premium, Negro divisions were broken up and sent to several forts. But Huachuca was in the desert, fifty miles from the nearest town. There was plenty of room. That's why several of the men in her boyfriend's unit found it odd. Yet when Lawson's boyfriend tried to locate his friend, he was ordered to drop it, that to pursue it any further might result in consequences for him.

The joke among the black soldiers was the ten were a spook patrol on a secret mission and only operated at night behind enemy lines. Then one time, several black officers, fed up with second-class treatment, attempted what other officers had done at other bases. These men tried to storm the white officers club, and a fight between them and the MPs resulted.

The story went that one of the MPs, a muscular cracker who liked any excuse to beat a burr head, walloped on a captain with his billy club. As the Negro captain fought back, the MP was supposed to have said something to the effect that if he didn't fly right, he'd be number twenty-one. But Lawson didn't know the name of this captain or the MP, and her boyfriend was subsequently shipped out to Australia.

Yates had confirmed that the confrontation had occurred; it had been covered in various newspapers. Thereafter the rumor started, but then numerous rumors had sprung from other racial incidents at bases. So what was real anymore? This one had seemed more solid. Though maybe Virgil Crimpshaw was right and she was simply hungry to break a big story and was willing to build this into a mystery.

But when she was in Philadelphia interviewing colored WACs, the Pullman porter angle had surfaced. One of the women had heard that one of the missing men had been in the porter's union. Of course she'd heard this from her hairdresser who got it Lord knew how, but Yates was hooked. She'd called the Brotherhood and inquired but the helpful functionary on the other end of the line said he knew of no such connection. Coming out on the train to New York, she asked some of the porters on the train and only got negative head shakes.

Virgil Crimpshaw had been a break. Yates found out he'd be at the Double V Committee meeting she was covering. She laughed brusquely, standing at the street corner. He could have been humoring her simply to keep on her good side.

She mulled this over as an emerald green Buick pulled away from the curb across the street. The car then drove past her and made a right on Amsterdam. She noticed two white men sitting in the vehicle. Whites weren't strangers in Harlem, particularly when it came to the nightclub scene. There was something about the two that made her zero in on them. She walked along, trying to decipher what it was.

"Hey, you didn't even hear me come up, did you?"

Startled, Yates turned toward the man who was talking to her.

"Good to see you, Silas," she said, hugging him. She looked around. "Where'd you come from?"

He pointed toward a barbershop across the street. "I was sitting in there shooting the breeze and saw you walking by like you were in some kind of fog. It was sure good seeing you the other night."

"Same here." She and Crimpshaw had gone to the Cobalt Room in the East Village for dinner and she'd been pleasantly surprised to see her cousin Silas Mayhew tending bar. Last time they'd been in touch, he'd been working at a slaughterhouse in Chicago.

They strolled down 127th Street. "So, how's your work going? I read your stuff a lot, you know."

"That's sweet of you, Silas. It's going pretty good. I think I might even collect my articles and see if I can publish them as a book."

Mayhew paused to cup his hands and light a Lucky Strike. "You'd be in tall cotton, then. That'd be great, Alma."

"What?"

"Well," he began, "It's none of my business what with you being a grown woman and plenty more sophisticated than me, seeing as how you've been to this place and that."

"But..."

"Virgil Crimphaw is a skirt chaser." Mayhew took the cigarette out of the corner of his mouth and shook the butt end at her. "I know something about him."

She touched his arm. "I'll be careful. Say, let's go to the zoo or something, huh? Every time I'm in New York it's always to come to Harlem and it's always on business." Maybe some of Crimpshaw's impulsiveness was starting to rub off on her.

He checked his watch. "Sure. Why not? I've never been and I've been living here more than a year."

As the two walked toward the subway, it clicked for Yates what had it been about those two white men in the Buick. It was their haircuts; very short, very Army.

CHAPTER FOUR

May 1943 - Washington, D.C.

Colonel Snow reread the report from his operatives, Palmer and Birch. The two had followed the colored girl reporter to a hotel frequented by Pullman Porters and watched her depart. They were certain she'd gone to see Bascome, probing into his brother's death. A subsequent visit the two paid on Bascome later that day assured them he did nothing to encourage her investigation.

A sneer played with the colonel's lower face as he put the report back in its file folder. He hoped their "visit" with Bascome had left him mobile. Snow was not like his peers in their assessment, or rather, their noblesse oblige when it came to the Negro race. He was not so dismissive of the black press as he knew his two men in New York were. Snow had done his own checking into Alma Yates' background. Like a lot of modern colored women, she and her ilk had been pushed by her parents to do better than their forebears had done.

A tomboy from Waycross, Georgia, she'd shown brightness and eagerness early. Her mother had wanted her to become a school teacher, but Yates had her own mind. She did two years at Spellman, working nights, and jumped at the chance to work as a summer intern at the Pittsburgh Courier. He could tell in just the crisp type recounting her young life she had the same hunger for something else nesting in her that took him, long ago, from the small patch that was the family farm in Arkansas City, Kansas.

The hunger carried him on the battlefields of World War I from a scared shitless private to seasoned sergeant in command of doughboys in the Meuse-Argonne. He'd found that something to satisfy that need. It wasn't the killing, but the plotting, the strategy and craft you developed to keep you and your men alive amidst the majesty of slaughter. That native cunning was noticed and after the Great War he was recruited into the Cipher Bureau where his sharp mind found yet another plateau to attain. And so it went. Now he was a commander in X-2, the manipulators behind the intelligence operations of the armed forces.

He'd decided, before becoming a soldier, despite the pleadings and threats of his father, to never be a sod buster. He couldn't see getting up before dawn to plow and plant and fret and scrimp to raise crops and cattle only to repeat that process over and over again until the grave. What kind of life was that? Honor in hard work his old man, a straight-backed Pentecostal lay preacher would hammer at again and again. Him sitting and smoking his pipe in the rocking chair his father had made, contemplating crop cycles and the lord's infinite unknowable. His pa was stiff-neck proud of the land, the gift from a father who'd fought the Indians for the dirt plot and spilled more blood of the renegade Red Legs after the Civil War to keep the farm.

For the first time he could ever remember his father had cursed. He'd screamed at the young man, his hair already turning white and not yet eighteen, who literally and figuratively turned his back on his heritage as he left for the depot to report for basics. His mother, arms around his younger sister, Claire, silently crying in the doorway.

The movieola in his mind flickered and went dark at a knock on the door. Snow quietly said, "Enter," and calmly placed the file on Alma Yates underneath some others. His guest was too observant for him to leave it in plain sight.

Madison Clay entered and saluted.

"At ease, Sergeant. Have a seat."

"Thank you, sir." Clay folded his six four frame onto the old-fashioned school house chair.

Snow had already removed a file from his organized pile. He laid it flat, his fingers, like spider's legs, straddling the thin cardboard. "This will be a most curious experience, for someone such as yourself."

"I'll do my best, sir." The tall man sat ramrod straight, no emotion obvious on his angular features.

"Of that, I have no doubt, sergeant. Of course, the ironic part is that outside of the two of us, and a few others you'll never meet, no one will no of this operation."

"That's as it should be."

Snow opened the file. "But a shame nonetheless. Particularly when Negro leaders are decrying the War Department's manufactured impediments to using the colored man in combat."

Clay didn't respond, didn't blink.

Snow went through the motions of reviewing the material before him, but he knew it cold. There was no one better suited for this assignment than Clay. Even the rednecks in the branch had to admit that. Clay had a Ph.D. in chemistry from Tuskegee, spoke four other languages, and had fought in Spain with the Abraham Lincoln Brigade. He'd been one of 100 black Americans along with some 3,200 whites from the Sates that had done so.

It was that premature anti-fascist activity that had earned him and the others files compiled by that prancing queen J. Edgar Hoover and his FBI. In particular, Hoover was adamant that the 100 Negroes be hauled before Congress and charged with sedition. He was virtually pathological, Snow had observed more than once, in his hatred of any black who dared raise his head above the rabble.

From the man's own comments and memos Snow had seen, Hoover intensely believed that a black messiah would rise up and portend the demise of white civilization as God and Walter P. Chrysler knew it. That's why Hoover had been so fervent in hounding Marcus Garvey and A. Philip Randolph, the union head. But his mania produced copious entries, and thus when Snow was scouring around to fill this slot, he was pleased that ball licker Hoover was so thorough in the information he'd compiled on Clay.

Almost, he prided himself, as complete as the dossier Snow had amassed on Hoover, the Jew hating Henry Ford, Eleanor Roosevelt's lesbian dalliances, and many others. It all came back to the plotting.

"You were saying, colonel?"

"You will depart at 0100 hours tomorrow by special troop transport from our hanger at National. You will fly to RAF group headquarters in Uxbridge, outside of London, and from there change planes for Egypt. Once there you will acquire your Senegalese passport and other papers establishing your new identity. Then you will be placed aboard the freighter El Farouk with Algerian registry that will take you to Tunis."

"Beside the pilots, am I the only one on that plane?"

"Yes, why?"

"Just wondering," he said evenly.

Snow was troubled, was that an ironic comment? Was he saying something about him being a Negro and no whites would want to be with him in such close quarters?

After two months of concentrated training and observing the man, he still could not get an accurate fix on the sergeant. One of his strongest traits was the ability to read people, to get a sense of what they wanted. For if you knew what they wanted, you knew how to control them. But Clay, since the inception, had manifested neither surprise nor gratitude at being plucked out of the hell of Camp Van Dorn in Centerville, Mississippi. The sergeant had already been in two serious dust ups with white soldiers, and Snow found him beaten and untreated in the brig. He was silent but not sullen, like he was awaiting purpose. As if he only lived from moment to moment. That could make him dangerous to the enemy, and possibly to

39

Snow if he survived this assignment.

"Is it's clear how you report?"

"Yes, I've committed to memory where the short wave is located and I know how to use one."

"If the radio is found?" Snow pressed.

Unwavering he responded. "Then I better be on the run. Because that will mean the operation is compromised, and my identity has been exposed."

"What would you do to survive?" Snow asked.

"Whatever was in my power," Clay said. His tranquil demeanor slipped momentarily and there was a glimpse of a will forged in the furnace of adversity. Then it went away, the composed expression Clay presented to the world back in place.

Snow appreciated the man's candor. So there was something he wanted after all. "I can't emphasize how important this mission is, Clay. If you can glean the information we believe is to be available in the French embassy, you will have done a great service to your country. Operation Torch has been successful in penetrating that part of Northern Africa, but the job is not complete."

"Too bad my country will never be aware of my actions. It would do so much," he added in what might have been a wistful tone.

"Yes, that is a shame." He closed the file folder, indicating the meeting was at an end. "Anything else, sergeant?"

"No."

"Your dismissed then. Get some rest."

Clay stood, saluted and left the room. Snow interlaced his fingers. He glowered at the door the other man had just gone through. The colonel was as much worried about the success of the operation as he was figuring out what to do with Clay should he return. Surely the Negro didn't expect a career in the intelligence bureaus? Maybe J. Edgar could use him to spy on some of these loud mouths like Ranon Bowlden or this new fellow, Elijah Poole who was now calling himself Elijah Muhammad. He was running around the east coast spouting some sort of crazy religion mixed in with race pride, calling the white man the blue-eyed devil and what not. But Snow didn't really believe that was the kind of work Clay would want to do. No, he decided, Clay would have to be handled just like Yates was going to have to be dealt with if she persisted. These new Negroes were getting to be a handful, he reasoned. Too many of them wanted too much too fast. Everybody had to know their place, and the role they played. Yes, he would make sure of that as far as Miss Yates and the self-possessed Madison Clay were concerned if he had to.

Chapter Five

May 1943 - Somewhere over the Atlantic

Clay stretched his long legs, stifling a yawn as the transport plane, a converted Flying Fortress medium bomber, rumbled across the Atlantic. Being in the plane had got him reflecting on several of his friends training at Tuskegee. These men had now gone through the pilots training program back there in Oklahoma. From what he understood, the men had trained and trained, more than ready to join the air war. The Spookwaffe they wryly called themselves, taking the power away from whites who would use it derogatorily.

Yet it seemed no matter how hard they trained or how much they prepared, nobody was going to forget they were black. There was a certain irony to it, Clay surmised. Whites feared blacks who were armed and ready to fight more than they feared dying far from home on foreign soil. Or so it seemed to him, having surreptitiously seen the recent casualty figures tallied from the European and Pacific theaters. You would think, he fantasized, that whites would be overjoyed at the opportunity to shove Negro bodies into the frontlines. They made such good targets against the virgin snows of the French countryside. A wan smile worked its way on and off Clay's face at his gallows humor. He stretched again and let the steady growling of the plane's engine and the vibration drumming through his body, lulling him to sleep.

Maybe he'd come up with a slogan for his imagined campaign. Something catchy like he heard the baritone announcer extolling Ovaltine during Terry and the Pirates on the radio. After all, Marcus Garvey had taken money from the Klan since they both shared the same goal, sending black folks back to Africa. Clay was sure he could sell virulent racists like Senator Bilbo to go along with the idea from this angle of saving white lives. Though the drawback would be Bilbo would insist that the Negro troops not be armed, thus not even giving them a decent chance.

And that's what it came down to, a chance to fight and die like a white man. Clay grunted. Surely there was something instructive about the black man's experience in America that after being enslaved and maltreated, lied to and cheated, the promise of Reconstruction dangled in front of him and taken away, that he kept on going. Was it fortitude or madness? Clay didn't know the answer anymore than why it was since his days of playing cowboys and Indians, he was the sharpest when there was a gun, even a toy replica, in his hand. It was not that he loved violence for its own sake. For him the gun was a symbol. It stood for not only how his ancestors had been oppressed, but how one gained their freedom. If they made the choice.

Not, he'd reasoned he was never going to be a flat out revolutionary like Kwame Nkrumah. He'd met the Ghanaian who at the time was studying in the U.S. at a conference sponsored by several leftist organizations where Ranon Bowlden was the keynote speaker. Nkrumah was a bold and visionary man who kept the liberation of his country and the whole of Africa forefront in all that he did. But Clay knew the objective conditions, to use the Marxist phrase, in America were different. Clay could not see an America as the mighty example of the worker's state. He could see black people getting their fair share, but only through concerted actions on many levels and much sacrifice. Yet he wasn't sure where he fit in all that.

For a while Clay thought he did when he made his parents happy getting his degree in chemistry. And he was on the path to being a college professor to help raise a generation of educated black minds. But he became restless. When the opportunity to soldier presented itself, he took hold of it with both hands. It brought him alive to engage in a fight for a cause he found worthwhile. That, it seemed, was his purpose on earth.

"You okay back there?" the co-pilot asked over the constant hum of the quadruple props.

"I'm fine."

"We might be hitting some bumpy weather, but don't worry, we know how to keep this crate out of the pond."

"No problem."

"Okay."

Decent man. He'd even offered his hand when Clay met the two at the hanger. That was unusual. The look of astonishment on the pilot's face was definitely more the usual since he'd been old enough to walk. Too bad there weren't more like the co-pilot. But if there were, Clay surmised, he wouldn't have the cool anger that kept him going. He let his lids close, the black and white image of the gray man, Colonel Snow floating before him.

Now that was man who he knew better than to turn his back on.

Some twelve hours later, the Fortress arrived at the RAF base at Uxbridge ahead of schedule, minutes ahead of a storm moving in.

"You can bunk down over there," the co-pilot pointed at a Quonset set aside from other structures. "And my orders also informed me that your transport to where ever the hell it is you're going next will meet you at," he checked his watch, "0500 hours, sergeant."

"Thank you." Clay stuck out his hand and the other man took it, shaking it eagerly. Rain pelted the men as they stood off to one side of the landing field. A quartet of Triumph Spitfires shimmering with a sheen of wetness and reflected light were parked in a row nearby. The pilot of the Fortress had taken off his helmet, glanced at Clay when he was exiting the plane with his Gladstone bag and duffle, and marched away.

"Where's the chow?" Clay asked.

The co-pilot looked like he'd been hit in the windpipe. "Over there," he pointed. He indicated a low building with a row of windows up high and parallel to the roof. That's where the pilot had headed.

"I'm hungry," Clay said, also making for the building. "Want to join me?"

"I've got to," the co-pilot began, "sure, why not," he finished. "Say, I'm Howard Leeds, by the way," he added, catching up to the taller man's strides.

"Pleasure, lieutenant, you already know my name."

"Yes, that's true," Leeds said. "But I don't know why we transported you here or for what purpose."

Clay didn't say anything.

"I didn't mean I wanted to know what your mission was, I meant," then he stopped himself.

"You meant why's a colored soldier, a noncom at that, in his civies, getting the hush-hush treatment."

"Yeah," Leeds grinned. Two British soldiers, dressed in mechanic's overalls, stepped out of a small hanger, set off from the larger ones. These two secured a doubled chain and three locks, and stepped past the other two. Neither said a word but glared at Clay and Leeds as the duo neared the mess hall.

Clay reached the double door first but pushed it open for Leeds. "After you."

The airman stepped inside, the din of plates and chatter like waves of the ocean rising to greet him. Clay eased in behind him and there was an audible change as the voices became more muted, then resumed their previous cadence.

"Let's find a seat, Lieutenant Leeds. Or if you prefer, I'm sure you could dine with your fellow officers."

"In for a penny," Leeds answered.

Clay swung his duffle off his shoulder and held it under a thick arm as they sought a spot. Clay was aware of the not-so-private memo sent by the Home Office in 1942 to the commander of the American forces in Europe, Dwight Eisenhower. In effect, the stance by the British allies was they would not import Jim Crow to John Bull. When it came to public places such as pubs and cafes, Negroes were allowed. If the U.S. military were to insist on restrictions, the bobbies wouldn't back their play.

Conversely, there were members of Parliament who were quite vocal in their views that coloreds should be confined to specific areas. Secretary of Foreign Affairs Anthony Eden had proposed a quota system when it came to colored personnel, at least when it came to the American blacks, entry into England. Underlying Eden's and some of his peers anxieties, was the old bugaboo of Negroes fraternizing with white women. On that score, they shared the sentiments of their cousins across the Atlantic.

But unlike their former subjects, the Brits were more in a quandary over race restrictions given that current subjects from Trinidad and Jamaica were also wearing British uniforms. And as this was officially a Limey base, Clay assumed a certain amount of civility would be in effect. But he was ready to be contradicted as well. He'd learned his lesson well at Camp Van Dorn. He kept a well-oiled Buck folding knife strapped to his ankle.

The two found a corner table. Clay noted there were two other blacks in the hall. These two he guessed were from the Islands, and they were eating with some other whites at a table near the exit. Coincidence? Or foresight just in case some foolishness, as his mother would say, broke out? Clay decided he should relax, and put his luggage down.

He and Leeds got some food, beef stew with large hunks of under-cooked potatoes plopped into the broth. Clay was aware of the bug-eyed stare the two were getting from the plane's pilot. No doubt he'd be having a stern talk with his co-pilot about the dangers of race mixing later. The two ate and talked about their lives before the war, and their plans afterward. Clay actually said little about himself, encouraging the eager lieutenant to do the jawing.

"I think it's going to be the wave of the future, Madison." Leeds tore off a hunk of rye bread and dipped it into his stew. "When the war is over, and all these GIs return home, they're going to want homes with detached garages and nine-to-five jobs. They'll pull little Suzie off the assembly line and marry her, and raise their children." He ate his soaked bread. "And then they'll want to rest."

"Not go to the movies or bowling?"

"Sure, sure they'll want to do that too. But I'm telling you, these units my fiancé's brother has in mind will be the cat's pajama's."

"A radio, a record player and the television gizmo built all together in one big box?"

"Yep," Leeds said with conviction. "You don't have everything spread out all over the living room, taking up sitting space and all that. This way it's nice and neat, and would be where the old Philco used to be."

"What would people watch on this television?"

Leeds was momentarily perplexed but then answered. "Newsreels about our exploits in the war."

Both men laughed and drank their coffee. Later, a Captain Orville of the RAF introduced himself to Clay and got him situated. The Quonset was a storehouse, but had several bunks and footlockers in it for sleeping use.

"My orders were to separate you from the general populace, sergeant," Orville said in his crisp accent. "Not, I might add as a matter of segregation, but having to do with you not in any way compromising your operation. Mums the word and all that, right?"

"It would seem." Clay stuck his bags under the bunk. There was an overhead light with a tin cowl, and a short stack of pulp magazines on the bed. "I'll be fine, captain."

"Your pilot will contact you directly." Orville looked as if an exotic taste landed on his tongue. "Very interesting, very interesting indeed," he said, more to himself than to the other man.

Clay wasn't sure what he was getting at and the captain didn't elaborate. He saluted as did Clay.

Going through his reading material, Clay was reminded when he heard Orville's lilt of a chap he soldiered with in Spain fighting Franco's Nacionalistas. This man had been a member of the British Communist Party. Yet unlike some of the Americans he'd known in the Party state side, this Joe wasn't long winded and self-righteous. He was a warm, humorous man who believed in fighting for a world without barriers. That man, McAlister, lay dying after a particularly wrenching engagement, his intestines giving off precious body heat that vaporized around Clay's face. They had to leave him where he fell, near the Ebro River as the faschiste advanced.

"Carry on, comrade," McAllister had told him and quite this life.

And Clay was trying to keep that promise. After a while, he was absorbed in a Doc Savage story, one about a scientist who devised a way to decapitate people yet keep them alive as mindless slaves. He knew that sleep was not going to be easy. It was the naps he'd taken coming over and the time difference. His body was fighting his brain, which was trying to command it to shut down for its own good. Somewhere around one in the morning, he finally was overtaken by slumber.

Clay came fully awake, his knife open and in his hand at the creak of the door's hinges. He'd purposefully chosen a bunk set back from the door in case there was an attack. Artificial light backlit a lone form in the doorway. Clay was already on his feet, advancing.

"Whoa, the figure said, "I'm on your side, always have been."

"Step closer," Clay ordered.

"Sure, man of bronze." The woman stepped in close. She smiled up at the figuring looming over him. "You haven't forgotten me that quick, have you?"

"Janet," Clay breathed huskily.

The sturdily built black woman with short curly hair winked at him, and put her arms around his thick neck. She was about medium height, her breasts on the small size for Clay's tastes. Her hips were wide, her legs heavy like that of a well-conditioned mare. But it wasn't Janet Bragg's body that sent men lusting after her. She was funny and brave, and was at home in an afterhours joint on Amsterdam Avenue or behind the controls of a Ford Tri-Motor.

"Long time, Clay." She kissed him, then playfully bit his lip as their faces parted.

"What the hell are you?" Clay began, "I'll be damned, you're my transportation to Egypt?"

"Thas' right boss, I sho is." She rolled her eyes in an imitation of a shuck and jive red cap a la Mantan Morland.

Clay checked his watch. "It's only a quarter to four."

"Now you getting the hint."

Clay propped one of the footlockers under the knob to secure the door.

"For a second there, I was worried one too many shells had gone off near that big head of yours." Bragg sat on Clay's bunk, working her calve-length boots off.

"Let me get that for you, madam." Clay bent down, and she extended her leg. His hand massaged the back of her calve, and she leaned back, enjoying the attention.

"You're a pretty smooth customer, aren't you?"

46

"Only when I see you, and that ain't to damned often." He plucked her boot off, cognizant that romance was fine, but the clock was against them – business was business. Clay leaned his long body across the cot and the woman he'd trusted his life to in the past.

"Let's not be hasty," She kissed him forcefully, her tongue searching for his. "You know I like to ease back on that stick nice and steady, ol' pardner. Lessin' the ship stall out on me."

"That's never happened." He pushed down on her, their legs intertwining like rope.

"Oh, I've never known you to boast," she snickered. "Getting a little long in the tooth, huh?"

"My days may be getting shorter," he rasped, "but I still have the fire, Janet. Ever since that day you banked that DeHaviland out of the sun, and strafed Mussolini's troops.

"Everything is combat with you, isn't it, Clay? Blood and honor."

He held her face in his knotted fingers, their eyes examining each other. "Sometimes I just don't know. It's like sometimes I've been here before, yet I always come back."

"Enough with the philosophizing, professor." She put her arms around his neck again.

"There you go." They kissed again and soon made love underneath the rough covers of the confining bunk. They got so carried away, the couple wound up on the floor. Bragg was on her knees, bent forward and gripping the side of the bunk, Clay inserting himself behind her. He nibbled on her back as she whispered his name.

Later a cooling Bragg lay on the cot, Clay sitting on the edge, breathing hard. "Goddamn. Maybe you do have a right to crow," she whispered.

"It's you that brings the beast out in me." He thumped his chest with his fist and got up. Clay indicated for her to get up too. He then draped the spotted sheet on the bunk. "Sorry, m'lady, but it is only meager accommodations I can offer you today."

"We've done it in a trench, with mortars going off, Clay. By comparison, this is the Ritz." She stood naked before him, her earthy body arousing him all over once more.

"Come here." Clay laid down.

"It's almost time."

"I know, I only want to hold you once more, close so I can hear your heart."

She put her head back and laughed softly. "You don't let that guard down often, do you, Clay?"

"Never." He held out his hand and she took it. They snuggled, Clay drawing the army blanket up around her shoulders. Two minutes past five they reluctantly got dressed and went out to the airfield.

"That's the plane?"

"A beauty, isn't she? A Vindicator, more or less. And they stuck a Brewster Buccaneer 1,600 horsepower engine in it. It's faster than the Kraut's Stukas."

Wheeled out for takeoff from the previously padlocked hanger was the sleek attack plane, silver-blue in the overcast light. The dihedral slant of the wings began about one third of the way back from the fuselage. Clay estimated the plane was about thirty-five feet long, the wing span maybe forty feet. Compact and efficient looking, there were no markings on it whatsoever.

"Everybody's going to be shooting at us if we're seen," Clay fretted. "We're a plane without a country."

Bragg slapped him on the back. "You're missing the point, Smilin' Jack. What the hell is a German flyboy gonna make of two smokes in a plane? And a woman at the controls of that plane on nobody's registry?"

"What, that's supposed to give us the element of surprise?"

Bragg didn't answer. She'd already walked off to do some last minute checks of the plane. At 0517 hundred hours, man and woman were air born, Clay riding in the co-pilot seat situated some five feet behind the aviatrix. She had the canopy pulled back, the wet wind making their nostrils flare as the powerful machine climbed toward its cruising altitude.

"So how the hell did Snow get you in on this?" Clay asked. Bragg took the plane in a semi-circle and arced the hybrid machine eastward.

"That little matter of running guns to your pal, the emperor. Seems I was supposed to have a few licenses and permits in order to do so." She laughed, each knowing she would have supplied the arms to Haile Selassie, the leader of Ethiopia and his doomed fight against Mussolini's incursions no matter what the obstacles.

"So now I have to work off errands for Uncle Sam to pay for my sins. That or they'll be building me a woman's wing at Leavenworth."

"That son-of-a-bitch knows too much about colored folks' business," Clay declared, venom in his voice.

She glanced back at him but didn't say anything. They flew on.

Clay stared at the control panel over her shoulder. "Where the hell's the radio?"

"That's what I like about you, honey, always on the mark."

"No fooling, Janet. You mean we're up here with no way to get help if something goes wrong?"

"Hey, that's insulting."

"Now..."

Bragg said, "That's your Colonel Snow. Radio transmissions can be traced, lover boy, you know that. As far as our country or anybody else, we're just two spades out for a romp."

"Yeah, and I bet Snow will have it arranged that if we're shot down, the plane will come up stolen."

"Good thing we got parachutes, ain't it?"

"Shit," Clay enunciated.

She asked, "You still remember how to use one?"

"Don't worry, I will when I have to."

Bragg cracked up again. "You're a brick." She pulled back on the controls and the plane effortlessly roared forward like a rock out of a slingshot. The Vindicator went through a hanging of clouds rippled with oranges, under lit by the rising sun. She got above the mass and leveled the plane off. Clay was suddenly aware that his lungs felt pinched, the air getting thinner. He put his oxygen mask to his mouth and took in several deep gulfs. Bragg was unaffected, as if she were indeed part hawk as she'd proclaimed more than once to him.

"What about our range?" Clay wondered. "Where do we set down for re-fueling?"

"Don't worry, we got an extra fuel tank under that iron firm backside of yours."

"But that's not enough."

"You think too much, brother Clay. I got that covered. And we got this." Her thumb flipped the top if the control stick, revealing the gun button.

"I didn't see ports for the fifty calibers in the wings," Clay said.

"There's little plates, the barrels of the machine guns slide in and out."

"Devious."

"I wouldn't have it any other way."

"You're tougher than a west Texas boot, baby."

"Ain't I?" she smiled.

The duo went on, the day stretching out before them. In the distance, the thundering of ack-ack guns cut the silence, though neither saw any plumes or flashes. Their journey continued on. Clay could tell from the position of the sun that Bragg was heading them on a southwest course that would take them over Spain.

"Don't tell me we're going to be crossing the Axis supply lines?"

"That's not my plan, gate. We're going to swing east again, do some wiggle and waggle, and set down on one of those Greek Islands you always see on a picture post cards at the Walgreen's. It's a stronghold of guerrilla forces, including a few of our mates from the old days."

"Yeah, I hear the partisans have been really giving it to the German's Army Group E. But I understand too, there are already rumblings between the ELAS and the EDES in exile in Cairo."

"Naturally the goddamn Brits have been sneaking in their agents through their Special Operations Executive to back up the government EDES. There's bad feelings festering, Clay. Old debts are getting mixed in with hardened political lines. People who've been united against a common enemy are starting to sharpen their knives to plunge into their cousin's ribs."

"And they say we're like crabs in a barrel," Clay cracked, trying to sound funny.

"At least they got something to fight for. Black folks keep chasing a dream of justice, Clay. But land and freedom, those are real."

"Now who's a philosopher?"

"Yeah, yeah," she said.

And so it went until Bragg banked the plane through another set of clouds and a string of islands, more atolls than anything, came into view.

"We're near Crete, aren't we?"

"Yep," she said tersely, taking the plane lower.

The Germans, though thinly spread in occupied Greece, given their need to maintain a strong presence in Russia, maintained airstrips on the north coast of the big island and no doubt scanned the skies regularly for unwelcome visitors. The Vindicator's engine wound down and Bragg aimed the aircraft toward a particular mass. She swooped over one of the small islands, Milos, that Clay recognized.

"I hope they're expecting us."

"Me too," she answered.

He couldn't tell if she was kidding or not. The plane descended and for a moment, it looked as if she were heading them straight for the side of a low mountain range.

"Ah, Janet."

Bragg bore down and the usually composed Clay could feel his upper teeth grinding into his lower lip. The plane veered upward and vaulted over the mountain and it was if they'd flown into a storybook illustration. There was a fulmination of greens and browns and it was like a lost valley in one of the pulps he'd been reading. The plane leveled then resumed its descent. She was preparing to land.

"Say, Janet, where's the airstrip?"

"Around here some where."

And then it appeared. From their height, the gap between a thick parallel stand of drooping trees was not evident. But as the plane got closer, the spacing became more pronounced. A roadway obviously cleared and maintained by human hands, appeared and was the apparent destination of the plane. It dead-ended at the mountain.

"Is that going to be long enough?"

Bragg snorted. "Isn't that what I asked you last night? Now hush, you don't want me to miss." She cut the engine way back and Clay assumed it was going to stall out. Maybe that was her scheme, to dead stick the plane and glide to the ground. But the engine held, the propeller sputtering from being starved for fuel. Branches broke off against the canopy's safety glass and disturbed birds launched themselves into flight. The Vindicator dropped suddenly; Clay's stomach feeling like it was dividing in two.

But Bragg knew what she was doing and it was if the plane were on guide wires as it neither drifted too much to the left nor right as it dropped onto the rough path. They bumped along, the backwash of the prop sending dust, rocks and small lizards all about. The mountain in front of them was starting to fill too much of Clay's vision for his comfort. But he'd be damned if he'd admit any more trepidation to the woman. The plane suddenly wrenched to one side and screeched to a halt, one of the wings slicing into a sickly olive tree. They came to a halt mere yards from the rock face.

"Need to pee?" She slid back the canopy, and unlimbered herself from her harness.

"I'm fine," he lied, his bladder trembling. Clay also unbuckled. There was a sound of dry leaves crunching and he looked over. From among the trees stepped several men and two women. Each of them either carried bolt-action rifles or Czech machine guns, grease guns they were called because of their round bodies. The guerrillas were dressed in civilian clothes that were mixed with coats recycled from the crushed Greek First Army. One face beamed up at him, and it took Clay a few moments to recognize the features. This man was more grizzled and weathered since last he'd seen him.

"Constantine," the tall man boomed, glad to be standing once more. He stepped out onto the wing and then onto the ground.

"Captain Chicago," the other man chortled, as if announcing a radio

51

show.

The two hugged and laughed. "So you've made your way into yet another war," Clay said.

"As have you."

Bragg was on the wing and one of the other men held out a hand to help her down. She ignored the gesture and easily jumped to the ground.

"Mademoiselle Bragg. Still the most beautiful woman I know who can fly or kill with the best of them." Constantine Maydorakas clicked his heels and bowed slightly as if at a cotillion.

"I need a drink." She clapped him on the shoulder and they also hugged.

"We have wine, bread, some dried figs and K and C-rations. The latter two thanks to a air drop from one of your Liberator Express planes on its way to Alexandria." Maydorakas led the new arrivals back through the trees. In his Greek accent he'd ordered the plane rolled back and hidden with loose tree limbs from view overhead.

Clay and Bragg followed their friend and his freedom fighters into an area set back near the low mountains. There were numerous tents and several more personnel were about. Maydorakas took them to a three-legged table propped against an outcropping.

"Help me with the goods," he asked Clay. He went into a nearby tent and the other man followed. Inside a number of crates were piled up, and there was ersatz spread around. Many of the wooden boxes were marked with the familiar stenciled red cross. Maydorakas pointed at one of the crates. "The lid is loose, the food is in there."

Clay did as directed and fetched some of the K-rations. He held them in one large hand against his chest. From a corner, his friend plucked loose a bottle among others. He grinned and tossed it to Clay who caught it effortlessly.

"From the Rhineland," he announced, translating the label from its native German.

"Booty from an encounter with a Nazi skiff," Maydorakas said. "Stuff included frankfurters and beans, and cans of ham and eggs too."

"What, no chitlins?" Clay joked.

"Maybe when the black man is accepted into this war, my friend." Maydorakas clapped him on the back and they rejoined the others.

Food and conversation flowed from English to Greek while some of the freedom fighters remained on guard duty near the makeshift landing strip.

"So has Uncle Joe been sending you anything more than copies of his glorious speeches?" Clay spread some bullion paste on to a hunk of baguette.

Maydorakas tossed a tin of tooth powder to one of the men. The light abrasive was used to clean out the barrels of the rifles. A functioning weapon was much more important than hygiene in war. "For my money," the resistance leader began, "General Karpov would be much better for the proletarian paradise were he to lead Russia after the war." Maydorakas was leaning against a eucalyptus tree and pried the lid off a can of with his knife.

Clay chewed and swallowed. "The hero of the defense of Stalingrad will be lucky to get a mention in the official version when this is all over."

"Soviet or your American history?" Maydorakas posed

"On that we don't have an argument," Clay agreed, "The sacrifice and the courage of the Russian people and army probably isn't going to be on the lips of a lot of school kids back home. It ain't like the newsreels play up just how important the allied victory has been for the Soviets to win on the winter front."

One of the women asked Maydorakas something in Greek, and he spoke to her briefly.

"You know the only reason he asks is because we don't want to see you hung out to dry, Constantine." Bragg sipped some of her wine. "Right now everything is lovey-dovey between the west and east against Hirohito and Hitler. But none of us believe a couple of Hollywood movies about how great the Russian peasants are is really the sign that this pact will last."

One of the other resistance fighters, who understood some English, spoke in Greek to the others, explaining what Bragg had said.

Maydorakas added in English, "I know, Janet. Winston Churchill in particular has long regarded Greece as the private beach of the British. The members of our political wing, the EAM, have been hearing the rumblings among the Union Jacks about returning Greece to the old ways." He stood. "But we have to fight this fight first."

"So will that blood thirsty idiot Stalin help you?" Clay asked as Maydorakas went back in the tent for more wine. "If only to spread his influence."

"He's no Lenin," one of the other soldiers said.

"When this horror is at an end," Maydorakas began, stepping back out, "it will be a race between the capitalists and Bolsheviks for the spoils and for territory.

"All the more reason why that son-of-a-bitch can't abandon you,"

Bragg emphasized.

"If we were loyal proletarians, maybe." He handed a fresh bottle to one of his fellows and another to Clay. "But Bulgaria and Yugoslavia and us, I'm afraid, are too independent minded in our ideas of a worker state to appeal to the "Man of steel" in Moscow. I actually think one should hear from what unions and social groups have to say."

"But you know some of these Greek Nazi quislings will invariably be used by the west to move against you if it comes to that," Clay observed.

"I also think we should line those self-serving traitors up now, and either imprison them or shoot them," Maydorakas added. "But then, I'd be accused of Stalinism, wouldn't I?"

Bragg smiled and Clay poured his friend more wine. There was more drinking and several more political strategies were discussed and analyzed, some discarded and others modified. They also rolled out barrels of aviation fuel from a secreted cache in a cave that included more supplies, a short wave and a partially assembled Russian Katushya rocket launcher.

"For bringing down the iron buzzards," Maydorakas said, kicking at a steel strut of the launcher.

Bragg's plane was tanked up and wheeled into position. The moon was a silver dirk in the frigid, dry sky as the two prepared for take-off.

"When I see you again, we'll have giros and rice sitting in front of the Acropolis, the free flag of a true democratic Greece waving overhead."

He didn't have the gumption to tell his friend he'd given up hoping for the best years ago. For now, it was enough to survive. "I'll see you in the funny papers, Constantine." The two embraced and both hoped it wouldn't be the last they'd see each other. That the capriciousness of war and the duplicitous nature of transient allies wouldn't consume them like a runaway fire.

Bragg and Maydorakas also said their goodbyes. Soon the pair were winging through the dark blanket shrouding the Mediterranean.

"Too many battles on too many fronts, Janet." Clay tried to relax in his seat. But unease had gripped him, and wouldn't be solved by shifting in his seat.

"I know," she banked the plane north. "What do we have to do so our friends win like in the serials?"

"Be more ruthless than our enemies," he said sincerely. Clay wasn't sure he completely believed his words, but he was willing to seriously entertain the idea. "Aren't we heading in the wrong direction for Egypt?"

"Just in case the ratzis are patrolling," she answered. "This way if we're spotted, they'll think, maybe, we've been flying over and not pin point where we took off. I'll circle back around, and come in from the east"

"Smart and a fine brown frame," he said joyfully. "I sometimes wish things had been different for us, Janet." She didn't say anything and he figured he'd gone too far, getting under her skin. Bragg wasn't much on romance or making like a housewife in some cramped apartment. The same desire that had given her the spine to perceiver despite all manner of shit from whites who sabotaged her training planes and tests, was the same drive that kept her foot loose. She was her own woman, and would not be confined by conventionalities.

The "Yes," came so softly from her, Clay at first assumed it was a trick of the whining engine his mind was playing on him.

"But we just weren't cut out for that kind of life, Clay. Now after all this, I can't tell you if it chose us or we simply carved it out of nothing," she continued, her voice firmer in its gravity. "But this is what has turned out for us. And there's no getting that chicken back in the coop, is there?"

"No, baby, there isn't" His big hand reached out in the dimness of the cockpit and he could feel her hand, reaching back for his. Their fingertips touched, and in that briefest of a diaphanous moment, Clay was at peace.

The flight hummed along, the smoothness of Bragg's handling and the dreamy quality of the darkness they sped through had a calming effect on him. It was if he'd been on this journey for a very long time, its purpose and goals lost in the murkiness of time and distance.

"We've got company."

Bragg's statement brought him fully aware, his pulse rate stepping up. Now he heard the other motor too. Its rpms in a lower register but the throatiness of the new arrival suggested much in the way of reserve power.

"A Messerschmitt." The discernable snick of her thumb flipping the head of her stick open was like breaking ice.

Clay saw glints of the opposing aircraft as it climbed, going at an up angle from where their plane was.

"The Messer's getting another look to make sure." Bragg's voice tight as piano wire. "The unmarked bit's got him stymied."

He knew better than to talk and disrupt her concentration. He knew from previous experiences that Bragg was having this conversation with herself. This was zero hour and she needed to be in rhythm with her machine.

"Come on, goddammit, come on." The modified Vindicator throttled up and into a looping right as the Messerschmitt turned, its guns blaring. The synchronized flashes illuminated the ship's underbelly as if it were a phantom conveyance that only materialized when dealing death.

Clay's jaw clamped with fear and the excitement of the confrontation, his chest rising and falling in a steady pace matching the Messerchmidt's blazing 20mm maschinengewehrs. He leaned forward, his fingers gripping each side of Brag's seat as if he were a teenager again, seeing Frankenstein up there on the Dakota's screen from the colored section in the balcony. He always wished the monster would rip the heads off those villagers seeking to destroy him.

Her own 50-calibers seared the space between the two planes, causing the German airman to break off sharply. But not before the unmistakable ping-ping of bullets finding purchase in alloy echoed across to them. "The hidden wing guns suckered him." Bragg's lips were drawn back against her teeth in a skull's grin. Rather than leap forward, she eased back on the controls and sent the plane downward into the black.

"Make him chase us," she declared. The Messerchmidt did as she predicted, and Clay looked around to see the craft gaining on them, his guns clattering.

Clay heard that telltale sound again and worried that whatever the hell Bragg was trying to do, they'd be spiraling into the deep sea before she could pull it off. There was another burst from the Messerchmidt but Bragg had been anticipating this. The Vindicator's shell shuddered as the plane suddenly jerked and tore into a vicious turn that sent it on its side, like a car taking a curb very fast on two wheels.

He braced for the inevitable when Bragg soared the plane around and the Messerchmidt's belly was exposed to her guns. Without mercy or hesitation, she let lose with a volley that ripped into the vulnerable plane. The bullets ignited the fuel tank and the Third Reich's airplane and pilot were consumed in an incandescent burst of reds and yellows. The plane scraps plummeted like seeds spewed from a giant's mouth.

"That was something," Clay said by way of understatement.

She rubbed the edge of her palm against her cool forehead. "I'm sure glad that trick worked. Herbert taught me that one, but this is the first time I've ever had to actually try it."

She referred to Herbert Fauntleroy Julian, the Black Eagle. He was the first Negro aviator, barnstormer and diplomat-without-portfolio. Julian had been in command of Salasie's meager air force when Clay and

Bragg had fought against Mussolini in Ethiopia.

"Yeah, I," Clay began but stopped when the now familiar drone of a Messerchmidt greeted their ears once again.

"Two man patrol, and he's on us, Clay." Bragg attacked the controls with fervor, trying to get the bird to vault upward even as the enemy swooped down on them.

Oddly, Clay wondered where the hell this second plane had been when his countryman was getting shot up. That was how his mind worked, calm and methodical, even as the Messerchmidt's twin machine guns cut into the Vindicator's fuselage and canopy.

CHAPTER SIX

August 1944 – Belgium

Giabretto awoke and like a somnambulant, made his way to the latrine to relive himself. He then started back across the compound, idly scratching his belly. He stopped to stretch as a large open truck made its way along what the men had affectionately named Broadway, the main artery of their base camp.

Removable sides had fenced in the flatbed's cargo area. It was an old Indiana model with bad springs and it bounced along fiercely. The headlights were cat-eyed, that is taped so as only to allow a slit of light out of each lens to lessen being spotted overhead.

Riding in the back were black soldiers. Despite the urgent dismay worming its way through Giabretto, he couldn't make his legs run. He stood planted as the truck loped past. Each face of the human cargo were drawn and alert. Each man looked around suspiciously, staring everywhere and especially at the corners of buildings and tents. It was as if they were POWs, and being paraded before the enemy on their way to internment camps. As if they weren't wearing the uniform of their country, and in the company of fellow Americans.

Rooted on his leaden feet, he saw a profile in the ashen light up on that truck's platform that he'd hoped not to see ever again. It was Silas Mayhew. And he knew that Giabretto was an act, that he wasn't white. Fortunately, Mayhew, like the others, was too consumed in looking everywhere to particularly notice the crooner.

Giabretto watched the rear of the truck recede, but not too much. It slowed, then turned at the row of tents that'd been pitched in the last two days. When some of the company had been ordered to do so, none of their commanders had told them why or offered explanations. But he did recall some of the C.O.s looked vexed about the whole matter. And each of them had their mouths pressed firmly into place as if drawn by Milton Caniff.

"Yep, McCloy's goddamn memo has been put into effect," a voice suddenly proclaimed at his side.

Crazily, Giabretto conjured that the speaker was a boastful Walter

White, head of the NAACP, and he'd suddenly appeared in occupied Belgium, his bony pale hand on his shoulder. He blinked and it was Sergeant Robeson.

"Who?" he managed.

"John McCloy, head of the War Department's Committee of Negro Troop Policy," Robeson explained. "Back in March, he sent a note to Secretary of War Stinson going on about how the colored boys have to be activated as combat troops as soon as possible." Robeson regarded Giabretto as if appraising him for a new suit. "Don't tell me you haven't been keeping up on this, gate?"

Giabretto was too terrified to respond. He mumbled unintelligibly and wandered back to the barracks. The sly look on Robeson's face stayed with him, and he trembled with the effort to turn around and go beat that expression off the man's face. He got back inside and shambled to his bunk. He was in his skivvies and he estimated how long it would take him to get dressed, throw a few items into his duffle, and bolt out of there.

He smiled crookedly at the idea. Where would he go? Italy? He held his hand up. Limbering up for his solo on the piano, he danced the fingers of the hand in front of his face, boring in on them. How lightly golden they shined, how long and slender ending in pinkish fingernails they were.

What was just a different kind of gig he was playing, okay?

Giabretto lowered his fingers tinkling the invisible eighty-eights. What if he went AWOL? Maybe he could stay here in Belgium, hide out in the countryside with the help of a wiling and plump mademoiselle? Pass himself off as a frog or Belgumite or whatever the fuck these cats called themselves around here. Of course the fact he didn't speak a lick of French might be a handicap, but not for long. He was good at picking up the cues, at blending into his surroundings. Too goddamn bad the chameleon was in danger of discovery.

Well, he resolved, his extended engagement wasn't closed due to circumstances just yet. The colored troops would be segregated as far as their living conditions. The commander, Major Foster, was a cornpone Confederate from Chattanooga. Giabretto had no fears that this creaking Johnny Reb had suddenly awaken one night to the virtues of Negro soldierhood. That somehow the mountains upon mountains of articles, radio shows soap box oratory and pamphlets put out by black leaders on the justification of sending jigs into harm's way had suddenly made a dent in his wooly skull.

Like many of his ilk, Foster sincerely believed that Negroes, at best, functioned at 60 percent of your average white man's intelligence. Was it any wonder, he reminded himself as he formulated his plan, that several bases had seen rioting given the intractability of ofay fixations. And was it also any wonder there wouldn't be more blood spilled in the name of racial ignorance over here, by the allies and the axis, before this business was through?

Giabretto got dressed. The rest of the squad was stirring and he wanted to sneak out like a chicken thief.

"What's up?" Grady Langford piped up, yawning and scratching at the sides of his head with stubby fingers as he sat up.

"You hear that truck a few minutes ago?" He hated doing this, but he was in a tight spot.

"Yeah, so?" Langford was a light sleeper. He swung his legs over the side of his bunk, and rubbed the gauze wrapped over his wound. He'd been lucky and the German's bullet had passed cleanly through the fleshy part.

In his best Amos n' Andy he said, "The coon squad done jitterbugged in, Mr. Bones."

Langford's body stiffened. "Shit," he drew out in a hiss like steam out of a busted radiator pipe. "How many?"

He felt queasy but pressed on. "Truck load, including a snowball at the wheel."

"Shit," Langford swore again as if that word summed up the entirety of the situation. "We better tell the squad."

"Look, I was just on my way to talk with Foster about this."

"Shouldn't we get a couple more of us to go with you?" Langford said. "But there ain't much we can do, Gil. 'Cept make sure them shines stay on their side of camp."

"What about mess, what about where we play cards away from the officers?"

"Yeah, yeah," Langford replied, working a kink out of his neck. "We gotta make sure there's two shifts for chow, sumptin' like that."

"And what if some of them have to do KP duty? You want a spade cooking your food, and peeling your potatoes." Giabretto was sickened to play so much to the man's irrationality, but he had to get out of there. If he could keep him complaining about the Negro problem, then all the better for him to skirt away. He tried mightily not to conjure up his grandfather, shaking his head in contempt and embarrassment.

"Look," he said in the gap of words from the other man who was attempting to absorb this news. "You talk to the others and I'll see what kind of mood Foster is in."

"Yeah," Langford wagged his head in agreement. "He might be having one of his Old Granddad mornings."

"Be back in a jiffy," Giabretto lied some more. And he was gone out the rear and making a beeline for Lieutenant O'Connor's tent. As he did, he remembered reading an article in the colored magazine, We Also Serve, about the Red Ball Express. The squad had been formed out of the 25th Regiment service unit. This was a trucking ordinance unit made up of a majority of blacks and their reputation was outstanding, even among the whites.

The hotshots with the Express were known to drive thirty, forty miles an hour at night, over all kinds of terrain and conditions, with those damned blackout lights. Of course no matter how good they did their jobs here, Giabretto reflected, it wouldn't mean squat back home. How many boots was some cross-country outfit going to hire to haul their rigs? The Red Ballers could be ferrying lit dynamite from here to Berlin, not dropping one stick, and the white bosses, wouldn't even clap them on the back for a job well done.

"Ah, Lieutenant, it's PFC Giabretto, sir." He stood at the entrance to the tent, a double-sized number to accommodate a map table. It should be in a separate designated command center, but space was a premium. "Could I have a minute?"

"Come on," he answered from within.

Giabretto entered to find the young Virginia Military Academy graduate shaving. He was in his khakis and a ribbed undershirt. The lieutenant was a good-sized man, a wide expanse of chest and shoulders that had served him well as a college halfback. He had a fragment of a mirror nailed to one of the tent poles and was using water in an empty toothpaste tin. Except for a movie Giabretto saw with Brian Donlevy, nobody really used water inside their helmet. That was a sure way to have mold creeping around your head.

"What's on your mind, private?" O'Connor's cheeks were baby bottom pink, his whiskers wispy and indistinct like moss. It seemed to Giabretto the man could let his bread grow a week and no one would notice. And what the hell did it matter whether you were neat like you were going to the office or a nightclub anyway? It didn't make any difference when the Mauser's bullet tore half your face off.

"I want to volunteer for that spotter job, Lieutenant O'Connor."

The youngish man, he couldn't be more than two years older than Giabretto, worked his Schick at a tough spot on his chin. It seemed to Giabretto he'd flay the area raw if he wasn't careful. He rinsed out his razor and wiped at the residue of lather on his face. "Why are you so eager for the assignment, Giabretto? You get along well with your squad members?"

"I do sir, I get along fine."

O'Connor looked around and Giabretto handed him his shirt which had been draped on the man's cot. "Thanks," he said, slipping it on. "Frankly I had a couple of others in mind. Malcontents in fact."

"But I want the gig, I mean the job sir."

"That's right, you were some kind of singer before the war." He shook a finger at the man, remembering something from civilian life. "My girl's sister said you were dreamier than that skinny little guy with the bow tie, what's his name?"

"Sinatra."

"Yeah," he chuckled. "Lizzy, that's the sister, says you got the boxer's build of that other spaghetti bender, Martino or Martini I think it is. Personally, I think he's more manly. Anyway she was crazy over this song of yours, My Masquerade." He started to button up his shirt then glanced up, uncomfortable. "Say, I didn't mean anything by that, it's just, well, you know, just a term."

Like porch monkey and dinge. "I understand, sir. About the need for a spotter, Lieutenant?"

O'Connor unbuckled his pants to tuck in his shirt. "Why? It's going to be lonely duty."

"I, ah," he started, with the right amount of emotion he estimated. He'd had a couple of screen tests and remembered the advice of a casting director to let it roll off you slow and natural. "I got some rough news from home yesterday."

There'd been mail call and Giabretto had indeed received two letters. One was from his agent inquiring about a check that had finally come in from Paul Whiteman. The other had been from an older dame he'd gone around with in St. Louis. She was the secretary for a talent scout there, one of those free thinkers, and had been very anatomically explicit in how she planned to celebrate his return from the service. Importantly, her letter was addressed in female script in case O'Connor asked about it later.

"What, your folks?"

"No, not that." He looked at his feet, trying mightily to get what that chick had written out of his head, both of them. He was getting aroused and that would definitely not go along with the story he was laying on the loot. "I know it's not a new story, kind'a pathetic really." He looked up and gave him the hound dog, exactly as he'd been coached in one of the screen tests. Not too much otherwise he'd resent the act.

"A Dear John letter." The lieutenant walked to the tent flap and chucked the grayish water out of the tin.

"That's right, sir. She's not only leaving me, she's already become engaged to some guy, some 4-Fer, working swing with her at Lockheed out in Los Angeles." He guessed the part about the chump not being fit for service would grate on the lieutenant, the product of a father and uncle who attended military academies.

"This wouldn't be because we now have some of the Red Ballers here with us till they get back with their unit?"

This flustered Giabretto momentarily. What was the right answer this white man, who was from Boston, but who'd gone to soldier school in the south, wanted to hear? "Nope," he ventured. "I've sung with colored musicians, sir. Those ol' boys don't bother me and I don't bother them."

O'Connor rubbed a hand on his squarish chin, gauging Giabretto. "You are pretty handy with a rifle, and that might come in handy." Since the report from their patrol on the possible presence of German tanks was raised in the enemy camp, Captain Foster had been going on about confirming that suspicion.

The idea was to plant a lone GI along the main crossroads that led to Malmedy and Bastogne, in a high tree and if the panzers suddenly came rumbling along, alert the base to be prepared to defend or retreat. Either way, the information would be useful to command since it was known the Nazis were running ahead of their supply lines. The Germans were thin on heavy equipment after their defeat in Stalingrad. There shouldn't be anymore than four to seven tanks in this sector according to advanced reports. If there were more, and they were heading to other contested parts of Belgium, the knowledge could well save thousands of GI's lives.

"So you want to be alone?"

"That's right, sir. You got it exactly."

"I'm going to talk to Foster this morning about it anyway. Let's see what he has to say."

He knew better than to push it and simply said, "Okay." He figured the fact he'd asked for the post would go a long way with him. As to Foster, who knew how that blue-blooded redneck decided anything in what was left of his mind? But he couldn't help but add, "Ask anyone, and they'll tell you what a light sleeper I am."

"I got it, Giabretto."

"Right." He stepped out of the tent and into the face of a black sergeant. He was a couple of inches over the singer's height and was wide like the grill of a Hudson. There was gray at his temples but nothing on him looked soft, least of which was his expression. They stood glaring at each other for several blinks, neither man doing much to get out of the way of the other.

"This the Lieutenant's quarters?" His voice was thick with the South. Giabretto automatically pegged it as Arkansas or Georgia. "Sure is." He moved past and the sergeant announced himself as Giabretto went back to the barracks.

"Lieutenant, I'm Pickett, sir."

"I've heard about you, sergeant," the young officer answered.

"Well, it's like this; I want to ensure my men are treated decently."

That was all Giabretto heard as he stepped away quickly and headed back to the barracks.

"We should keep our heads about us, that's what we should do." Weitz, a lankly soldier who was a comic book artist from New York, was saying when he stepped inside.

Waving his hand dismissively, Bassett said, "It figures you'd say that."

"What does that mean?" Knowing perfectly well what he meant but damned if he was going to let it go.

"Now look, it's no good for us to tear at each other," Langford chimed in.

"Oh it's we now." Weitz went back on his heels, hunching his muscular upper arms. He turned his head to the side and barked, "What do you say, Arcardo?"

Arcardo was willowy, moody and had managed to already duck one court martial. "We're supposed to be fighting Otto and Tojo, aren't we?" He got out of his bunk and leaned against the front door. His lidded eyes betrayed nothing, but the men knew he was someone who backed up his words with action. What they didn't know was he had a brother who was badly beaten in June last year in Los Angeles when navy sailors, soldiers and civilian whites descended on East Los Angeles for some 10 days beating up Mexican-Americans and some Negroes wearing zoot suits, often stripping the young pachucos of their attire. Zooters wore long draped coats and pants that ballooned at the hips and tapered at the ankle complimented with wide brimmed hats like that favored by bandleader Cab Calloway.

Ostensibly the servicemen were doing their patriotic duty to rid the city of the Mexican gangster element. There had been a sensational trial the year before the attacks involving Zoot suited members of the 38tth Street gang falsely charged with a murder in what became known as the

Sleepy Lagoon case. Various civil rights groups, and the Communist Party, had come to the defense of the youths.

Arcardo, who once belonged to the 38th Street gang, folded his arms and waited.

"Let's just get dressed and get some chow," Giabretto suggested. "Some of them colored boys don't roll their eyes and mumble. I've heard some tough stories from a few incidents at bases. But the good thing is O'Connor won't let it go by like Foster will."

"But the old crab out ranks him," Langford pointed out.

"Sure, that's right," Weitz said. "But you'd have to count on me and Arcardo not saying anything too."

"Nobody's talking about anything nutty, Weitz," Barney Childs said. "I'm only interested in making sure we keep everything separate, that's all. That's how it is back home, and how it should be here."

Weitz didn't have to strain his imagination to hear what his uncle, the socialist sewing factory organizer, would say. "Don't you think it's awfully funny, Ross, that we're fighting for democracy over here but not back in the States?"

Another man, Williams, jumped into the discussion. "That's not the same thing, Weitz. Negroes got the rights we got, only in their own areas."

This got a response and on it went over their breakfast of powdered eggs and scrapple. Giabretto was glad, since it meant no one was discussing their personal business. The talk quieted down when several of the black soldiers entered and found a spot where they could congregate by themselves after getting their food.

"Aw, hell," Bassett groused. He gobbled down a mouthful of Scrapple.

"Relax," Weitz reminded him. "Seems to me they got as much right to shed blood fighting the fuckin' fascists as any of us."

Langford said loudly, "You think one of them's got the Star of David underneath his shirt?"

"I think," Weitz began, and he pointed with his butter knife. "You like to hear your yap a little too much."

"Maybe you'd like to give me speech lessons?" Langford cocked his head.

"Maybe." Weitz let his tongue show as he rubbed it against the bottom of his front teeth. "You've got all kinds of opinions don't you, Grady? Handed down from one generation to the next I bet."

The other man sat very rigid. "Don't push me, Weitz."

"Say it, Grady, say what you really want to say."

"You two," Giabretto interjected, "let's simmer down. This isn't helping any of us to be fighting amongst ourselves."

"You ain't got to be talking' down to me, Weitz," Langford said. Anger stretching his mouth thin. "I may not be from New York and read like you have, but I know what's right and what's wrong."

"And it's wrong for a Negro to hold up their end in this war, Grady?" Williams calmly folded his toast in half over a spread of eggs and Scrapple and ate heartily.

"I figured you was on my side in this here skirmish, cousin." Langford stared hard at Weitz.

Williams retorted. "I guess they ain't gonna erect a statue of me in Harlem, Grady, but the way I see it, every man that can, should. Period."

With the sides not so sharply drawn, the conversation eventually wound around to the latest dogface cartoon of Bill Mauldin's in the Stars and Stripes. But several times, Weitz and Langford exchanged looks that could be interpreted as challenging or hate. Giabretto pretended he was at ease but his insides were twisted like paper.

He was constantly looking up to see who among the black troops was entering or exiting. If Mayhew before came in, he'd be trapped. Giabretto was squirming like he used to do beetles with his mother's hat pins.

The robust colored sergeant with a head built like it was quarried from limestone strode into the mess. Robeson had come in with him and the two talked and nodded solemnly. It was his own guilty paranoia he knew, but Giabretto was convinced the two must be talking about him. The black noncom shook hands with the white one and went to get his food.

"I wouldn't want to be sharing a bunkhouse with that field hand," Bassett observed.

"You wouldn't know if he'd eat you or stab you," Langford joked viciously.

The men laughed, even Weitz shook his head ruefully. Then the door opened again and Giabretto saw Silas Mayhew step inside.

CHAPTER SEVEN

Corporal Silas Mayhew lit the Lucky Strike with his Zippo and slipped the pack back into the pocket of his fatigues. While he inhaled, he dug the scene. Nothing but a roomful of grays. His pals from the outfit were of course clustered together in one section. He blew out smoke and admired Sergeant Mayhew who heaped the grub on his plate as if it were his mama's cooking. He had to give it to that tough-hided Rattler, it could be raining jerry bombs and he'd be shouting where was his flask.

Not aware of it until then, he was holding onto the Zippo tightly. He gazed at it fondly, wishing he was with the girl that had given him the thing as a going away present. This Zippo was gold finished, not the usual silver-metal veneer. He fooled with the instrument as he picked up his tray. The filigree delicately machined in its surface comforted him.

Mayhew, the cigarette skewered at an angle from his sardonic mouth, sauntered to get his food.

"Lay some hen fruit on me, slip." He wasn't much for jive talk, but figured he'd give the gray boys a show.

The sweaty gap-toothed cook gawked at the newcomer, the eggs dripping off on the end of the spatula.

"Those'll do." Mayhew got the rest of his food and went over to the table with the others. The plan Pickett had laid out was a few at a time of the squad would come in and eat. If any scuffling broke out, the others, some making sure they loitered near the entrance, would signal for the rest and they'd come running.

"Everything's on the level so far, brother Mayhew," Lenny Jones whispered as he went past the taller man.

"Solid."

Jones had finished his breakfast and had left a space for the corporal. He sat next to Sergeant Pickett, and ground out his smoke with his shoe. "What you think, sarge?"

Pickett wiped crumbs and grease from his chin with his blacksmith's hands. "That if our own country men don't kill us, the food they serve up sure as hell will." Belying his complaint, he spooned in more oatmeal. "Look, some of these ofays pretend they ain't never been around no colored folk before, but you and I both know a many of them got suckled at mammy's tit."

"Even a cow can let a baby wolf drink her milk," Mayhew glumly said. "But that cub grows up, sarge. And you know it don't have much in the way of memory." He had some of his food. "But the pack has been thinned, Deacon Mayhew. The white man has found out, once again, that he can bleed and die too." He showed his blunt teeth, grinning at the corporeal. "They need us to be targets for a while now."

Mayhew pushed his tray aside and lit another cigarette. "We been fighting this war way before we got over here, sarge," He observed. "More than half our boys should be flying or manning ships or marching in the infantry. Who knows that better than you, what with the shit you went through over here in World War I?"

If Pickett had a comment, he resisted making it in favor of more oatmeal.

Mayhew blew three concentric smoke rings, watching them float upward to gracefully dissipate as the vapor caressed a bare light bulb. He took in the room again, noting the eyes darting his way. Some of the whites were bold, not averting their gaze in the least when their eyes met. And others gave quick glances at the black men, then pretended to be interested in their food.

One of those who'd suddenly lowered his head caused Mayhew to frown. Now why was that? Why be any more or less concerned with this gray than the other ofays in the room? He tipped his head up to try and see the man over the assortment of the tops of heads, but the man was going out of his way to avoid looking up.

Could be, Mayhew ventured silently, that this fella had been in one of the jazz bands he'd seen after hours at the Apex in Chi or Minton's on west 118th in New York. Mayhew had fist worked as a bartender at Minton's when ex-band leader Teddy Hill took over the place in 1940 before getting the gig at the Cobalt. Just for kicks, Mayhew, decided, he'd find out who this shrinking violet was. Probably some pale face who used to hang out with the boots, smoke some reefer with them, and now was embarrassed to let on he even knew any blacks.

"I'm going for a stroll." He started walking toward the table where the man sat who seemed especially eager not to be seen. And as he got closer, a familiarity gnawed at him.

"Don't be foolish," Pickett rumbled.

"Never." Mayhew walked down an aisle, trying to get a better look at the dark haired object of his curiosity. Of course several whites gave him the bug eye as he walked past, but he was used to their scrutiny. It didn't faze him. Somebody stuck out their leg but he effortlessly sidestepped the crude attempt to trip him.

Nearing the table, that clammy feeling worked its way along his shoulder blades. He knew this guy. The soldier was fidgeting something fierce and Mayhew was going have his answer.

"The latrine ain't this way, boy."

The soldier who filled the passageway may have been as wide as Pickett, but was flabby where the sergeant was defined. And he was that particular hue of pallid white man with the colorless eyes to go along with his bleached features. Behind him, Mayhew heard boots scrambling and the man he'd been heading for took off like a naked woman was calling his name.

But Mayhew caught a good glimpse of him as he escaped. "I'll be horse whipped," he murmured. Then the oakie stepped into his view again. The man scooted out of the mess hall through a swing door that flapped loudly.

"Did you hear me?" The big man repeated himself. Bench legs scraped against the plywood floor and several more whites rose.

Mayhew wasn't about to flinch. Ben Webster coaxed Cottontail out of his sax as his heart kept beat. "Yeah, I got your drift."

The corn husker glowered. "That some of that Harlem jive?"

"Make of it what you will." Pickett eased back a half-step to give his punch more landing power. Some of his squad were coming over. More whites got up and the chatter notched up too. Bodies jostled in the aisle, dark and light faces keen with anticipation.

"Everything was just fine until you shines showed up," a voice blared. The din got louder. Somebody shoved one of the Red Ballers and he upset a tray, knocking it to the floor.

Pickett edged his way to Mayhew and the dust bowler. "What seems to be the problem?"

"I'm lookin' at it."

"You need glasses, or can't you see these stripes on my arm, son." Pickett squared off in front of the other man, Mayhew moving to the side.

"You don't give me no orders," the big private squawked.

"We don't take no orders from jigs," someone else yelled.

Slowly, Pickett said, "I better get a salute or I bring you up for insubordination."

"I don't think so, snowball." He shoved the sergeant.

Pickett hit him hard enough to stagger him. The raw boned noncom then simply followed that with an upper cut that draped the farm boy across trays of food on a table. He lay half on, and half off in a listless spread eagle position.

Time slowed.

Then a fist collided with the side of Mayhew's face, and the fireworks show replaced Webster's drums in his head. He leaped and the rumble was full on. The black soldiers were sorely outnumbered but they were up against it and had to give out better than they got. Sergeant Levi Pickett carried two GIs who'd clambered on his back into a wall, knocking one of them off like a shingle falling from a roof. The second one wrapped his forearms around Pickett' windpipe and his eyes teared up as his air was constricted.

With his steam shovel-like hands, Pickett clawed at the man's arms and his strength was such he pried the goof loose, his triceps trembling with the effort. Pickett then lifted the man over his head like a sack of potatoes, and tossed him into his fellows, bowling a couple over.

Nobody was trading racial insults as the participants were focused on attacking or defending themselves. Mayhew went down under a rain of blows and for an instant he considered what it was going to be like on the other side. But he managed to punch a man in the nut sack and he felt much better, watching the mug double over. This gave him an opening and he crawled under the table, getting his wind back

Crawling, he encountered a pair of legs and latched onto the owner's ankles. The man tipped over, the back of his head barely missing the corner of the table. Mayhew came up swinging and caught one flush on his eye. Dazed, he went wobbly but managed to keep his legs working. If he went down again, he wasn't sure he'd be getting up. The horror of being stomped to death terrified him and simultaneously propelled him on.

Pickett plowed bodies aside as he came to the aid of one of his men who three whites had pinned on a table and were beating. He'd just thrown off the first man when twin rifle shots cracked above the melee.

Lieutenant O'Connor lowered the carbine, holding it at half-mast. "The pillow fight's over, girls." Several white soldiers, including Sergeant Robeson, were standing near him, some with M-1s or brandishing their service .45s.

"They started it," a white soldier complained.

The black soldiers grumbled and Pickett, bleeding from the top of his head, his sleeve torn, stepped forward. "That's a goddamn lie. This private struck me," he pointed at the farm boy, who was sitting on the floor, holding his face in his hands. "I struck him back as is my right."

O'Connor and Robeson exchanged nervous looks. "Until we get this straightened out, I'm restricting you Red Ballers to a specific section, and specific hours in the mess and showers."

"No matter where we go," Mayhew said, "we always got our friend Jim Crow."

A few of the black soldiers chuckled and O'Connor added.

"Just remember, if we had the room, I'd throw all your black asses in the cooler." He jerked the rifle at he doorway. "Let's go, double time."

"Yeah, that's fair," Mayhew grumbled. He rubbed the swelling on his face, glad his bridge work hadn't been damaged.

"You disappointed me, Pickett," O'Connor griped as the big sergeant filed past.

What might have been a smile came and went across the man's mouth. "Sorry, Lieutenant, but I just couldn't disappoint myself. I got some injured, and I figure as an officer and a gentleman, you'll have the medic come to see about 'em."

O'Connor's face reddened while he glared at the man's back as he and another black soldier helped one of their men to his feet. This man winced and he appeared to have a broken arm. "I'll see to it, sergeant," he said quietly.

Outside, Mayhew didn't expect to see the escaped man. No, he couldn't take that chance, Mayhew reasoned, grinning crookedly. Assessing the soreness settling into his jaw, he recalled the last time he'd seen Giabretto. A night spot, that's where it was.

"It's on me, man. Least I can do for you." Mayhew put ice in a tumbler and poured some smoky-colored whiskey.

"Thanks." The singer sat at the bar of the Cobalt Room, his voice tired, his shoulders sagging. It was well past three in the morning, and only these two and the palsy janitor Cooper remained. He was asleep in the storeroom and Mayhew would wake him to finish locking up the club.

Giabretto enjoyed his drink and touched the glass to his brow.

"Three sets," Mayhew said, eyeing the crooner. He'd poured himself a beer. "You believe in giving them their money's worth."

Giabretto spread his arms wide. "Want to have them hold onto something for me when I get back. I go in start of next month and plan to throw one hell of a going away night."

Mayhew shook his head. "More power to you."

They clinked bottle to glass. "Just be careful."

"Don't you worry about that, Silas; I'm not going to let one of those goosesteppers creep up on me."

Mayhew fooled with something below the bar. "They're not the only ones you're gonna have to be hep about." He turned to busy himself arranging bottles.

Giabretto's features went slack. "What do you mean?"

Mayhew stared at him full on. "You know."

"Know what?"

"That you're passin'. But listen," he added, "it means nothing to me. This world is hard on colored folks, man. So if you can slip by, well, what's it to me or anybody else?"

"I," Giabretto began, "I don't know what you're talking about, Silas. Passing for what? Italian?"

"That's good," Mayhew set his beer down. "Most people don't know, Gil, so don't go getting' all excited. You got them buffaloed."

"I still don't," Giabretto stammered.

"I've watched you operate on the dames when they buy you drinks and wink and get all mushy with you here at the bar," Mayhew said. "I wasn't trying to spy or anything like that, but you can't help but notice the kind of women you get eating out of your hand. And the lines you use, and reuse."

Giabretto wasn't interested in compliments. "What are you saying, Silas?"

"See," the bartender said, "there you go."

His hand closed tightly over the rim of his glass. "I don't get you."

Mayhew pointed at his ear. "I can't help but hear it. I guess when you get excited or angry or just not concentrating on it if you're thinking about what you and some broad are going to be doing when you leave."

"Silas," he burst out, not worrying if he woke the janitor or not.

"The black comes out in you, Gil. That baritone of yours makes them girls cream. But, I don't know, maybe because you sound like a fella I knew back home or maybe once or twice I, I don't know, saw the way you looked at me when you caught me looking at you in the mirror." He shrugged. "Or how you avoided them Italians from that Free Italy society or what ever it was we had in here one night. But like I said, you be careful around them ofays, Gil. No matter whose uniform they're wearing. Make sure you don't do anything to let your self slip."

Giabretto remained fixed on Mayhew but also needed his drink. He downed the rest of the booze. The crooner got off the stool and said, "That's crazy, man. You must be on hop or something. All you Negroes do that stuff. My mother and father are both from the old country."

Mayhew stacked his gasses. "Would that be Alabama or Louisiana?"

Giabretto picked up the glass and Mayhew instinctively put up his arm. But he got control of himself and set it back down just so. Giabretto smoothed his loosened tie, did an about face, and walked out of the Cobalt Room for good.

Life sure was a funny thing Mayhew remarked to himself while he felt the tenderness of his jaw. Yeah, Giabretto was going to stay white and all right. The corporal lit another Lucky Strike. What a war, black man had to get his head beat in for the chance to get his head blown off by the krauts or the Japs.

"If that ain't nuts, then I don't know what is," he lamented aloud. He enjoyed the rest of his cigarette.

Chapter Eight

June 1943 – Harlem

Alma Yates shifted in her seat as the speaker's voice rose in fervor. "This Harlem Patriot's Rally is one more example of the kind of foolishness that has made temporal allies of disparate men such as A. Philip Randolph, Walter White and the muddled-head Stalinists running the New York Communist Party." The speaker shook a flyer in his hand announcing the upcoming event.

There was tepid applause that Yates understood was akin to a standing ovation among the very serious Socialist Workers Vanguard. The speaker, a compact welterweight of a black man with large glasses, went on in the front part of the room. "More and more, these efforts retard the real work that has to be done. How long will Negro misleaders pursue these polices of naiveté, of echoing the pronouncements of the warmongers and their flowery talk of fighting and dying for the preservation of human liberties in Europe?"

The speaker paused and had a sip of water. Yates, who was sitting in the back, noted that the majority of the audience was white. But, she supposed whimsically, that only meant to the SWV they had to redouble their work to reach all the Negroes who'd been duped by Roosevelt or the Urban League. Of course if the Vanguard really wanted to organize the black workers, they'd go to the night spots and bars they hung out in after hours. But if members of the organization actually cut loose now and then, where would the revolution be?

"If the Negro lives a life on the margins in the north," the speaker railed, "the south is pure hell. Can a black man or woman sit in the same room with a white in Memphis or Jackson to hear a pretty speech about the benefits of democracy? Or what about a Negro in the south who tries to exercise his right to vote? Does he have a chance to do so at the polling place without getting his head caved in or having to answer qualifying questions like who were the founding members of the Committees of Correspondence?"

A few select snickers rose from the gathered. The lithe man stalked about, drawing energy from the meager showing of emotion. "The great and vaunted Democratic Party, the friend of the Negro." Mocking a preacher, he stopped and thrust his hands heavenward. "Oh what a friend we have in the president's party, isn't that so?" He lowered his hands. "It's the Democrats who control the state governments in the south. Stand on the fourteenth and fifteenth Amendments extolling Negro rights with these chicken-stealing politicians, and I can assure you you'll get fourteen or fifteen bullets in you for your trouble."

Yates made sure to write his words down exactly. Not everything the SWV proclaimed was off the mark.

"You're not with the Daily Worker are you?" The questioner was a dour looking young women, her blonde hair cut short and in black slacks and a checked coat.

"The other enemy, the Pittsburgh Courier," Yates admitted. "Seriously, I'm not here to do a hatchet job on the Vanguard. I want to fully explore the different attitudes toward the war and whether we should be in the fight overseas."

The girl wasn't listening. She was making a concerted effort to read Yates' shorthand upside down.

"Satisfied?"

The withering stare the reporter got in return didn't faze Yates. She blithely continued to make her notes, recording her encounter with the stern insurrectionist. Her would-be interrogator sneered and turned back around to share some muted words with her companion.

Yates was pleasantly surprised when the speaker finished not with the SWV's pat and vacuous permanent revolution refrain, but put forward several concrete steps he wanted his members to debate and to ultimately implement a strategy.

"It's fine to hone our rhetoric and be prepared to verbally counter the Stalinists and do-good liberals, the mammies and the Uncle Toms, that's what's always been expected of us. But we have to popularize our message, and I don't mean dumb it down." The man pushed his glasses back on his nose, sweat slicked his angular features. He reached into his suit pocket and took out a pamphlet.

"When we print up our tracts, it's not enough that we sell them at our meetings or rallies. We have to be able to take them into beauty parlors, barber shops and cafes."

Yates witnessed real astonishment on the faces of some of the true believers. The speaker was dancing close to perfidiousness and he and his audience were both aware and aroused by the titillation.

"The question, dear comrades, is not the rightness of our course, but how we convince others of joining us in the journey. Here we are in

Harlem and we have members who come as far as Scarsdale to be with us. That's all well and good, but two blocks up is where we have to be reaching out to the masses, if we want to keep our movement vital and strong."

This time there was no polite clapping or head nodding. This time he had their full attention. Some, Yates wrote, were probably sharpening their knives.

The speaker shook the pamphlet beside his glistening face. "We have to rework and retool some of our writings so that we can reach, not appeal to the lowest rung you understand, but reach out to our brethren and sisterhood. There are lessons informed by the arguments that went on between the artists and writers during the Harlem Renaissance. That of depicting the pretensions of the bourgeois, the Ideal Negro, versus romanticized street life. I'm not making an argument for vulgarity, but I am making one for simplicity and directness."

He soon finished up and the forty minutes of questions and comments following his talk had to be the liveliest the SWV hall had seen for some time Yates conjectured. She scribbled relentlessly and was glad to give her hand a rest when the meeting was finally called to a close. That was after it was moved, seconded and there was consensus that the proposal of Inez, the name used by the woman who'd been curious about Yates, was accepted. Essentially she sided with the speaker and reiterated his point that if the Socialist Workers wanted to move the masses, they had to reevaluate how they outreached and spoke to them.

Inez was huddled with some others as Yates walked over to the speaker. The reporter doubted if the young woman was really named Inez anymore than she believed the nom de guerre used by the inspirational speaker.

"I'm glad to see you've lived up to your writings, Mr. Johnson."

The wiry built individual dabbed at his lined face with a black and white polka dot handkerchief. If he had a horn, he could have been a jazz musician catching his breath between sets. "A reporter from the establishment press."

"That's the first time I've heard the Negro news referred to in those terms."

He bowed slightly then snapped upright. "Then let's say the not radical press, would that be more accurate?"

"As long as I can use your real name in my article, professor."

The man calling himself Johnson grinned as he cleaned the lenses of his glasses with his sopping handkerchief. "You understand why we use aliases?"

"I suspect J. Edger, the DuPonts and the Chrysler brothers already have all they need to know about you and the SWV in their files."

He twitched his squared-up shoulders. "So you've read some of the articles in our newspaper?"

"I have."

He flashed teeth. "You read the piece I wrote about IBM?"

"No, can't say I saw that one."

"I'll give you a copy before you go. It lays out what I think are some interesting facts about the system of tabulation patented by Herman Hollerith and its use by the Nazis in keeping count of the Jews."

"Are you saying an American company is aiding the Germans?"

"For monopoly profits, yes. You might want to look up some information on a German company called I.G. Farber, their investors have an interesting genealogy."

She wrote down the names. "But if we could set back to you and the Vanguard."

"I'd like you to mention we use the aliases to keep from being harassed in our regular jobs by the capitalists we expose."

"Shall I add the word swine?"

"If you wish." His smile was inviting with a hint of a guardedness hovering at the edges.

"I know you came from humble roots, Professor Bowlden, but when's the last time you hung out with the working class you radicals are always romanticizing?"

"I enjoy a domino game down at Byrd's Grill quite regularly, Miss...?"

She filled him in on her name and what she was working on. "That's what brought me to the Socialist Workers. My editor is interested in explaining to our readers the specifics of your split with the Communist Party and others who should be your brethren on the war question."

Ranon C. Bowlden, who once taught at Wilberforce, and who went by the pen name Adam Johnson, motioned toward a Cathedral window overlooking the street below. The two sat down, dust motes like blind butterflies flitting about them. Some of the people had left the room and others were rearranging the chairs and lifting several long tables back into place. This large room, which served as library and meeting area, was one of four the SWV maintained on a third floor walk-up over a laundry on 123rd Street. Around the corner was the Harlem Swing Club. And looking down on the street, Yates had seen several musicians walking toward the club. It was Saturday afternoon, and they'd be rehearsing for tonight's set.

The headliner was bandleader Earl "Fatha" Hines, and Crimpshaw was taking her. She was certainly seeing a lot of him.

"We're not opposed to knocking heads, Miss Yates. As you must know, several of us served in Spain."

"Yes, I know, Professor –"

Impatiently he waved and said, "You might as well call me RC, everybody does."

"Okay," she wrote that in her pad. "As I was saying, I know you were wounded in Spain in the Ebro River Campaign. I believe you were an ambulance driver."

He nodded and crossed his legs. "Yes," he drew out. "Dear comrades of mine, men and women, lost their lives in that damnable skirmish. His gaze took him far beyond the walls for a few moments. "Mind?" he asked, having produced a pipe.

"No, go right ahead." Her father smoked a pipe and she always found the aroma comforting.

"Well," he puffed as he got his pipe going, "We believed then we were on a righteous cause as we do now, Miss Yates."

"Even though a lot of people, black and white, label you as un-patriotic? A bunch of yellow reds who'd rather flap their gums while innocent women and children are ground under the iron heel?"

"Or how about what Rankin of Mississippi has said?"

She notched her head. "What was that?"

"He said that Japanese fifth columnists had been fomenting Negro resentment through organizations like the ACLU and the NAACP. Clearly Negroes could not be voicing their own demands to be let into first class hotels, or restaurants and picture shows in his home state and Washington, D.C." He uncrossed his legs. "Imagine that."

Not to be sidetracked she pressed on. "What about it, RC?"

"I don't pretend that what's going on in Europe and the Pacific is not horrendous and can't simply be wished away by withering analysis or sharply-worded speeches."

"Are you coming by later?" The young woman named Ingrid butted in. "Some of us want to work out a plan for what you were talking about in a redirection of our outreach." She purposely didn't look at Yates. But the reporter was sure she wanted this to be in the article. The Socialist Vanguard were a close-mouthed bunch, but they like their rivals in the Communist Party understood the value of free press.

RC confirmed that he would, and the young woman left.

"Then what do you hope to accomplish?" Yates asked.

"Wake up the masses," he answered straight-faced. "Short of that," he acknowledged, "at least raise the contradictions so that our would-be Negro saviors have to step up the fight here at home."

"Some things take priority, RC. The world could go to hell while we only get whites mad at us for being isolationists." She stuck the end of her pen at him. It was one of those new Biro's, from Argentina, and was called a ballpoint. The salesman at Greene's Stationary had been quite ecstatic in his explanation of the marvelous mechanics of the pen. Basically the Biro brothers, one of whom had a background in journalism, figured out a way to use quick drying newspaper-type ink in a handy container. It clogged now and then, but Yates liked it better than a leaky fountain pen.

"Or worse," she added, "agents of the Nazis, black fascists dupes."

"As some have labeled the SWV." RC mined his pipe, which had gone out, with a crusted wire. "That doesn't in any way deflect the correctness of our position."

"And why you'll actively organize against the Patriot's Rally? You know perfectly well, RC, that to the outside world, the perception is not of one road to freedom versus another, but of a bunch of college-educated white kids like Inez messing where they don't belong. Hasn't there been enough of this with the nasty public feud between Garvey, DuBois and Randolph?"

"True, that's why it's imperative we do better at reaching the black folk we see as our base. You know as well as I there are plenty of coloreds who are at best ambivalent about the war and your paper's Double V Campaign. Plenty of people barely making it by wondering why the hell they should be so hot and eager to be a busboy in uniform when that's all they've got to look forward to now as a civilian."

"But that's the point," she persisted, "just as we struggle for our full and equal rights to be men and women in society, we must break down those same barriers within the armed forces. That wall is cracking, RC, and soon Negro troops will be seeing action in the theaters of war."

"So much for the objective press," he jibbed. "That may not be as glorious an undertaking as you think it will be, Miss Yates. Choking on your own blood is not much of an art, or something necessarily you want to aspire to."

She was going to answer when two uniformed cops came through the door. One was white, the other black, and both built like stevedores. Each had their nightsticks out. The white one had a scar along the ridge of his nose. He rapped the end of his billy club against the back of a chair.

"I came to borrow a book," this one said jocularly.

A stout woman with a missing pinky finger spoke up. "We're not a public library, Milikan, or don't you remember me telling you that before?"

"Have you now?" the cop replied, walking toward her then veering off to peer at the shelves. Yates kept writing.

"Whatchu doin', girlie?" The other cop, the black one, joined in.

"I'm writing this down for my paper."

"What would that be, the Coon Tribune?" The black cop laughed, looking at Milikan for his endorsement.

Milikan had stopped tapping his club. "She ain't kiddin'," I've seen her around. I wouldn't forgot those legs."

"Why thank you, officer, Milikan is it?" Doing her best to keep any quiver out of her voice. Yates stood. "And what's yours, officer?" Her efficient Brio was poised to record just like she'd learned in dictation class.

"I don't have to tell you troublemakers shit," The black one spat. He pounded over to Yates. "You better give me that."

"Or what?"

"This isn't some bookie joint you're rousting," RC said, also on his feet "You need to be careful what you say and do around here." Smoke from his pipe filtered about his head like he was casting a spell.

Milikan scratched an eyebrow with the chewed end of his club. "Is that a fact?"

"It is."

"Hogwash. Give me that." The belligerent black cop grabbed at Yates' pad, and she snatched it away. He raised his baton over her head. "You better watch yourself, bitch."

She flinched but refused to look away. She wasn't going to give him the satisfaction. "I can still write from a hospital bed."

The large woman and several of the other Vanguard members didn't back down. "Go on, wail on her and see how it's going to run in the colored and white press."

"Nobody reads your commie rags." The cop lowered his club but he glared at Yates like a junkyard dog would a Porterhouse in a butcher's window.

"I told you, Olson, I've seen her around, she's legit." Milikan had stepped closer, his back to him, watching the others in the room. "We better go."

"I ain't scared of a bunch of over-educated Bolsheviks. They're the ones stirring up all this who-rah."

Yates said, "What exactly would that be, Officer Olson?"

Gary Phillips

"You don't know what you're foolin' with, girlie." He shook the end on the nightstick at her. "It's you book worms that got these silly ideas stirring up colored folk. Making everybody excitable when they shouldn't be."

"You mean us darkies should be happy to clean between our toes and lift that bale, boss? Like you?" RC leaned against the window, his arms crossed and his pipe going again.

Olson had his big arms loose at his sides and he was eager to use them. Milikan was in motion. "You just make sure you keep the peace," he declared, going through the door. His partner lingered a few moments more then he too started for the exit. "Next time we're going to have a real conversation about what you agitators do around here."

"Let's," RC said.

Olson left and audible sighs escaped from several of the party members as the cop's heels descended to the street.

"So you know this Milikan?" Yates had put her pen down so no one would notice that her hand was shaking.

"Oh yes, he's looking out for our every interest."

"He ever rough up some of your members?"

"He's usually just content to give us a hard time but never anything physical."

"Until this Olson?"

"Yes, he hasn't been with him before. Nothing worse than the field nigger who has to do more bad than the white man so he can get his scraps."

"Maybe the precinct figured Milikan was getting too friendly with you bomb throwers." Yates made some more notes.

"You could ask them. The desk sergeant doesn't regularly supply us with information."

Yates smiled. "Even Walter White wouldn't want you messed over by the cops, RC."

He also grinned.

Yates asked a few more questions. and got a number to reach him at if she had any more. On Wednesday, she was leaving for Los Angeles to interview Kenneth Washington and Charlotta Bass, who respectively ran the two largest Negro newspaper on the West Coast.

But at the moment, as she said her goodbyes, she had her appointment at Leonelle's Emporium of Excellence on Lexington to get her hair and nails done. They used the products from Madame C.J. Walker's company that Yates much preferred. Shampoos and relaxers allowed her to have her hair combed out to a moderate length without lye and the use of a hot comb. Yet with enough kink in it so that she didn't feel she was imitating the standards of white beauty like Lana Turner on a Life magazine cover.

And of course the side benefits of time spent at a beauty parlor was hearing about neighborhood gossip, and putting something down on the numbers when the runner came by. Virgil Crimpshaw wasn't exactly her ideal man, but he made his own way, did good for the Negro people, and did know how to show a girl a good time and not just take her to a boxing match. Hell, she had the right to cut lose every once and a blue moon. For one night, the cause could wait while Fatha Hines coaxed melodies from his eighty-eights.

She might even let Crimpshaw get more than a kiss tonight. She laughed at her reflection in the plate glass of a nickelodeon. Lord have mercy, what had the big city done to her?

CHAPTER NINE

May 1943 - The Mediterranean

A bullet creased a red trail across Clay's leg as Bragg screamed the Vindicator into a sharp turn. Glass was at his feet from the fractured canopy, and his teeth ground as he watched the Messerchmidt's guns bore down on them yet again. The Nazi pilot was adept in handling his aircraft, and he replicated Bragg's escape maneuvers easily.

Her face was drained of color, and the muscles stood out like cable on her exposed forearms as she worked to keep them alive. The needle on the engine's tachometer jerked upward in register as Bragg revved the machine viciously. The plane whipped forward, the pursuit plane also pouring it on. Bragg suddenly shoved the controls forward and the plane lurched like a car on a roller coaster. Clay's head hit the top of what was left of the canopy's frame. The body of the aircraft shuddered, and he wouldn't have been too surprised if the thing started popping its rivets at that moment.

The Vindicator sped downward at an angle, the black depthless carpet of ocean spreading before them. The German's machine guns roared once again, and part of the tail was chewed up in a flurry of rounds. Bragg kept going, the water getting closer and closer. Clay was pretty sure the plane hadn't been rigged to be a submarine like he'd seen once in a Superman cartoon. At this speed they'd be busted apart like crockery tossed on the floor when they collided with the water. Flesh and metal parts would be fused together, and spread over the Mediterranean's surface to eventually sink from memory.

The plane continued its descent, the Messerchmidt continuing to sear the air between them with hot rounds. More bullets tore into the fuselage, and the altimeter was blown apart. A sliver of flying glass lodged into Bragg's cheek but she didn't notice. Clay prepared himself mentally for impact when she expertly cut back on the acceleration. The underside of the Vindicator skimmed across the water as the plane righted itself. The enemy pilot had naturally pulled up by then, assuming that Bragg must have been dead at the controls.

Bragg rocketed the Vindicator skyward, looping the craft so that a tip of its right wing dipped in the sea. She thumbed her guns and caught the Messerchmidt toward its front end as he'd adjusted his altitude and was diving toward her to finish the job. The pilot goosed his plane to get out of the line of fire, but his engine cut out and he stalled. The luck had been on their side. Some of Bragg's bullets had done their damage well.

The Messerchmidt slapped onto the water with a thunderclap as the propeller sputtered and caught. One of its wings crimped and partially tore loose. Bragg banked back around and could see the pilot slide the canopy back, struggling to get out of his harness as bubbles gurgled around his now useless sky hunter.

She had her thumb in position on the gun button but didn't depress it. The man had gotten himself loose as his aircraft slipped away beneath him. He treaded water and looked up at the Vindicator as Bragg brought it back around one last time. He saluted the adversary who bested him as the Vindicator, an oily plume piping from it, zoomed overhead. His lone shivering form became smaller and smaller until it disappeared in the big, dark sea as Bragg and Clay continued on their journey.

"We're losing oil," she announced, tapping the corresponding gauge and sniffing the air, the smell evident. "It's steady but not drastic. We may be able to get to Egypt before the engine seizes."

"I like your optimism." The cold air blowing in on them made him rigid all over.

Bragg picked a part up that had come off. She turned it this way and that, then tossed it out of the plane and kept flying.

Clay wasn't even going to ask, he was busy enough trying to stay warm. But he couldn't help but say, "Maybe I can plug it."

Both eyebrows touching the edge of her helmet, she glared back at him. "Always volunteering for that hazardous duty, ain't you?"

"Keeps me spry." He fished around and found a rag under his seat. Bragg handed him a screwdriver and Clay undid his harness. He slid back the canopy and started to clamber out onto the wing. The oil's smoke trail came from the right front. There was a gust of wind and the plane shimmed as Bragg rode the currents. Clay nearly lost his tool and balance.

"Sorry, mate, I'll do my best to hold 'er steady."

"I'd appreciate that." He put the greasy rag and the screwdriver in his mouth, as he needed to use both of his hands to hold on. Bragg eased back on the throttle to lessen her speed and he got out on the wing.

"It's probably going to be toward the cowling, probably underneath," she told him.

Finding purchase where he could on the airplane, foot over foot, Clay went forward. He slipped but didn't let go. By smell and squinting, Clay located the source of the leakage. As Bragg had predicted, there was a jagged hole punched through the plane's lower body at the seam of the cowling as it encircled the engine housing.

"You okay?"

"Ugh," he answered, bending down, the rag and screwdriver still in his mouth. Cautiously, like a blind spider, he let his right hand reach across the wing while he held onto the plane's body with his left.

"Careful," Bragg unnecessarily warned him.

The plane droned along, Bragg flying it as smooth as she could. Clay squatted, having to let go of the body of the plane, his palms flat on the frigid surface of the wing. Momentarily he had the fearful sensation the plane would buck, and he'd futilely be clawing air as he fell hundreds of feet to the liquid earth below. He managed to go flat and then belly crawl over to the wing's end. The smoke from the burning oil made him gag, and he had to shut his eyes. He opened them again, and knew he had to get closer to reach that goddamned hole. Clay inched his upper body out from the wing, the rag and screwdriver now in his right hand. He was on his side, his left hand holding onto a portion of the canopy next to Bragg.

Then the plane hit an air pocket. The plane's body torqued like a clutch let out too quickly. "Shit," he said as he lost his grip and slid toward the tip of the wing. The rag and screwdriver blew away.

"Clay," Bragg hollered. She turned the craft so that it was angled in such a way that the left wing was pointing downward, the right one up. Clay's legs dangled as he held on, gripping the edge.

"Can you get back on?"

"Don't you think I'm trying?" Clay swung his left leg up, trying to get his knee onto the wing. He failed, the stinging wind taunting him with its superiority. The plane soared along and Bragg gently brought it back level. Clay wormed his body back on the wing and again on his stomach and crawled back to the main section.

"Here," Bragg said, handing him a Phillips screwdriver. "I've got a toolkit up front here."

He took the screwdriver and this time had to tear part of his sleeve off. He got it in the hole, the oily fumes hot and greasy on his arm. Clay stuffed the cloth in tight with the rounded end of the screwdriver. Breathing with effort, he climbed back into his seat behind the pilot.

"You certainly have style, Mr. Clay."

"Heh." He conjured up a weak grin while he got his nerves under

85

control.

The sun was bright and very few clouds were out by the time they made their approach to the airfield outside Alexandria, Egypt. The engine had run completely dry of oil and the pistons had seized with a loud clank in the engine block. But the intervention of the rag had, according to Bragg, kept the dam back just enough to get them here.

"Strap in, baby," Bragg said lightly. "I'm going to have to dead stick us in, and it's gonna be rougher than making love with a porcupine."

"Now I know why we had to stop going around together. I couldn't take the excitement."

She cackled and swooshed down through the breezeless air toward a concrete strip lined with two shacks and a jeep set on end. A goat was tethered to one of the shacks and the creature idly watched as the plane approached too fast and sinking too quick for the runway.

Bragg rode the stick and it shook violently in her hands. "Get ready, big daddy."

"I'm not worried if you aren't"

"I'm scared to death, darling." Bragg brought he Vindicator in, the wing's ailerons and the tail's elevators were flapped up as the sleek craft swooped low. Blue smoke and sparks seeped out of the air scoop.

The door to one of the shacks was thrown open and a man, dressed in the garb of fellahin, pounded out of the lean to with urgency.

The airplane came down roughly onto the runway. The wing clipped the recently vacated shack, sending planks everywhere. The goat, tied on the other side of the strip to the other shack, kept chewing. The plane bounced up and down, and the whole of it vibrated as if they were in a cement mixer. It came down again and Bragg was cussing while she applied the brakes. The tires screeched like bats and the plane's momentum continued to carry it forward swiftly.

"Motherfucker," she swore. "They're gonna give."

"What's gonna give?" Clay asked and immediately got his answer.

One of the landing struts buckled and snapped. The Vindicator dropped on one side and now the wing was scrapping along the runway. Sparks as big as basketballs spewed from underneath the scraping metal. The plane's body then hiccupped again and it turned on the lowered wing like a toreador doing his number. The aircraft spun in two complete circles and the tail end slammed into the upended jeep, causing them to slow but not stop. Then as if shoved by an invisible titan, the Vindicator skidded backwards into a mound of earth and sand off the airstrip. They came to a halt, dirt showering them.

"Talk about style," Clay wheezed. Wrestling himself free he and

Bragg were applauded. He twisted around to see peasants atop camels, an Egyptian in khakis at the wheel of a jeep and beside him, an RAF officer stood.

"Excellent," the officer complimented, touching his sandy-colored moustache. "You Yanks don't believe in doing anything quietly, do you?" Clay and Bragg stumbled over to his jeep. The officer introduced himself as Major Archer. After a meal that included pineapple from South Africa, Australian Bully beef and warm Guinness, the two retired to bed, another cot, this in a bunker converted to an ammo dump.

"I'll try not to get you too heated tonight, silky smooth." Bragg winked, patting a case of grenades nearby.

Clay's shoulder was bruised from the crack up, but the blood seemed to be flowing just right elsewhere. "Anybody ever tell you, you're the screwiest broad ever?"

Bragg threw back her head and laughed heartily while she took off her torn blouse. And when they made love it was with a fierce intensity for who knew if they would ever see each other again. The following morning, a light fog drifted in off the Mediterranean as she walked him toward the steamer that would take him west to Tunisia. The boat flew under a Swiss registry and its crew a tossed salad of men from New Zealand to Tibet.

She easily carried his duffle and he his Gladstone. At the dock, Major Archer waited.

"Best of luck to you, old stick." He stuck out his hand and Clay took it. "Thanks for the clothes and the gun."

His permanent smile left his face. "It's not what you might think, Mr. Clay. If the Vichy or jerries get onto you, well," he hesitated, "let's say the plight of a black man, a spy at that, in their hands would make those bloody Boers doings the kiddie hour, eh?"

Bragg nervously looked at Clay as the major moved out of earshot. "Look, maybe the crash caved in another soft spot in my head, but you better make sure your big ol' mule skinin' self comes back, here?"

He pulled her close, momentary regret causing a loss of words. Then he spoke, "Glad it was you ferrying me on this trip." They kissed. "I'll see you, Janet. We'll drink gin sours and eat pigs feet sandwiches at La Bagatelle while Satchmo blows out the windows in a free France." They kissed again.

"Then we'll have to see about freeing Harlem."

He shook a finger at her, smiling. Clay hugged her tight for goodbye and for reasons he was afraid to name. He boarded the freighter and watched her, hands on hips, standing on the dock watching him on deck.

The boat chugged into open water.

Later, he lay on his back in his upper bunk, staring at a dented bulkhead plate. There were two photos taped to the wall next to him. One was a portrait of tough guy actor Humphrey Bogart in trademark trench coat and rain spotted hat. Next to that was Field Marshal Kesselring, chief of the Luffwaffe in the Mediterranean. There were small pricks in this one from the darts that had been thrown at it at some point.

He was worn out, but true sleep wouldn't come. In a fitful half-awake state, Janet Bragg flew a chrome-skinned rocket plane, like something out of a Flash Gordon comic strip. She was happy as she made her flying machine do loop-the-loops and barrel rolls as she zoomed across the skyways. There was a seat next to her in the enclosed cabin, but she was alone at the controls.

CHAPTER TEN

July 1943 - Los Angeles

"Girl, you just don't know." Brenda Collins laughed from her belly and clapped Alma Yates on the knee. The Pacific Electric "red car" trolley swayed on its tracks as the train left the docks area of Long Beach and crossed over to San Pedro in L.A. proper. "I know I probably shouldn't say this, but thank God for Tojo, honey." She chortled again and a briny wind whipped through the open window. The riveter's good humor was infectious, and several other graveyard shift workers smiled or nodded ascent.

"Now don't you go writin' me like I'm some kind of sab-a-toor. Shit," she exclaimed, "I sure got enough problems without the G-Men comin' down on me." She chuckled. "Aw, hell, I'm too tired and too sore to fuss anyway."

Yates did her best to make her notes as the car clacked along, the ride particularly bumpy. "How long have you been working at Todd Ship yards, Brenda?"

"Feels like twenty years," she said, massaging a bulging biceps. "Getting so firm up here might be hard for me to get a date on Saturday night."

"I like my women strong like my coffee," a male voice peeled from the rear of the car." There were several bursts of laughter.

Collins twisted her lips as if she were chewing on a cupcake. "Careful, Ray, I might have to take you serious." She turned back to Yates, "All I mean is, what with people like that there Randolph fella, you know, the porter union man, stirring up stuff in Washington and the shortage they got of mens in these plants, girl, my days of cleaning up Miss Anne's house is over." She made a cutting motion with the flat of her hand.

She wrote the woman's comment. "At least for the time being."

"Huh?" She was suddenly sitting forward.

"Nothing, I, forget what I said. Tell me what it's like in the yard."

"I'll get to that." She shook a finger at the reporter. Her nail was split along one side, the flesh underneath purple and bruised. "What about the other thing you mentioned?"

The trolley wound its way in a northwest direction. "I didn't mean it like it sounded, Brenda. I've talked to women in Detroit and Oakland, and some of them are worried that after the war, that you know, when the men return, what about their jobs on the assembly line?" Damn, why hadn't she kept her big mouth shut?

Collins' anger left her as easily as it had come upon her. "Yeah, yeah, I hadn't figured that before. Yeah."

Yates felt bad. "Brenda, it will be different, I know it will when the soldiers return. That's what we want, what the Double V is all about."

"I ain't workin' to set up a good thing for all them, honey. I know they doin' they duty, but ain't I doin' it too?"

"Yes, you are." Yates wrote some more, compelled to tell this part of the story the best way she could for the women like her. Providence had given them a chance and it seemed that precarious opportunity could take that job away like her job at the Courier?

"Well," Collins sat forward, her hands clasped together between her legs. "You sure done got me to thinkin', that's for sure. Maybe I'll check out one of those meetings they been passin' out flyers about."

"Who's this?"

Her toothy smile showed her gold canine. "Loose lips can sink my ship." She winked. "Now get on with your questions, okay?"

"So what's it like putting together those big ships?"

"I was scared, scared like you don't know what when I first got there in February. But like I said, it was a damn sight better than being on my knees scrubbing and putting up with the missus mess and them little, you know, pinches and what not from the mister when she ain't around. Him bein' a big fan of dark meat." Her laugh this time wasn't humorous.

Yates nodded. "How'd you get the job at the shipyards?"

"A friend of mine, Jean, she'd seen this handbill at her church and we was off to the races."

"Todd advertised jobs in the colored neighborhoods?"

Collins got her good-natured laugh back. "Hell naw. I think she said it was this radical group of lawyers, the ACU or something like that and the Eagle newspaper. They had a meeting informing us we should go down and apply for these jobs since it was the law now that they had to hire us. Said Roosevelt himself had made it so. They said if the bosses at Todd raised some sand, they'd sue 'em, sue 'em good."

"I'm going to interview Mrs. Bass too," Yates added.

"That's good, she's done a lot with that newspaper of her's for the colored. Them and the Sentinel. I know you can tell I ain't much on book reading, but I do read them things pretty regularly."

"What's it been like working there?" The trolley came to a stop as a load of trucks went past on Alameda.

"The money really makes the difference. Too bad it don't mean them ofays ain't a better cut above."

"Like what?"

"I'm not telling you anything new, 'cause you said you been going around the country talking and interviewing people all over the place."

"But your story is part of this too, Brenda."

She grinned, her metal lunch pail sliding beneath her seat as the trolley pitched forward again. "I like that," she confided as she took in a breath. "Look, I know some people think we got it made out here in L.A., how it ain't like 'Bama or 'Sippi. Now to an extent that's true, but in many ways, it's just the same only more spread out."

"Give me an example, Brenda."

Collins leaned forward. "Okay, I got a juicy one for your paper." She pointed a dirty nail over her left shoulder. "Where I live in Watts, right next door in Compton did you know the Kluxers got them a council or klavern or whatever the hell they call they little gatherings."

"They're active at Todd?"

"Hell, I don't know for sure, but the word is that more than the line crew, a few supervisors have a hood in hanging in their closet."

"Have there been incidents at work?"

She poked a thumb into her breastbone. "We got notes, you know, run off on the Duplicator in purple ink, tellin' us that niggers better not get to happy building boats. That soon we would be on those boats shipped back to Africa. It was signed the KKK."

Yates purposely didn't use her shorthand for this passage. She wrote in longhand, making sure to record Collins' words exactly. "What happened then?"

"We had us a meeting. Jean, my girlfriend that got me the job? She called this Jewish fella over at the ACLU, that's the ones, a lawyer, and he came out and talked with the owners. There was a lot of shouting is what I hear. Anyway the Eagle and the Sentinel both carried articles about it and I got quoted in those too."

"Were there reprisals?"

"If you mean did we get them looks and mumblings, yeah. Even got into a shoving match with this dust bowl broad, but they knew other eyes were lookin' in on them so nothing got too nasty. See Jean and a couple of others have been recruited." She winked broadly.

Yates lowered her voice. "You mean the Communist Party?" The trolley had stopped to take on two passengers. The newcomers were good-sized white men in working clothes that looked too new.

Yates got a twinge, the memory of those two in the Buick in Harlem. But these men had regular haircuts and were talking about a local boxing match at the Olympic Auditorium. They certainly didn't seem to be paying the two of them any attention.

Collins said, "Oh they's a few of them working down at Todd. Fact, they be workin' harder and longer than a lot of the others if you ask me."

"Anything for Uncle Joe," Yates quipped.

"Yeah, well, what I meant was that my friends joined Miss Bethune's National Council of Negro Women. They have a pretty active chapter through several churches 'round here what with more of us women gettin' out in the work world."

"Oh," she said and wrote more.

Collins explained how she learned to weld seams in bulkheads and the thrill of finishing an aircraft carrier and her current work on the SS Tom Paine, a Liberty ship. This was the name given to freighters designed for emergency construction by the Maritime Commission.

"Ugly ducklings, Roosevelt calls 'em." Collins added. "But it's important work, we're doing. These ships are used to break what they call blockades bringing medicines and food and what not to all kinds of people."

"Yes, that's true," Yates agreed.

"We get what they call pre-fabricated parts, you know, sections that have been put together at other yards, and we slapped the Tom Paine together under 45 days, working double shifts and Saturdays." Collins animatedly talked with her hands. "I heard about this one Liberty ship, the SS Robert E. Peary? They put that together in four and a half days. Of course it was lots smaller than the Paine. Ours was full-sized, four hundred and forty-one feet long and fifty-six feet wide. It can carry nine thousand tons of cargo and you can put planes and tanks on her deck."

"That's something, Brenda."

"You doggone right it is, sister." She slapped Yates' kneecap. Momentarily, she turned and looked out the window as the red car carried them across a portion of the awakening city. "Now how is that fair to mothball us after all we done for the sailors and soldiers and flyboys overseas?" Her question was a frosted mist of breath on the trolley's glass. She returned attention to Yates. "You know you should talk to Jean. She got a cousin or some sort of relation that's one of them

Red Tails."

"A Tuskegee airman?"

"Sho is. Her aunt got a letter from him, they saw action over this island," she shook her head, reproaching herself. "Penta, Panama, no that wasn't it."

"Pantelleria," Yates offered, "near Italy. My paper like the other Negro outlets got reports. We're all very excited about this. Seems there was quite a dogfight led by A-Train Dryden against twelve Nazi aircraft."

"Jean's cousin bagged one of those birds," she said joyfully. "Now that's somethin', ain't it?"

"You damn right it is." The women laughed in unison.

The two got off at Collins' stop on Avalon near 110th Street. A man in a Nash passed by, honking his horn at the woman who waved back. Yates finished her interview as Collins got out of her work clothes in a small back house she rented behind a fourplex with water cracks. She thanked her and put the steno pad away in her purse.

"You think theys just gonna kick us out on the streets when the men come back?" Collins was in her bathrobe, a hand on her hip.

"I don't really know, Brenda. But I think it would be a good idea for you and Jean and whoever else to talk with the National Council people and maybe even the ACLU. Seems to me there's going to be a lot of scuffling by everybody to find work once the war is over."

"Honey the door's been opened a little, and I damned sure ain't going to be pushed back outside."

"I hear you."

CHAPTER ELEVEN

Yates had some tea with Collins, thanked her and walked to Central Avenue where she caught a Yellow Car, the intra-urban trolley, to her hotel room at the Dunbar Hotel on Central Avenue. Exiting the place was singer Billy Eckstein. Like she'd seen on photos and posters, he was handsome, his caramel skin smooth and unblemished. The crooner was dressed sharp in blue serge and his tie was loosened about his open collar maroon shirt. A burning cigarette dangled from beneath his pencil thin mustache. The smoke coiling about his face that was partially shaded by a Turf Club-style Stetson.

"Say, good looking, don't tell me you just getting in." He stopped and gave her the once over.

"Looks like you haven't been in yet."

"I wouldn't say that."

"Cute." Yates kept moving, aware he watched her go.

"If you aren't too busy, I'm singing down at the Barrel House tonight. You know, the joint that Johnny Otis owns."

She didn't, but said, "We'll see." He wasn't her type but it gave her a tingle to flirt.

"Seeing is right." And he bounced off, humming. He then got into a cream yellow Cadillac at the curb and wheeled away.

Yates yawned and crossed the lobby. There was an announcement on the wall reminding everyone to save their bacon fat and take the cans to collection centers. The lard was used in the manufacture of nitroglycerine. She got into the elevator and yawned some more. Yates had her own sleep to catch up on, and then other appointments to keep.

"Going up," the elevator operator said, sliding the cage's door shut. Leaning next to his stool was a case containing a sax.

"Where do you play?"

"The Crystal Tea Room, the Downbeat, sometimes my grandma's garage just for the mice and termites."

They both had a laugh and Yates got out on the fourth floor and went down the crisp runner to her room that was off around the bend. She passed by a window at the end of the hall, and absently noted it was cracked open. The slight breeze felt invigorating.

Out on the fire escape landing, the crew cut man was a statue still crouching beneath the sill. He waited soundlessly until he heard the key in the lock and Yates entered her room. He'd been a half-minute ahead of getting out of her room. He hoped he'd put everything back like it was. Snow had already warned him and Palmer to be careful. That they shouldn't underestimate the target just because she was a dame, Negro or not. Good thing he'd spotted her out the window in her room overlooking the Avenue. Birch waited some more, praying that nobody came along the alley the fire escape looked out onto.

He let three sweeps of the minute hand of his Timex go past then eased back into the hallway. He didn't dare close the sash for fear of it drawing Yates' attention. He figured it was better to be seen going out the front than from the side.

Still, white men were known to shack up for a night with a bronze princess now and then he rationalized, smiling to himself. Shit, he knew Palmer had. And dollars to donuts, that devious bastard Snow probably had those pictures of that too. Birch paused, lit an Old Gold, descended the stairs, and walked casually through the lobby and into the street.

That evening, Alma Yates, Kenneth Washington and Loren Miller, a reporter for the California Eagle, exited Alex Lovejoy's restaurant on the Avenue.

"Nothing like a catfish dinner," Miller enthused as he picked between his teeth with the end of a matchbook cover.

"Yes, it was good," Yates agreed.

A late model Lincoln Cabriolet convertible rolled past, dodging around a trolley. Entertainer Bill 'Bojangles' Robinson was driving.

"It sure is different out here," Yates remarked, watching the dancer and actor go by.

"Well, it's not like Mr. Robinson or any other colored show person can get a room in Beverly Hills any more than I can," Washington noted. "The sun might shine on our version of Jim Crow, but it prevails."

"Hey, coozahn," the Creole barber said, greeting the trio standing in the doorway of Le Petite Barbershop and Process Parlor

"Back at you, coozahn," Miller replied. The reporter and the barber let their fingers slide across the others then pulled back their arms slowly.

The three continued walking along the avenue, toward the Sentinel,

Washington's newspaper, at 42nd Street. At the corner of 40th, Miller tipped his hat at his companions. "I've got an appointment over at Golden State."

"Big story?" Washington asked.

Miller smiled. "You'll just have to read about it in our pages, Ken." He shook Yates' hand. "I'll call you later. Maybe you, May and me can go over to Shepp's tonight. Wynonie Harris and his band are playing there tonight."

"Okay, I'm going to see Mrs. Bass then I'll be back at the Dunbar typing up my notes."

"Excellent," Miller said.

"Say hello to brother Houston for me," Washington called out, referring to Ivan Houston, the head of the company Miller was heading toward. "Tell him I expect to see him at the Hall this Sunday."

"I will, Ken." Miller touched the brim of his hat again and headed west on 40th Street to the offices of the Golden State Mutual life insurance company. One of many black-owned enterprise on or adjacent to the Stem, as the denizens called Central Avenue.

"Good man," Kenneth Washington said. "You know he's taken the bar exam and will know soon whether he passed."

"I'd heard that," She'd also heard that Miller was lining up some backers to buy the Eagle with the blessing of its board, but kept that to herself.

The two soon arrived in front of the Sentinel's offices. A tall man some six feet five in a wrinkled gabardine suit bolted over the sidewalk in front of them, snatching open the door in one clean jerk.

"What's the rush, Henley?"

"Soldier on leave died in police custody at the 77th, boss," the telephone pole shot back. "I'm gonna get the mother on the phone." With that, he ducked inside with a hop, the top of his head barely missing the doorjamb.

Washington looked down at the ground as if searching for something then back at her. "Not the first such incident."

"Yes," she commiserated,

"What's it going to be like when our boys see action, upholding the flag on foreign soil, then come back here expecting their just rewards?"

She didn't have an answer.

"Better go and get started on my next editorial. It was a pleasure meeting you, Miss Yates."

She headed toward the offices of the rival paper, the California Eagle. It was also on the Avenue, some blocks back south, past Lovejoy's. As she walked past people at fruit stands and newsstands, the questionable death of the soldier was being talked about vociferously.

"Those bastards ought to get what's coming to them," a man proclaimed in a loud plaid sport coat.

"This shit's got to stop," uttered another.

By the time she got to the Eagle's offices, Yates knew that Mrs. Bass was going to be too busy to see her. This was a breaking story and the time for chitchat would have to be rescheduled. Nonetheless, Mrs. Bass came out to see her.

"Depending on how it goes around here," the diminutive and blockish Mrs. Bass was saying, "I'll come over to the Dunbar." She looked at her wristwatch. "How about we meet in the bar downstairs, the Turban Room around six? If I'm not there by fifteen after, it'll be because the story is hot."

"Or the town is," Yates said.

She was envious that she couldn't play a part in reporting the story. This was what the black press was all about. Under-staffed and always hovering near debt, it was an entity that could be counted on to go into action when an incident like this came about.

The white press couldn't be depended on to dig for the facts when it was a Negro dying at the hands of the law. Sure they were all part of the vaunted Fourth Estate, but the darker members knew when their peers at the L.A. Times and the Herald Examiner gathered around the coffee pot, baseball scores were more likely to be bandied about than who was going to be doing the follow up to one more shine killing.

Back in her room, she broke out her portable Underwood and composed another dispatch. She had her typewriter on a table next to a window overlooking Central Avenue. Yates worked in the soldier's killing from the radio report she'd tuned in to on KGFJ, the white-owned but black-themed station in town. The man's name was Harold Soames, and he'd been in the Army Quartermaster Corp, part of the 3418th Trucking Company, which had a high percentage of Negroes in it. He'd trained at Fort Carson in Colorado, and had been on tap to be shipped with his unit to the European Theater. That was to have been late Sunday night. Now he had all the time in the world.

Yates rolled her sheet and carbon out of the carriage. She separated the two and put the pages of her story together, then she got up, stretched and yawned. It wasn't yet sundown, but it seemed her room had trapped the heat of the day and wasn't letting it out. She leaned out the window to the patter of wage earners walking to and fro along the avenue. Some of them were just getting off work, and others lining up to catch the bus or trolley to start swing shifts. Many were heading toward the airplane parts plants in the Valley or nearby at the Goodyear rubber factory further south at Florence on Central.

It was a pleasing feel against her grimy skin as the warm air-cooled blowing in from the ocean. A man in stained khakis, a metal lunch pail tucked under an arm, whistled at her as he strolled past. Yates watched him go on, wondering what Crimpshaw was up to at that moment. Considering a long distance call, she checked her watch and remembered her tentative appointment with Charlotta Bass.

Hurrying, she bathed, powdered and hustled downstairs to the basement and the Turban Room. It was four after six and a cadre of regulars were already taking up space. It was comfortable but not too crowded. Yates looked around but didn't see Mrs. Bass. She decided to have a beer. Yates wasn't due to take a train out of L.A. to Oakland till Monday, so she'd catch up to Mrs. Bass if she didn't see her tonight. Besides, she wanted to soak in more local flavor for her stories from the coast.

The bar was upholstered on its sides, and had a yellowed marble top. There were appliqués adorning its stuffed surface. A closer inspection by Yates of the handiwork revealed that the images were stylized representations of jazz musicians playing their instruments. Twisted narrow notes danced around the hepsters. She caught snatches of talk, some of it about Soames. Yates found a perch and signaled for the bartender.

"What can I do you for, miss?" The bartender was handsome, above medium height, wavy hair and walked with a limp.

"A Schlitz?"

"Got Pabst or Hamms."

"Make it a Pabst and make it two, Sipsy," Mrs. Bass said behind Yates. She sat beside her, where the bar curved.

"Sure thing, Mrs. Bass." He went to fill the order.

Yates stifled a yawn. "How's it going?"

"I feel as tired as you sound, young lady."

"I'm sorry, still on New York time."

Mrs. Bass put her elbows on the bar, hunching her small shoulders. "I've read some of your articles, Alma, I like them. I'm glad the Courier could afford to send you around the country to make your snap shots of our people. Ollie Harrington, an old friend, stopped through on his way overseas. He's both a writer and an illustrator, and will be chronicling what it's like over there."

"I've seen his work in the Amsterdam News and the Daily

Worker."

The older woman winked. "As always, Ollie was close-mouthed, but I figure some of his fellow travelers were helping foot the bill for his latest excursion."

Yates chuckled. "Well, it did take several fish frys and a few special Sundays at several of Pittsburgh's larger churches to supplement my travel expenses. And those preachers have been good enough to pass the plate recently for the cause."

"How well I know how tight it is."

Sipsy returned with their cans of beer, each partially wrapped in a paper napkin. "There you go, ladies."

Mrs. Bass had produced a dollar bill. "Let me get this. I'm a cheap date, one's my limit." The barkeep took the bill.

"Thanks." They clicked the cans together. "So what have learned about Soames' death?" Over the publishers shoulder, Yates spied a twitchy man anxiously patting his pockets down for a cigarette.

Bass noted Yates' expression and glanced around. "That's "Smoke Ring" Harris, erratic, but a good newspaperman."

"He looks like he's going to blow his top unless he gets a cigarette."

"All kind of clouds follow him," she said, but didn't elaborate. She had a dainty sip of her beer and set the can down, satisfied.

"Police Chief Hohman, it will come as no surprise to you, has not returned my calls. Nor can we get much from the desk sergeant who is supposed to have such knowledge."

Yates leaned closer. "But you have your sources?"

"Just because your paper is on the other side of the map, doesn't mean I've lost my head."

"Who am I going to tell, Mrs. Bass? I'm on special assignment."

"Uh-huh," and she had another lady-like sip of her beer while she adjusted her cat eyeglasses. "I'll put it this way, there are a couple of numbers I can call to get the low down, sometimes," she said. "Soames was picked up by a patrol car on Hyperion, not what you'd call an area frequented by the Negro population."

"What was he doing there?"

"Still trying to find that out. We do know he had a swollen eye and busted lower lip by the time they got him to the division." Yates recognized trombonist and singer Trummy Young as he entered, an Oriental looking woman on his arm. She couldn't be Japanese she knew, as that population on the west coast had been forcibly sent to relocation camps. She was still trying to figure out what the woman was as Mrs. Bass continued.

"We think from some scuttlebutt on the street, that Soames was that way." She flipped her hand back and forth in the air.

Yates' brow crinkled. "What, he liked to fly?"

Charlotta Bass' bulldog frame shook and it was a moment before the younger woman realized she was chortling. "I'm sorry, I guess this might be a little out of your bailiwick."

"I'm not green, Mrs. Bass." There was more invective in her voice than she intended.

"I know you're not." She patted the younger woman's hand. "Even though we don't get to play much more than butlers, maids and bugged eyed cabbies, the taste of Hollywood affects even us poor colored folk."

Irritated, Yates remarked, "If you're trying to confuse me on this Soames business, you've succeeded." She swallowed an amount of her Pabst.

Mrs. Bass straightened up on the stool. "This street that Soames was picked up on is a part of town where the boys walk with a lightness in their shoes. Friends of friends, follow me?

She stared at the cherubic face of the woman then finally understood. "You mean," she whispered, "he liked other men?"

"That's the skinny." She had another delicate sample of her beer. "So it's not too hard to imagine one of these square head cops we have on the force cruising the area, looking for a noggin to bash, then seeing this black GI strolling along. Or God forbid, doing something else in a doorway or window.

Then how does Soames wind up at the 77th? Wouldn't this part of town you're telling me about be another precinct or division as you call them?"

"It's not uncommon for the cops to move a prisoner around from station house to station house. That way it's harder for the family to find him, particularly after they've worked him over." She had more of her Pabst. "But we'll get to the bottom of it," she declared confidently.

Yates leaned on both her forearms. "That's the difference between you and Mr. Washington of the Sentinel," Yates observed.

Bass' body did a brief shake again. "He likes to be called Colonel. Makes him feel like he's keeping up with the legacy of Harrison Gray Otis of the L.A. Times."

"That's honorary, isn't it?"

"He wasn't rough riding with Teddy Roosevelt up San Juan Hill." Mrs. Bass had some more ale.

Yates also drank and let some time stretch out. "I bet you've asked some of your," and she duplicated Mrs. Bass' hand gesture, "entertainment friends who are like that what they've heard about Soames."

Mrs. Bass dipped her head. "You're not saying that those artist types are all ah...sissies, are you?"

Yates mused, "They're more tolerant. They move in many circles. And some of these seem to be concentric around you, Mrs. Bass. The Sentinel is pushing for the door to open; you seem to want a different kind of house the door is attached to."

"Nice turn of phrase."

"I also heard Vice-president Henry Wallace takes and returns your calls."

"People say all kinds of things."

"There are a lot of people who say many things about you, Mrs. Bass, friends, admirers and adversaries."

She shrugged economically. "Just trying to do my job."

Yates let more time and silence elapse. "Have you ever asked the vice-president or any of your other interesting friends about anything funny at Fort Huachuca?"

"Oh," she said over the lip of the can at her mouth, "what would that be?"

Two soldiers, Army, came into the Turban Room. One had already been drinking and leaned against his pal. The tipsy one, a corporeal, had a garrison cap precariously tucked on his clean-cut head. His sunken eyes were bleary and unfocused, the whites red from crying. The other one, taller, wider, a handsome sergeant with clear brown eyes, and a trim mustache, had his cap tucked and folded around his belt. A cigarette dangled from the corner of his mustached mouth.

"I'm telling you, Levi," the loaded one lisped, "Les' you and me drive real quiet like over to the 77th, and put a short round in the brain pan of that ofay cop, man." He whipped his body around, taking in the room. "Whole goddamn town is full of date palms and hillbillies."

"That won't bring Harold back." The other man flicked ash from his smoke. His eyes steady on something.

"Don't I know it," the inebriated man shook his head, and put a hand to his face. "But they gotta be show they fuck with one of the 34-18, they fuck with all of us." He had to lean on the bar to hold himself up. "Them crackers got to be taught, man, you know that. Shit, you've cut your share of--"

"Hush." The sergeant grabbed his friend and the two went past Yates and Mrs. Bass. The sergeant noticed Yates and winked at her as he dragged his morose friend into the depths of the bar.

Yates watched the sergeant's broad back recede from her view. She liked the way the material of his shirt sheathed his muscles like it had been sewn right on him. She let her eyes go lower. Then quickly she turned her head, catching sight of herself in the bar's mirror. She didn't look man hungry. And good girls didn't think about that kind of thing. She got back to her topic. "I'm sure you've heard something about it. Several of these men were probably from California, since you're right next door to Arizona," Yates said.

As if she were a scolding schoolteacher, Mrs. Bass stared at her over the rim of her glasses. "Are you actively digging into this?" She used an index finger to push her cheaters back on her nose.

The younger woman told her about her talk with the Pullman porter in Harlem. And the two white men she'd spotted coming out of the apartment house. "I also talked with my editor about it."

"Over the phone," Mrs. Bass lashed out and gripped Yates' arm with a strength belying her compact body.

"Sure, of course," she stammered, reflexively pulling her arm away.

Mrs. Bass blew a silent whistle through parted lips. "Before or after your talk with this Bascome?"

"Before and after. Once I got wind of the rumor, obviously I'd discuss it with my boss."

"What did he tell you? After talking with the porter?"

Yates made an exasperated gesture. "That he'd been hearing about or following some such rumors since before Prohibition. He told me there'd been a story going around during the influenza epidemic that there was a special branch of the government injecting black rabble rousers with the disease."

"Another one, ladies?" Sipsy leaned across the bar.

Mrs. Bass held her can up. "No thanks, we're still nursing these."

"Let me know." And he went away to take care of other patrons.

The Eagle's publisher pointed. "Come on, it's more private over here."

Yates followed her to a side archway that was a spacious alcove of candlelight and booths. Two sets of couple were in there pitching woo and Yates felt self-conscious.

"Don't worry, a lot of people think I'm a bulldagger anyway. Her body shook again with mirth. She slid her squat form across the Leatherette seat and Yates sat opposite. Taped on the wall between them was a silk-screened fight poster announcing middleweight boxer Tiger Flowers in a bout against Kid Gavilan at the Olympic Auditorium next month.

"You keep doing the stories you're doing, Alma. This other matter is nothing to fool around with. As mama used to say, that's white folks business."

"The possible death of Negroes under any suspicious circumstances is the business of the black press. Our mission is to look where the white folks want us to avert our eyes, to dare to shine the light into dark corners. That's our charge, our duty to our people and to the finest traditions of the Fourth Estate."

Mrs. Bass lowered her head and wagged it from side-to-side. "I still give that speech."

"As well you should." There was a smack and a deep voice said, "Aw, baby."

"Baby nothin'", the woman who'd slapped her paramour raged, "Claudia saw you and that tramp Lisa tipping out of the Rooster's Nest last night."

"Do you still believe it?" Yates asked.

The man pleaded, "That wasn't me, baby. You know I was workin' the double shift."

"Oh, you were workin' the double shift all right." She threw the candle globe at him and it burst into piece against the wall. She rushed toward the exit. The man, a large individual with cheaply conked hair, was at her heels. He was holding a bedraggled bowler in his meat hook of a mitt.

"What choice do I have?" Bass answered.

"Rhonda, listen to me, you know there ain't nobody but you, girl. Nobody." He took a moment to appreciate Yates as he ran after his girlfriend.

Yates sat back, her palms pointing toward the ceiling, waiting.

"This is no joke, Alma." Mrs. Bass swirled the beer in the can.

"Have you been warned? Followed?"

"That comes with the territory. Either it's a visit from the police red squad one week or it's one of J. Edgar's girl scouts the next. And yes, they tail me. I've gotten pretty good at spotting the players they rotate in and out of the line-up."

"But you've heard about this particular incident, haven't you?"

"You were right, Alma. Two of those young men came from right around here. Hell, Roy Nelson, that's one of the fellas, worked a couple of summers at the Eagle in high school. That's how I heard the story." This time, she drank a sizeable amount of her beer.

Yates asked, "What happened?"

"Roy's people got an official notice from the Army stating that their son, while in the performance of his duty, was killed in a explosion at the ordinance depot at Fort Bragg."

Yates stroked her chin. "But how could he be in North Carolina when he was supposed to be at Huachuca in the Arizona desert?"

"There's that, but people do get transferred. There's a black township called Lake Spring not far from the camp in North Carolina. We had a report from one of our stringers that there had indeed been an explosion on base at the time that Roy was said to have been accidentally killed."

"Then I don't understand." Sipsy had sent one of the waitresses over and she was sweeping up the pieces of glass.

"A week or so after the official letter and us running a story in our weekly about this tragedy, a man comes to see me."

Yates got a chill.

Mrs. Bass placed the can aside as if it were a captured chess piece. "It was Roy's father, Horace. He works down at Goodyear and he came by after work. He's a big man, Alma, but he was shaking like a little kid before his first haircut. There was something he just had to tell me. He didn't know where else to go with it, but he was going to bust if he didn't."

Yates felt a thud behind her eye, and fought to get her heart beat settled down.

Mrs. Bass went on, her voice low, her manner guarded. "Horace told me that Roy had snuck home to see this filly of his that works at the gas company. It was his first time in love or at least he thought so. She's a few years older than him, more experienced if you catch my meaning." She got a sour twist to her mouth like she'd swallowed salt.

"He went AWOL? And this was when?"

"Three weeks prior to the explosion at Fort Bragg."

"And he stopped in to see his folks too?"

"His mother would have slapped the black off him if she'd know he'd tip-toed back into town for some R & R. Or whatever you young'ins are calling it these days. But he did stop in to see his dad for a loan 'cause he wanted to show this woman a good time before he got back to Fort Huachuca."

"So at that point he was still there?"

"That's just it, Alma. Roy told him the reason he could sneak away was because him and some other colored GIs had been selected for special duty. They were separated from the other soldiers and given their own barracks away from the base. They had their own food, got to listen to the radio, read magazines, even got beer one night he boasted. No maneuvers, just a half hour of calisthenics in the morning, and every other day a five-mile march, but no field packs."

"For what?"

"He didn't know. He told his dad he had to sign some papers, and that soon the observation period would be over. He didn't go on, but said the reason he could get away was because they were left alone a lot and he was able to take the chance."

"Get back to L.A. Make sure no other cock-a-doodle-do was in his henhouse," Yates snickered.

Mrs. Bass nodded. "He came in Friday evening and was gone by that Saturday night. Harold told me Roy didn't want to leave till Sunday. But his father convinced him to get while the getting was good. That he had to do what was right and finish his service."

"How'd Roy get back? His father took him?"

"That was the funny thing too," she said. "He bolts from this secret barracks of his, figuring to hop a freight. He runs across this working Dodge pick-up at a boarded-up gas station. Now essentially being a good church going boy, he leaves a note and promises to return the vehicle. Which he does by the way."

Yates rubbed at her temple. "Like the truck was waiting there for him?"

"That's my emphasis," the Eagle's publisher retorted. "Harold assumed it was intervention from the good Lord."

"So Roy's father thinks his son was killed in Arizona?"

"He's not sure and neither am I, Alma. But some kind of monkey business is going on, that's for sure."

"What else, Mrs. Bass? This is very interesting, but what is it that made you not pursue this further?"

"Pursuing it further is what got me spooked, if you will allow me the expression." A loop-sided grin rolled along her mouth.

"They came to see you? Who?"

"Hold on, hold on," the other woman held up both hands. "Eyes and ears, okay?"

"Yes of course, I'm sorry. But it's just--"

"This isn't a Torchy Brown adventure, Alma," Mrs. Bass said.

Yates nodded. The older woman referred to a strip featuring an independent Negro woman written and drawn by a black woman, cartoonist Jackie Ormes. Torchy had originated in the Courier and ran in other Negro papers, though Ormes hadn't produced a new one in some time. "But I feel this is something that runs deep."

Mrs. Bass stared off. "I wish I'd learned to drink more." She sighed and Yates waited. "Okay," the older woman began, "I promised Harold I would keep his confidence. He didn't know what to do and neither did I."

"You knew," Yates declared.

"But not how and keep my word, Alma. You know the black press is much less about the vaunted ideal of objectivity and more about being the advocates for our people's aspirations."

"Don't I know." Yates put the can to her lips. "Anyway, you're making the argument for getting to the bottom of this, Mrs. Bass."

"See? Ain't I good to you, baby?" The man and woman who'd been fighting returned. They made kissy faces at each other as he walked behind her, his hands lovingly on her shoulders.

"Come on," Mrs. Bass said, rising.

Yates followed and they eased their way through the now crowded lounge. The late master of the drums Chick Webb could be heard pounding the skins on the juke.

"The woman was Filipino." Mrs. Bass told her when they'd gotten outside.

"Was I that obvious back in the bar?"

"I was sizing you up, but you weren't the only one giving Trummy and his date the Barney Google."

They crossed the street, several people saying hi to the activist publisher.

"How are you, Ellis?" Mrs. Bass said to one and "See you at the meeting next Thursday," to a tall woman.

"So what is it you're going to show me, Mrs. Bass?" Yates asked as they went along.

By way of an answer she said, "Of course my natural nosey nose got he best of me and I had to try and find out what happened out there in the desert."

"You sent a reporter out to the fort?" Despite her chunky small build, Yates had to work to keep up with the hard charging Charlotta Bass. As she's assumed, they were heading to the Eagle's offices.

"I figured that would be a lost cause, and tip off whoever was the mastermind that we had a line on it."

"What is it?" Yates huffed as they crossed in front of a used car lot. A row of recently washed Buick grills grinned their chrome teeth like a harlot's come-on.

"You tell me." They arrived at the offices. The name and eagle head logo of the newspaper painted boldly in brown and gold on the large plate glass window. Inside, several desk lamps were on attesting to a skeletal crew at work on the Soames story.

"This way." Mrs. Bass cut to the left and they entered the building through a side door half way down. The two stood in a short hallway seeped in the peculiar nose-tickling odor of photo processing chemicals. Yates followed Mrs. Bass down the hall to a door in need of varnish. On it was the publisher's modest name plate. They entered the unlocked door and the lights were clicked on.

"Lock it." Mrs. Bass directed Yates and opened another door to a small room and went inside.

Yates turned the anchor knob to secure the door. She could hear Mrs. Bass moving items around then she re-emerged with a Dictaphone and set it on her busy desk. She unwrapped a cylinder and set it in the machine. She then adjusted the funnel and beckoned Yates to come over. "Make yourself comfortable."

She switched the device on and remained standing. "This was recorded by me," her recorded voice announced. Yates heard a phone ring and a receiver being lifted.

"That you, Mrs. Bass?" A male voice asked tentatively. It was a white man.

"Go on, sir." the publisher responded.

"I'm only doing this because I owe--"

"No names, sir," Mrs. Bass admonished on the wax cylinder.

"Yes, yes of course, nerves you know."

"About the matter you have knowledge of."

"As I tried to relay through channels, I can't, that is, I won't substantiate this if I should find myself hauled before a court or some committee on the Hill."

Mrs. Bass said, "I understand."

"Good. In the fall of 1939 I was ordered by my supervisor to do a series of tests with dogs and cats, typical household pets you see." There was a gap and the faint sound of a door opening and closing was heard. "I exposed the animals to varying degrees of the emissions." Another gap. "You understand what I'm saying?"

Yates looked at Mrs. Bass who stared grimly at the Dictaphone.

"You mean something about radioactivity?"

"Very good, Mrs. Bass, you're on the right track. Microwave research is an offshoot of the Department's ongoing work to better our radar systems. You see microwaves lie between the infrared and radio range."

"We don't have much time. If you could get to the soldiers at Huachuca"

His response was unintelligible.

"Sir?"

"It was more; well, to see, to chart the reactions to their bodies given the varying intensity and times of exposures."

"You're not talking about the animals now, are you?"

"No, Mrs. Bass, I'm not."

"Let's be very clear here, can we, sir? You're saying the United States Army--"

"The project was initiated higher and more secret than that particular branch actually. Something called X-2 section, of which I know little else."

"My point," she said sharply, "is that officials of this government willingly used its own citizens as test subjects in an experiment they seemingly had no specific knowledge about."

The man breathed heavily. "More or less, yes."

"To what purpose? Or was it enough they were black and therefore deemed expendable?"

"Building the right equipment and finding the correct calculation to boil the water molecules beneath the surface of ones skin," he said bluntly.

Yates tittered nervously. What was she to make of this?

The voice continued speaking. "Imagine an unseen stimulation of this peculiar wavelength of the cosmic spectrum? You can heat water or cook meat from within."

"Or kill people invisibly," Mrs. Bass gasped on the Dictaphone.

"Their liquefied brains running out of their ears." He added. There was another door opening and closing on the recording, this time much more distinct.

"Goodbye Mrs. Bass. I won't be calling again."

"What's it called?" She shouted.

"Sacrifice, Operation Sacrifice." The line clicked off. The rotating sound of the wax cylinder whizzed and cracked, filling the void left by the enormity of the man's words.

Yates finally said, "Is there anything to this man's Buck Rogers mumbo jumbo?" There was no easy way she could absorb what she'd heard. "I guess there must be," she said nervously, "why else have you hidden this recording away. But how did you follow up?"

"Relax, take it slow," Mrs. Bass advised. "It is a lot to take in, isn't it?"

"Mrs. Bass?" Yates was woozy and sucking in air.

"Yes I did do some checking into what the man on the other end of that phone told me." Mrs. Bass sat down heavily, as if gravity itself were conspiring against her.

"And you were threatened?"

"It only took a note under my door on a quiet Sunday morning."

Yates imagined the message had been filled with invectives and racial epithets.

"It simply read, stop or no paper. When I came to the office Monday, there was a stack of pulled ads from long time customers. From Golden State Mutual to the Barrel House club."

"Just like that?"

"Just like that. We don't make enough around here and God knows the staff has to do odd jobs elsewhere to put gravy on their kid's biscuits. But when we need to, the Eagle does soar." She smiled weakly at her clichéd homilies. "I'm not on a crusade, but it's what we have, it's all I have."

"What did you find out?"

"That's just it, nothing. I wasn't even off of first base, Alma. The most I did was make a visit to a professor friend at USC."

"A scientist?"

"Yes, he'd worked on a component used to get radar going in the '30s. He's an older gentleman and semi-retired. I was trying to get some background information on microwaves, and we had a pleasant tea and chat on campus. I made sure I didn't ask him anything too specific; I didn't want to get him involved."

"But," she spread her hands, "that was naive of me. The act of seeing him was enough I'm sure. Anyway the note followed and that's all there was to it."

"Has this office been searched?"

She looked around at the piles. "You tell me. I keep the cylinder on the move, Alma. From garage to hole in the elm tree to the abandoned refrigerator in the empty building."

"But it was here tonight."

"So were you."

Yates snorted. "So now I have the burden?"

"Pandora's box," Mrs. Bass observed. "I'm not telling you to lift the lid. Really, I will tell you in the sternest way not to pursue this now."

Yates slumped down in her chair, exhausted and exhilarated. "This man you had on the phone could have been jivin' you."

"The note, those pulled ads, that wasn't jive. No matter how you slice it, it's the real McCoy. Whatever the 'it,' is."

"Your advertisers I mean, they ever say anything to you?"

"We pretend as if nothing ever happened when they renewed. The world keeps spinning and Ella can still belt them out." Mrs. Bass blew out her breath as if under great exertion. "Here's what I think you ought to do, Alma, keep telling those good stories and--"

Both women jumped at a knock on the door. "Boss," someone said on the other side, "Joe Adams is here with some shots of Soames' body."

"Damn, Joe," Mrs. Bass grinned. "He's owns a barber shop and runs around like a fiend taking photos too. What a character." Then louder, "Tell him I'll be right there."

"We've got a joker like that, Yates said, glad to be able to talk about something light if only for a few moments. "Teeny Harris. He's always dressed to the nines and always behind the wheel of a new Caddy."

Mrs. Bass rose and put the cylinder away. She came over to the younger woman. Yates also got up. The publisher put a hand on the reporter's shoulder. "What I'd do is not pursue it, let it blow by you like used ration stamps. You go on telling our stories."

"But I can't turn my back on this."

"I'm not asking that." She took her hand away and started for the locked door. "If you go poking around, then who ever or what ever department is behind this will poke back, harder." Her pudgy hand was on the knob, the other turning the lock. "Listen more than ask, Alma. You've got a career and a life ahead of you. There's always a time for martyrs."

"Gather a little here and a little there. When you get to be my age, then maybe you'll be able to tell this story.

"And sacrifice," Yates reminded her.

"You have a duty to perform, Alma. Sometimes we do get to choose our battles." With that Mrs. Bass went into her newsroom.

Yates suddenly didn't feel like any gay catting. But she needed something to calm her so she could get some perspective on this damned thing. Whatever it was.

The two women wished each other well as the members of the Eagle's staff looked at the photos Joe Adams had taken. The photographer was a burly man with a freight handler's arms and a kind, open face. The pictures were matt black and whites freshly taken inside the coroner's facility. The prints glistened from just being squeegeed and excess chemical stop blotted onto the desk.

In the shots an obviously beaten Soames was laid out on a metal slab next to another colored corpse. Even in death, segregation prevailed. Or maybe it was only Negroes who died violently in the City of the Valley of Smokes. The undertaker was going to be awfully busy with Soames' face and upper body Yates estimated. A slow anger welled inside her, and she had a mind to ignore the sanguine advice of Mrs. Bass and go charging out of here to turn over every lead to discover the white men

110

behind this evil. She wanted to expose this wrong to the condemnation of the world.

Instead she stepped lightly into the cool night air and later had three martinis over the objections of the level-headed Loren Miller and his date.

CHAPTER 12

Bergen County, July, 1943

Crimpshaw ducked under the haymaker and shooting up chugged a solid right onto the chump's chin. The white man teetered back on his heels but he didn't fall over. His partner, an even beefier Hunkie in a too tight coat clacked his rabbit teeth together and brought his sap down toward the organizer's skull. He rolled his left shoulder, letting that part of his body absorb most of the blow. Still, pain bolted through his arm, making it temporarily useless.

"Nail this coon, Cornie," the one who'd thrown the looping punch cried.

"I go him, I got him," Cornie promised, wailing his home made blackjack. "You hold the jig still, hear me?"

The other man loped forward, going low to tackle Crimpshaw but he kicked this one in the throat as he came for him. The man coughed phlegm and blood and splayed out onto the wet grassy field of knee high weeds, dandelions and discarded car parts.

"Tricky bastard," Cornie declared, using his mallet of a fist to stun Crimpshaw with a jab to the gut. Cornie evidently had some boxing experience, and was using it with earnest. "Why don't you just take your warning and we can all get on with our day?" The sap twitched again and whistled toward Crimpshaw's leg, connecting.

Crimpshaw's knee suddenly couldn't support his weight and a mortal fear made his chest go cold. He didn't want to die in this goddamn dump at the hands of a couple of hired thugs. He didn't want to die before he had a chance to hold Alma in his arms one more time, her mouth on his.

Cornie got another shot in but this one invigorated Crimpshaw. He bent over as if hurt more than he was, allowing the base of his neck to be a target for the stocky man's thrasher.

"Oh, baby," the gorilla said happily.

As he brought the knocker down, Crimpshaw bulled forward, the notion of not seeing that beautiful Alma again giving him a second wind. The thing slapped him between the shoulder blades as he got his arms around the hired muscle and drove.

"Nigger," Cornie the sap wielder hollered, striking an off-balance hit on the other man's upper body.

"Nigger this, shit head." Crimpshaw suddenly stopped short rather than topple over with his attacker. Cornie's momentum kept him going and he slid onto his wide backside among the tall weeds. Knowing he couldn't give the other man an opening, Crimpshaw sprang and brought his foot down like stomping on a roach. His shoe came down on Cornie's surprised face, and there was a sound of cartilage crunching.

"Motherfucker." Blood trickling from his nostrils and onto his mouth. Cornie reached up and tried to get a hold of Crimpshaw's leg but was having trouble making the upper portion of his body cooperate. He weakly grabbed at the labor man's pant leg. "You, motherfucker," he repeated, as if invoking an ancestor.

Crimpshaw stomped on his face twice. Cornie was going to have to visit the dentist. There was a muffled moan and he turned to see the other goon trying to get up.

"Here, let me help you," Crimpshaw said, gripping the man's arm. The white moon face glared up at him and the Brotherhood of Sleeping Car Porters' lead organizer drilled a straight left into that groggy continence. The thug's body sagged to the earth, Crimpshaw pounded on the man's face with the bottom of his fist like rapping on a table for attention. The hood lay still, in a fetal position, his cheek fractured.

Crimpshaw had his hands on his knees, leaning over at the waist and breathing out of his mouth. His wind returned and he examined the inert forms. His shoulder where the blackjack had tagged him blazed in pain. One man, the one without the sap, had no identification on him. Though he did have a half filled ration stamp book imprinted with tanks in his shirt pocket. The other one had a cocktail napkin from the Hawk's Lounge on Flatbush Avenue in Brooklyn. A phone number was written on it in runny ink. He pocketed this and went to a knee next to the would be blackjack user.

"Hey, Mister Charley, can you hear me?" Like he'd seen in a Jimmy Cagney movie, Crimpshaw pulled the man up by his tie and slapped his face.

"Huh," the man slurred.

"I know you're stupid, but not deaf," Crimpshaw slapped him harder on general principals. "Who in the company put you up to this?" He asked politely.

"Fuck off, tar baby."

"Oh, I see." Crimpshaw let the man's tie go and looked around. He spied the pacifier nearby and plucked it off the ground. "Now what did you say?" He tapped the weighted end against his palm.

Sitting up, the man squinted, one red-rimmed eye steady on Crimpshaw's hands. His chest rose and fell rapidly, his shirt front stained crimson. "Nigger boy, get that look off your face, you'd be buying yourself a world of trouble."

"I've already got that, I'm black." Crimpshaw whacked him along the forehead, making him yelp in shock. "Now answer my goddamn question."

"You can't do this to a white man." But he didn't sound so sure.

For emphasis, Crimpshaw rapped the blackjack against the man's knees. Like a ventriloquist act, his partner lying face down in the weeds groaned. "What about it, tough guy? Who paid your light bill this month?"

The man put a hand to his mouth, assessing his odds. As if he could get up and run without receiving billiard ball-sized knots on his noggin. He said, "Krupp."

Alnon Krupp was one of the first vice presidents of the Pullman Car Company. He was headquartered out of Kansas City, Kansas, and had been the last hold out when the bosses had decided to finally recognize the union. But it was known that Krupp still went out of his way to torment the members and staff when ever and where ever he could.

"That kraut's in town, isn't he?"

The man glared.

Crimpshaw smiled and did a Cagney hitch of his pants. "Shit." And walloped him on top of his square head.

"Aw fuck." He held onto the sore spot with both hands as he rocked back and forth in his sitting position. "Cut it out, huh?"

"Any time you're ready, son."

"No more hitting, right? That goddamn thing hurts."

Crimpshaw cocked his head to one side. "Well?"

"The Alexandria, suite on the 17th floor."

He figured that. When Krupp had come into town with the other vice-presidents and the head boy to bargain the master contract, he'd stayed at the Alexandria. Crimpshaw had developed an informal information network among most of the shoeshine men and janitors working the midtown and upper west side hotels. Colored men like them were invisible to white folks and they said all kinds of things in their presence. Ofays tipped good, but the pride the Brotherhood elicited was priceless.

"Thanks, sport."

The man had gotten his confidence back and tried a move. He swung an arm out and upset the organizer's balance. Crimpshaw went down and the torpedo leapt on him, his fists flailing. But he had the blackjack and Crimpshaw went to work like Josh Gibson at the plate. He struck repeatedly even as a fist welted his lip. The bohunk went limp and Crimpshaw had to shove his heavy body off of him. He lay for a few moments gathering himself and then got to his feet.

The men had left the keys to their Hudson Pacemaker in the ignition. He got it going and let the brake out. Crimpshaw put the wheel-mounted standard shift into reverse with little grinding of the gears and soon righted the car onto the highway. The morning air was sharp with anthrite, and in the near distance three tall smoke stacks attested to the presence of a coal processing plant beyond the horizon.

Driving over the George Washington Bridge back into New York, Crimpshaw couldn't find a reason for the rough up. At the moment, the union wasn't in a huff with the Company, other than the usual grievances they had to handle.

He was starting to stiffen from his workout and Crimpshaw smirked self-confidently. Maybe he did like his chicken and waffles a little too much, but it was good to see he could still stand toe-to-toe when it mattered. Crimpshaw finished dabbing at his nose and jammed the bloody handkerchief in his coat pocket. He got back over to Manhattan and arrived at the Brotherhood offices on 129th Street.

"I told you about those crazy gals you take up with" Dorthea, A. Philip Randolph's executive assistant cracked upon seeing Crimpshaw's dishevelment as he breezed into the inner offices. A hand-cranked Spirit Duplicator was going in the front office as someone printed handbills.

"The Chief in?"

"He's on a call to Milton in Chicago, Virgil. He's going to be another fifteen minutes or so."

Crimpshaw hadn't stopped moving. "He'll want to know about this and so will Milton." Reaching Randolph's closed door, Dorthea released a small sigh as she continued to edit one of Randolph's letters. She was quite used to the ways of the excitable Mr. Crimpshaw who knocked rapidly and entered.

"Hold on, Milt, Virgil just stormed in here." Randolph, who maintained a reserved facade, nonetheless conveyed his displeasure at the unannounced intrusion. Crimpshaw marched over from the doorway. Randolph had his hand over the handset's mouthpiece, his alert eyes watchful and waiting.

Crimpshaw laid the news on him and any reprimand he was going to get for barging in went out the window.

"You hear that, Milton?" Randolph said to the man on the other end. He'd removed his hand when Crimpshaw mentioned Krupp. "Yes, yes, I'm not sure what to make of it either," he responded after a pause as he listened. "Let me and Virgil discuss this, and I'll get back to you." He nodded to the other one's answer and hung the phone up. "Take a load off, Virgil."

"Thanks, Chief."

"So, from the top if you please?"

"Okay —"

Randolph held up a hand. "You want some water?"

He waved it off and went on. "I'm coming out of my place this morning and these two bohunks are in front, leaning on their car big and white as all get out."

"Them or the car?"

It took a moment for Crimpshaw to understand that the reserved Randolph was making a joke. "One of them was smacking on a cannoli from the Italian place. Threw the wax paper it'd been wrapped in at me when I came down the steps."

As was his habit, Randolph made notes in his neat penmanship as Crimpshaw talked. "They tell you they were from Krupp then?"

"That's later." Crimpshaw now wished he'd asked for the water. His mouth was suddenly dry and the thirst was working its way into the bruised parts of his body. "So this bohunk—"

"How do you know that?"

"His accent is thicker than Rockefeller's wallet." The Chief could be a royal pain with his desire for details. "Anyway, this Hunky, he's the one that's been snackin', gets very close after he flicks the ball of paper at me. He says we gotta take a ride over to the meadowlands 'cause the grass smells so much sweeter out there.

"The other sumbitch is still leaning against the Hudson, arms folded, goofy grin on him as he watches his pal brace me."

"That's when the fight started?"

"No, that's when the tough one shows his sap but since my knees don't buckle, the one laying back opens up his jacket for a peek at the gat he's got nestled there."

"They didn't say anything to you on the way over to New Jersey?"

"Not much, mostly trying to get my goat. You know, going on how we're stirring up matters, how we're a bunch of communist instigators and so forth."

Randolph lifted an eyebrow. "That's the phrase he used?"

Crimpshaw rubbed his lower jaw. "Sure as shit, yeah, that's the words all right." It was a saying both knew Krupp used often about the Brotherhood. He then told him the rest and how he effected his getaway.

Randolph tented then inter-laced his fingers, his angular frame leaning back in his chair. "As far as I know, there's no Pullman Company meeting happening right now. At least not here in town."

Crimpshaw didn't have anything to say.

Randolph clicked on his intercom and asked Dorthea to check on the matter as fast as possible. "You better dump that car of theirs or you're sure to get pinched for stealing it."

"Yeah, I'll do that. But what do you want to do about Krupp?"

"This may be something he's doing on his own, a maverick action."

"I don't know, Chief, he's always been a tough nut, but the Pullman Company has been good to him. It doesn't seem to me he'd do this unless it was on orders from the very top."

Randolph considered the situation then said, "Maybe I'll have a conversation with him."

Crimpshaw knew he wasn't kidding. "Like he'd come clean?"

"He's always dealt with us like he had all the cards," Randolph pointed out. "To him, we're just a bunch of poor field hands and glorified butlers who can't possibly come out ahead of the white man in the end. And him in particular."

"He's so taken with himself he'll spill the beans?"

Randolph smoothed his tie. "He's let the cat out before. Remember that sticking point we had about hazard pay of seventy-five cents an hour during the marathon negotiation we had in Detroit?"

"Yeah, Krupp finally boils over and jumps up and yells at you they'd already agreed inside the company to give us sixty-five cents so why crow about another dime. But his patience was at an end." Crimpshaw spread his hands. "But this…"

"There was some kind of message he was trying to convey," Randolph commented. "When they took you out to the field, the one with the gun used the butt of it on you?"

"He sure did. I dropped to a knee and when he used it again on me I managed to knock it away into the weeds. And you can bet I wasn't going to give him a chance to go on a treasure hunt for it."

Randolph let his fingertips rest against his pursed mouth, his elbow propped on his desk's blotter. "You've been more than a soldier in our struggle, Virgil. Like you name sake, the Greek poet Publius Vergilius Maro, you've been a model for others and as Dante knew, our guide through this most Divine Comedy the American Negro has uniquely faced."

"You lost me there, Chief."

Randolph smiled thinly. "Do you think they meant to kill you out there today?"

"I think they meant to work me over good, maybe put me in the hospital. But if they wanted to croak me, why do it out there?"

Randolph looked at a point beyond the room. "Why indeed?"

Dorthea buzzed the intercom and Randolph answered it. "Even if it was a secret meeting, we'd have some hint about it through our spies, Phil. But so far nobody has heard about anything."

"Bear down on the office in Kansas City. See if there's some sort of rumble about Krupp."

"Like he's on the outs?" Crimpshaw cut in.

"Exactly. Check on that, will you, Dorthea?"

"Right away."

Crimpshaw looked up from his Elgin. "If it's okay, I promised to pick up this chick when she got back into town."

"The reporter?"

"Yeah, she's all right, Chief."

"Give her my regards. Tell her I'm expecting her Friday at two for the interview she wants to do with me. And just so it's on the record, we'll make a police report but of course expect little in the way of an investigation."

Crimpshaw was up again. "I'll see you tonight at the meeting at the Elks at 6:30."

"Don't fall down any manholes." He walked him to the door.

"I'll try not to." He left the offices and caught a cab to Grand Central Station. A Red Cap was walking by with a filled baggage cart.

"Renny," Crimpshaw called out.

"Gate, give me some skin, baby."

They slid their palms against each other's. Quickly Crimpshaw filled the man in on what he wanted.

"I'll see what I can shake loose. Ed goes on for the swing shift at the Alexandria and I'll have him put his peepers on this pale face you're askin' about."

"Solid, brother." He slipped him a fin and went inside the train station. He was ten minutes late and the train from Los Angeles was twenty minutes behind. By the time Alma Yates got off her car, he'd washed his face and combed his close-cropped hair. Except for the blood stains on his shirt, and his closed jacket covered these, and the grass stain on one knee, he looked presentable.

"Hey now," he said, waving as she entered from the tracks.

"Hey, yourself," she answered back. They came close and impulsively she dropped her bag and put her arms around his neck. He drew her close, tightening his strong arms around her compact waist. They kissed with a ferocity that amazed both of them.

"Well, now," Crimpshaw said appreciatively.

"Yes," she replied, looking at him.

"The rally," he declared. Seeing her triggered the association in his memory.

"What?"

"Come on, I got a call to make." He grabbed her bag and holding hands they found a phone booth. He called the Brotherhood offices and told Randolph his suspicions. The Chief said he'd make calls to the other endorsers to see if anything had happened to any of their people.

"Make sure I can reach you a little later, general."

Crimpshaw had a hand on Yates' hip who stood near him while he sat on the booth's stool. Her fingers fooled with the hair on the side of his head. "Oh course," He disconnected and the two walked across the massive concourse toward the 44th Street exit. Mid-afternoon light ghosted through the huge arched window giving the tile a gray, shimmering quality like they were gliding over layers of ice with secrets buried deep.

"Want to get some lunch at the Empire State Building? It's not far and the view from the café on the observation deck is something else," Crimpshaw said. Curiously he noted to himself, you could see over to the part of Jersey where the two had taken him this morning.

"That'd be fine," she lowered her head momentarily. "Good to see you, Virgil."

"Same here, Alma." They checked her bags. He squeezed her hand and they walked over to Fifth Avenue and the world's tallest building. In the elevator, the two exchanged goofy grins. In the restaurant, they got a table and ordered.

"So what is all this, Virgil?"

He told her about the incident as their food arrived.

"Oh my God, you okay?" She placed her hand on his, rubbing.

"I've had dust up worse than those two birds could hand out, baby."

"And why would this Krupp care about Negroes wanting to be in combat?" In the back of her mind, the crack and pop of the anxious man on the wax cylinder played.

Crimpshaw ate his meatloaf like a bear. "I know this, egg, Krupp see? I know down to his Aryan soul he ain't too far from getting behind the whole master race two-step. Alma. I wouldn't be surprised if he was some kind of fifth columnist or something."

A week ago she would have chastised him for being far-fetched. Now she wasn't so sure. "If anything, you'd think he'd be happy that black folk have been clamoring so much to get our chance to die." She picked at her chicken pot pie. It was too heavy and the weather too hot. And her stomach was aflutter anyway. But it wasn't the business at Fort Huachuca that was bothering her as they ate.

"Anything that shows unity on the part of colored folks would only make Krupp use the Pepto more, Alma. Anyway we'll get to the bottom of this. We ain't come this far to let the fat cats beat us at our own game. They forget, but this is out country too."

"That's what my cousin, Silas said."

"Smart man," Crimpshaw jested.

"He's going over, Virgil. He got his notice."

"Sorry to hear that."

"He said it was a relief. He figured it was only a matter of time and wanted it to be over with."

"It's just starting," Crimpshaw pointed out. He ate more in silence and finally said, "You think I'm chicken for not signing up?"

"You're no kid, kid." She smiled at him and it felt good inside, natural.

"You know what I mean."

"You dispatch two ruffians who might have been taking you for the proverbial ride then sit down to eat like you just stepped out of the barber shop. I don't think anyone questions your manhood, Virgil."

"I'm just worried that you do."

She leaned over and gave him a peck. "You're a cradle robber, you old man of thirty-three, but why the hell is this on your mind, Virgil?"

"Because before it didn't matter. Being glorified porters and stewards was one thing, but now, you can feel it, Alma." He put air in his chest. "You know we're going to see some action. And I don't want no son or daughter of mine thinking their old man was yellow when it counted."

"It seems to me you do your share of fighting on the home front."

"Yeah, yeah, that's what the Chief says too. But it ain't the same thing, Alma. Man has to, I don't know, he has to stand and be accounted for when it's this axis business, don't you think?"

"And what's going to be different for colored people once this is over, Virgil? White folks going to realize we love and hate like them?

Run scared and worry about our kid's teeth like they do? Or will they still see us as different, the other. Look at that," she continued, pointing at a poster adorning a curving wall.

On it was a gauche illustration of a Japanese soldier complete with his sun-visored cap. He had a machine pistol in one hand and carried over his shoulder, proud butt in the air, was a barely clad fearful white woman. The soldier's face was illustrated in an exaggerated way so that his Asiatic features had a particular demonic cast to them. The epicanthic folds of his eyes were angled up behind horn-rimmed glasses, and his ears were pointed. The bold-faced marquee type asked: "Defeat the Japs."

"You going to tell me that couldn't be a black man, drawn ape-like, with the same headline?"

Crimpshaw's face pinched. "I know, Alma, but this is more than that, and you know it. This is like after all the years of pushing against the big door with the brass door knobs, the heartache and bullshit, that day when we got word the Pullman Company recognized the union, that was a hell of a special day. We were men."

"You don't have to die to show me you're a man, Virgil."

"Death can be quick. It's living with the doubt that can eat you up."

"Like I said, I'm not ashamed of you Mr. Crimpshaw."

"I'm glad." He leaned across and kissed her. "But maybe I need to prove it to myself."

"I've got another battlefield in mind for you today, dough boy."

"Yeah?" And a piece of meatloaf fell off his fork.

At his place near Small's Paradise, they made noisy afternoon love. Outside the half open window, beyond the drawn shade, busses, trolleys and a fruit peddler went by with his pushcart.

"Blueeeeberrieessss...

"Stawwwwberrieesss...

"Blaaaaackberrieessss..."

Afterward, they lay side-by-side, the sheet up around both of them.

"They ain't even sure who the first Pullman porter was." Crimpshaw said apropos of no previous conversation between them.

He puffed on a dainty White Owl cigar.

"How's that?" she murmured, touching the cooling sweat on his hairless chest.

"The big Chicago fire of eighteen –"

"Seventy-one," she completed for him.

"Uh-huh," he kissed her shoulder. "Anyway, all them early records of the company were burned up so nobody knows who the cat was."

She breathed in deep, enjoying the smell of their bodies that floated about the room. "So you don't want to be unknown, Virgil? You want to come back home with a tunic full of medals?" She had a vision of her cousin in a torn uniform, steam and filtered sunlight all around him. But unlike the peaceful aura of the train station, this light gave her no warmth nor comfort. She shook it from her head as he spoke.

"You're pretty smart beside being beautiful."

"That's what all my boyfriends tell me."

"Huh?"

She laughed and he finally got the joke. They snuggled and soon were making love again. They moved from the bed to a chair. There she straddled him, riding him up and down slowly then faster and faster to the beat of a Harry Dial drum solo that invaded the room from somewhere.

"Stop, stop," an out of breath Crimpshaw pleaded as they reached their end. "You're gonna kill me."

She put her arms around him and they kissed intently. "Good work, soldier."

"Thanks, cap'n." He put his head back and moaned from exhaustion and pleasure.

Drowsily he watched Yates get up and put on her slip. She tossed the sheet over his still form in the chair and bounced into the bathroom. After using the facility, she stood at the sink washing her hands. In the mirror was a woman who had a choice to make. If this was a time to stand for your beliefs, then what about her? She couldn't let go of the secret experiment the man hinted at on the Dictaphone. Maybe it was all hooey, but she couldn't rationalize it away that easy.

Mrs. Bass had tried to warn her off, God Bless her. But she was too much a journalist to be able to sit on what might be the biggest story of the year. Yates smiled at the face in the mirror. How much of this was love for her people and how much was living out that unspoken wish she'd made several years ago to herself. That she could be the first colored reporter to win a Pulitzer? It was nuts, but it wasn't impossible. And this story about microwaves being used on colored troops could be it. If it were true and she could prove it.

She peered close at her reflection as Crimpshaw snored. "You're right, Virgil," she told herself, "it's living with the doubt that can eat you up."

CHAPTER 14

Tunis, North Africa
June, 1943

Madison Clay removed the empty bottle of Armagnac French Brandy as the two men in civilian clothes sat and smoked H. Upmann cigars. The taller one with the horse end ugly face was Swiss, a gear and sprockets salesman. He wore loose, ill-fitting clothes that always seemed haphazardly thrown onto his lanky frame. The other man was a wider six one, fair skin with sandy blonde hair and arctic lake blue eyes. His clothes, which mostly consisted of khakis and short-sleeved shirts, fit him as if tailored on Savile Row. His upper body was that of a man who put himself through regular conditioning. This one was Vaslov, an olive oil middleman of Serbian extraction.

The taller one had just told a joke to the other one in English and the two men howled with glee. "Boy, boy," Vaslov said in French to Clay, "I say, what is your name mister sour puss?" He looked at his companion and the two had a chuckle.

"Baku," sir," Clay replied in his Senegalese accented French. He gave them a big country grin to go with it.

"Just what is it about this job you don't like, eh, Baku?" His interlocutor went on. "You get food, your own quarters, and even sneak peeks at white thighs, isn't that so?" He tapped his buddy's knee with the back of his hand. "Yet you go around hour after hour, day in day out, for a month now with a look of, oh I don't know." He playfully drummed his chin with his fingers and glanced over at the tall man. "What would you say, Lenz?"

Lenz clucked his tongue. "I'd say this fellow has a problem with humility and fortitude, like we all do."

"Hmmm," the other one pretended to consider. "Could be he has too much on his mind, too many chores to attend to. You know these darkies can become worrisome if complicated tasks are required of them."

Clay stood with the bottle on the tray, his hands tightly gripping the silver server. "I'm simply trying to do my job the best way I can, boss man."

"Yes," the one built like a boxer drew out. He crossed his legs and leisurely tapped his cigar ash into an onyx ashtray. "What's your opinion of white men, Baku?"

"You're in charge, boss. You must be very happy that the Germans have been thrown out, aren't you?"

He glared at Clay's blank face.

Lenz took a deep pull on his cigar and exhaled a plume that obscured his elongated face. "Very happy indeed."

"Of course that must be so. I must get to my other duties now, if you please, good gentlemen."

"Really," the blonde bruiser put in. "Well, we wouldn't want to keep you from your work, now would we, Lenz?"

"No, we wouldn't."

Clay pivoted on his heels and started to walk away, but he knew this was coming.

"Ah, Baku," the blonde one cracked.

"Yes, sir."

"Be a good chap as the British say and bring me some of those wonderful Egyptian olives, would you?"

Clay had turned back but didn't move. The punch line had to be delivered.

"And make sure you pit them, understand, boy?"

"Completely." And with that, Clay walked the length of the room and stepped behind a curtain into the makeshift kitchen area of the Tom-Tom Klub. The watering hole was actually a big box of a space rigged together from packing crates, tin, girders from abandoned oil rigs, found lumber and the remains of a Junker 52. The plane had once been used to transport parts for Rommel's Afrika Korps. Windows had been cut into the slap-dash joint's sides but there was no glass, though mesh was tacked in place to keep the mosquito traffic to a minimum.

The plundered items included rugs, chairs and tables the routed Nazis had collected from Athens, Paris, and Poland with touches of Italian crystal, and been placed about to make it cozy. The partitioned section had been erected with heavy gauze curtain material and this constituted a sort of pantry where Clay and the two other men fetched snack food and napkins. The bar was a couple of doors upended on sawhorses manned by a stiff legged individual named Lom. He was Belgium and beside French spoke Italian, and liked to listen to his wireless that occasionally pulled in arias from God knew where. The club had no doors and on either end of its length, archways had been cut to allow entrances and breezes. When rain or the infrequent cold front moved in, drape material like that used for the pantry section could be dropped into place.

The outside of the club had been tar papered over and some enterprising type had painted the name of the place in bold Gothic letters over the northern entranceway. The whole of it was sandwiched between a fig merchant's stall and a knot of threadbare palm trees. All of this across a narrow street the width of an alley from the French embassy. Part of the third floor of the embassy had been destroyed by a tank blast in the recent battles for control in the city.

The Vichy staff of the embassy had been sent off to a prison camp in the mountains with their German masters for interrogation. This had happened a little over a month ago when the combined forces of the Americans and British had fought their way into Morocco, Algiers and Tunisia, heretofore French colonies occupied by the Germans and the Italians and administered by the Vichy. But the resolve of the Allies, the loyal French struggling from within the Vichy government and the fact that Rommel could not put as much material and men under his command fast enough, added up to a victory for the allies.

And during one of those interrogation sessions of the enemy, a phrase slipped. This eventually reached Colonel Snow, and Clay was put in motion for the very fact that he was black and would therefore be the least likely one to be suspected of being a spy.

The man with the doctorate in chemistry set the pitted olives down on the elegantly carved end table between the two men. He wondered if the piece of furniture had once graced the sitting room of a genteel madam or hard-working doctor in Prague or Warsaw.

"See, you can follow direction," the blonde one needled.

"Leave him alone, Vaslov, he's just trying to do his job," Lenz said. His manner betrayed his sudden weariness of the other's tedious low-grade torment.

Vaslov displayed mock astonishment. "What, have you been sleeping with?" He snapped his fingers. "Lena Horne again?"

"I'm simply too hot and too bored to inflict my unease on the help." Lenz plucked up an olive, examined it and then dropped it back into the bowl.

Lenz's drinking friend regarded him with an arched eyebrow. "You shouldn't show this ape anything but your contempt," he told him in English.

Clay had perfected not showing any emotion, any hint that he understood the language. He stood as if awaiting new orders.

"What I do and say is my concern, Vaslov," he replied. "My interests are fairly prosaic after all."

"The fate of the war is a destiny that affects your business," Vaslov snapped.

Lenz did a lethargic sieg heil "As you say."

"You shouldn't joke like that," the other man advised sternly.

"Or what? Major-General Alexander is going to come marching through the entrance and shoot me on the spot?" He grinned broadly. "I am unconcerned with what any and all of these powers do, Vaslov. I am concerned with the pallets of machine oil I have sitting on the dock and can't get transit papers for." He thumped his chest. "That's what concerns me."

He looked over at Clay. "You can go," but he said it in English, not French. Clay feigned not to understand. He was sure Vaslov hadn't made a slip.

"Sir?" He asked in French.

"Go away," Vaslov groused irritably in his fractured French. "This is man's talk, boy."

"Very good, sir." Back in the pantry area, Clay and Yusuf Wahid, a Berber, took a cigarette break.

"If the Nazis should return, my friend," the wiry Wahid began in his flawless French, "what will become of us?" He sat on a sack of apricots that in turn were stacked on a crate of powdered milk.

Clay said, "Their plight will be no better than that of the sons of pharaoh and their predecessors. They denied us our signs and Allah called them to account for their sins, for he is strict in punishment."

Wahid snickered, blowing smoke through his nostrils. "If only the German high command read the glorious qur'an, all would be resolved."

"Or Allah himself smite them down." He too lit a French Gauloises and blew streams toward the ceiling. Normally he didn't smoke, but did what he could do to fit in with the men.

"Careful, careful," Wahid shook his cigarette at him, "the Nazis aren't known for their sense of humor."

"Neither am I."

The curtain parted and Jean-Jacques, "John," Ali entered. As usual, the Congolese's white tunic and black pants were pressed just so, his shoes spit polished shined. "You're wanted, Baku. Monsieur Belmundo needs you to help set up the reception for the countess."

"She's not a countess, you idiot," Wahid reminded Ali,

"She's a white woman with money is all he needs to know," Clay cracked.

Gary Phillips

"Let's go," Ali repeated.

Clay winked at Wahid and the two departed. Lenz and Vaslov were in low conversation, and Lom was placing a tall tumbler before two British officers. In the corner mumbling into his beer was a bloated drunk named Klein. He swore he was a World War I veteran, a German pilot who'd racked up kills under the command of von Richthofen, the legendary Red Baron. Apparently this had been checked when the Allies took the city, and found to be hogwash as Klein still occupied his post. He was a fixture in the Tom-Tom Klub but as to how he wound up in Tunisia, Clay had yet to determine.

"You two need to get in step," Ali commented as they crossed over to he embassy and the servant's entrance on the side.

"You mean get on the winning team, Ali? Didn't your two and a half years in England endear you to defend Old Blighty?"

"You joke too much, Baku," the other man lectured.

"Funny," Clay quipped, "but other people tell me I'm too serious for their liking."

"Keep it up." Ali reached his hand over the gate and unlatched it from the other side. The two stepped into a compact garden and on toward the windowed double doors.

"Do you seriously believe some white woman is going to come along and recognize you for the genius you are and take you away from all this?" Clay took one last puff and tossed the butt away. Dammit, he was starting to enjoy smoking too much.

"I'm simply trying to instill in your thick Wolof head what is reality." The two were at the double doors. "At best the Brits, the Russians and the Americans will reach a stalemate with the Reich. I will make you a guarantee the welfare of our black assess are the last concern on their minds." He opened the doors. "Getting the French back in control here will be the least of your pickaninny worries."

"That's the first thing you've said that I agree with." Clay muttered to him as they entered the embassy.

"You two move this table over there and move the couch over there." Monsieur Belmundo was a tallish, portly Frenchman who favored gold colored ties and young dark boys. Not waifs, but teenagers, tough kids who'd been living off the land and had developed hard sinewy muscle to go with their beaten down world view. He liked, or so a bemused Wahid had further told Clay, to have the lads rough him up before he would beg, dinars or francs clenched between his teeth and on his knees, to be allowed to perform fellatio on the bristling youths.

"I've got to see about the parfaits," he croaked breathlessly after giving the pair more orders. "You two get busy." Belmundo started to leave. "Sweep the rug too," he called out as he darted away.

"What exactly is this reception about?" Clay asked in a low voice as they went about their tasks.

"Some friends of Madam Scirola from Tuscany." Ali grunted while he lifted his end of the rococo-styled couch. "Some of the members of Major-General Alexander's staff are also supposed to be here tonight as well."

"What the hell are Scirola's effete bourgeois pals doing here in Tunis? They get lost on their way to the fox hunt?" They set the couch into place.

"Why are you always so nasty about her?"

Clay sighed. "I know she's your dream girl, Ali, but her manner wears very thin with me."

"That's just it," Ali poked his finger in Clay's chest.

"What are you talking about?"

"You're no more a Wolof Senegalese tribe member than I am Joe Louis."

"You've got pussy on the brain."

"I do, that's true. But I know what I say, Baku Bahrim. Oh you smile inside when you fool all of us all right. But I know you're too, I don't know," he wagged a finger vigorously underneath Clay's nose. "Too much. okay?"

"Sure," he said. "Hope you don't mind, but I'm going to finish my work before I have to hear that priss Belmundo screech at me."

"Uh-huh," Ali huffed.

Crazily, he toyed with the idea that maybe like him, the Nazis had done the unexpected too. It wasn't that far-fetched that they had sought out, or it had been brought to their attention by some collaborator, how useful an educated black man could be. Ali might be their eyes and ears in hostile territory like he was, but where the original invisible man could exist without notice.

Clay and Ali finished readying the room and Ali went off to freshen up. Clay went into the kitchen where the chef and his assistant were preparing the food. When the Nazis had occupied Tunis, they'd left the kitchen staff intact. Conquering countries in the name of the Third Reich was one thing, a well fed stomach another. The smell was terrific.

"My good fellow," the chef, Alan Druillet, enthused at spotting the big man. "How goes the struggle, dark warrior?" With surgical precision, he removed the eyeball of a Red Mullet. Unlike the big screen version of the hefty, bearded chef, Druillet was medium height and well proportioned. His aquiline features were at odds with his deep-set eyes and as usual, he needed a shave.

"I'm happy if I get to sneak some of your delicious chocolate éclairs tonight." He patted his stomach and chastened himself for putting on a few pounds since being in Tunis.

Druillet showed his tobacco-stained teeth. "Of that, I'm sure we can accommodate you."

"Please leave, we have much work to do," Claude, the assistant chef said. He was a good-sized man who had the build and mannerisms of a ditch digger. He was jealous of his kitchen space and not particularly fond of the lower echelon help. "And Shana was looking for you anyway."

Druillet flexed his shoulders as he continued de-boning the Mullet. "She's needs some muscle on the third floor." He managed a lascivious grin while he looked up from his knife work. "I think you can manage that, no?"

"I'll try," Clay answered straight-faced.

"I'm sure you will mon ami, I'm sure you will." he said, executing a flourishing flick of his blade.

Clay climbed the stairs and found Shana Owens wrestling with the end of a support beam where the tank shell had done its work.

"It's about time," the Tunisian-British woman said in her lilting French. She's taken off her heels to get better footing. Clay leaned on a wall, enjoying watching the pretty woman in her maid's uniform and work gloves exert herself.

"What are you trying to do?" The roof creaked as Owens got the beam to move an inch.

"Belmundo wanted to see if a passageway to the guest bedroom could be cleared. He wants to impress his British masters as much as he used to impress his German ones that he has everything under control." She grunted and continued tugging.

"This is just my observation," he intoned clinically, "but if you keep messing with that beam, you're going to bring what remains of that part of the roof in."

Owens tugged on the beam again and plaster and lathes fell from the fractured ceiling. She stopped and examined her handiwork. "Then what's your suggestion, mister engineer?"

"Leave it alone."

She fumed at him.

"Fine." He came over. "We'll have to create a passageway beyond the beam, but it has to remain in place to hold up this fragile structure."

She was close to him, looking up at him. "Can you handle it?"

"Depends." They stood breathing in each other's air, Clay inclining his face toward her's but at the last moment, she broke away.

"We better get to work then."

"It would seem."

She smiled at him. Clay stepped over the beam and began to poke around in the fallen wood and plaster. "Making a passageway shouldn't be too hard, I can toss enough junk out of the way I think."

"Do you need me?"

He looked back. "Anything I say will get me in trouble, wouldn't it?"

"Maybe," she teased. Footsteps tromped up the stairs.

"Ah, there you are," Belmundo huffed. "I need you to clean the water closet on the second floor. The shitter backed up last night again."

Clay chuckled. "Run along now, run along." He made a shooing gesture.

"Pig," she growled and trudged off to her new filthy job.

Clay began lifting pieces of the roof and walls away and realized a passageway had already been cleared through the rubble. That once he moved a couple of stacks of waist high material, a tunnel was uncovered. The hole was definitely not an accident of formation. And upon reflection, the stacks in front of it were made to block the hole from casual inspection but also meant to be pulled out of the way. Maybe Ali had scored with Madam Scirola and they'd been using the back room as their love nest. Clay proceeded along like a miner exploring a new vein of gold.

Near the end, he was surprised to find an opening to his left before the room at the rear. He shifted some timber and was expecting it to collapse but it didn't. He looked closer and could see that someone had shored up this section with new pilings. He got down on his knees and was able to crawl through into an opening in the wall itself.

In the crawl space, he struck a match and saw by the flickering light a kerosene lamp, some loose foolscap, a pencil, a squat tumbler from the Tom-Tom Klub, and a radio set. The matched burned his fingers going out but he hardly noticed. Clay felt his way forward, careful not to disturb the placement of any of the items. He struck another match and could see the German lettering on the ID tag stamped on the side of the short wave. He followed a wire that disappeared into a small hole that had been punched out at the base of the lathes. No doubt the wire led to a small battery-powered generator that supplied the juice.

His light went out again and he had the foresight not to toss the match away. He stuck it in his pocket and lit a third. He found his first spent match and put that away too. He couldn't leave any evidence that he'd been here. On his fourth match, Clay took the top sheet of paper and folded it up and put that away in his back pocket. He could take the tumbler and using some cocoa powder from Druillet's pantry to raise a print on it. He couldn't get the prints from all the likely suspects. But this was a break through.

He got out and dusted himself off. Clay then grabbed the beam and yanked hard. Several hunks of plaster and wood noisily tumbled from the ceiling, making it even harder to get into the pile. He grimaced as he plucked several splinters out of his palm and heels of his hands. If he'd finished making the path to the rear room, that would have scared off the German agent.

"What the hell was that?" Belmundo demanded, hurrying up the stairs.

Apologetically Clay said, "I was trying to clear the way when the beam shifted and part of the roof fell in again."

"Fool, didn't you know you had to dig out slowly, not use that hulking strength of yours?"

"Sorry." Clay managed a hound dog look of contriteness.

"Ach" he surveyed the mess and then consulted his watch. "All right, we'll get back to this later. Go to the second floor and we'll move a few cots into the room the Germans used as their conference space. That will have to do."

"Very good, sir." And Clay went to do Belmundo's bidding before he had to sneak away and do Snow's. He got a break about half past six, the muezzin's call to evening prayer, the azaan, echoing from somewhere in this quarter. The Nazis had destroyed several mosques but there was no crushing a people's beliefs or will to practice them. Even though the British overlords had little use for the Islamic faith as did the previous occupiers of Tunisia, they at least didn't round up the faithful and shoot them for praising Allah.

And it was a good time for Clay to make his way to his radio with a dearth of the fellaheen about for a while. Back behind the embassy in the small garden he looked about and then went into the shrubbery that fronted the rear wall. He climbed up and over the wall and into more low foliage. He went onto all fours and crawled into the covering until he got to the particular base of a palm tree. He moved a plant previously dug up and extracted his short wave wrapped in burlap.

As he was setting up, he remembered the piece of paper he filched. Clay unfolded it and squinted at the impressions in the fading light. A surprised look contorted his features and he chanced lighting a match.

He stared hard at the markings, turning the paper to make sure he was right in his interpretation. He got his dry cell battery out and hooked it up to his set. He then got his headphones on and dialed the pre-set frequency.

There was interference but his signal cleared and was relayed to an outpost in Cairo then to another transmitter on a ship in the Atlantic then on to Snow in that office building near with no address.

"Clay," same the cold man's voice after 70 seconds of clicking the locator dial back and forth while fooling with the booster knob.

"I'm here. I'll make this brief. I've found the radio the infiltrator is using and more."

"What?" An unaccustomed excitement crept into his voice.

"A doodle of a kind of flying cigar with fins. And the designation A-6."

"It's not that much of a secret that Von Braun and Dornberger have been working on these pilotless bombs, Clay. The Luftwaffe has the V-1s, and these other rocket scientists are calling their's the V-2."

"But the V-2 is designated A-4 by the krauts. This would indicate a more advanced model."

He scoffed, "You're smart, Clay. But you can't be seriously suggesting they're constructing this new version in North Africa?"

"It would be the least suspected place," he pointed out. "And it could be a dual reason too. Maybe like the oil they need a resource that's plentiful here for their experiments."

"You've been drinking too much of that goddamn Limey warm beer. You just find our friend and neutralize him."

"Very well." He severed the connection and replaced the radio. He went back to the wall and started to go over but he heard voices on the other side He waited and listened.

"Of course not," the one voice said. He was sure that was the assistant chef, Claude.

There was a reply, but this one spoke quieter, more rushed. This one was worried about being discovered.

"Look, it's been going fine so far, hasn't it?" Claude chastised. "Then let's not get worried for no reason, shall we? We make the delivery tonight that we are obliged to do and so that is it."

Another husky reply that Clay, straining, couldn't tell whose voice it was, let alone if it belonged to a man or woman. But he could smell the cigarette smoke coming from both speakers.

"Enough, enough," Claude interjected, "it doesn't matter to me who pays as long as their money isn't in francs or lira." He laughed and the

132

two traipsed back inside the embassy.

Clay leapt and got hold of the edge of the eight-foot wall, using his upper body strength to pull himself up. He got a footing on the top then went over, in a crouching position, wary and waiting. Like Sherlock Holmes in one of those stories he kept re-reading by Conan Doyle, he scoured the ground for spent cigarette butts. He found one that was warm. It was a Gouleois, which told him nothing because everybody smoked that brand or the Turkish Murad or Helmars were plentiful as well. There was no lipstick on his evidence, but again, that didn't mean much.

"Baku, what are you doing?" Belmundo was at the open double windows, hands on his hips, impatiently tapping a foot.

"Checking for mines, sir," Clay answered, straightening up.

Belmundo blinked hard and pointed toward the interior of the embassy. "Get back to work."

"Right away, sir," Clay said, dusting off his hands and smiling slyly as he re-entered the embassy.

That evening the guests consisted of a Captain Montclair and his driver from Alexander's office, and Madam Scirola and two other women, Paula Funero and Nellie Leary, a Canadian by birth whose mother was Italian. An American, Major Ross, also stopped by. He was seeking directions to the central command headquarters. He'd flown in last night, he said, and found out command had been relocated. He asked to use the facilities and shortly returned to the study where the small and dour soiree was being held. As he was about to leave, he gave Clay the once over while he carried a tray of the tender Mullet and brie on C-ration crackers. One had to make do during wartime.

"Don't I know you boy?" he said in his East Texas twang. He was Clay's height and stared at him like pinning an exotic bug.

"He doesn't speak English, Major," a bemused Belmundo stated in his thick version of the language. "He's Senegalese and barely speaks French."

The major poked a thumb into Clay's chest while he addressed Belmundo. "This specimen of a buck looks like a boot black right off the watermelon truck from 'Bama. Fact, I pride myself on telling these boys apart, and I know'd I seen this one before." He put his face close to Clay's who maintained a confused expression.

"Not a bloody word," Madam Scirola said in her lightly accented English.

"Shit, pardon me, ladies," he said, "but I'd swear on a stack of Mister Johnson's bibles that this roustabout was at Camp Van Dorn in

Mississippi. I had to pass through there to get some replacement forced volunteers for paratroopers, and they was a'talkin' about his hard-headed black bastard it took eight MPs to take down one night."

Madam Scirola tensed.

"Well, sir," Major Ross continued, "I peered in on this superman as he lay restin' on his bunk in the brig and it shore looks to me this sharecropper is his twin."

In French, Clay asked to set down his tray and get on with his duties.

"Major?" Belmundo cocked his head slightly.

"Well that was frog he was speaking, that's for damned sure." He looked Clay up and down, frowning. "No English, huh?" It wasn't clear who he was talking to if anybody.

"Go on Baku," Belmundo ordered.

Clay set the tray down, aware that Annabella Scirola was also studying him, though the look wasn't from consternation. He started to walk out of the room, avoiding the major as it seemed like the natural reaction to project.

"Hey, nigger," the major suddenly shouted, "I'm coming for you," and he bounded at Clay.

Properly startled, Clay started at the man and asked the room was the American crazy. This got some snickering going and using his hand on the crown, Major Ross tamped his hat further down on his head.

"Okay, I know when I'm licked." He headed toward the exit then turned around. "You jus' make sure I don't catch your monkey ass walking down Elm Street, U.S.A., bud." And with that and Clay's feigned questioning expression, the major left.

The rest of the evening consisted of the soldiers making polite conversation and the women going on in varying degrees about the culture and pampering the war had spoiled for them.

"Yes, it's so sad that Il Duce has turned out to be a well-dressed thug," Funero lamented. "Early on, he had seemed genuine in wanting to preserve the paintings and sculptures of our people." She wrung her hands and then had another sip of wine.

Clay let his mask slip and a derisive sneer formed on his face. He caught himself and again took on his servant's mantle. He took a few glasses into the kitchen as an excuse to see what was up. There he encountered Claude at one of the cupboards. From the angle he was at, and given the open door, he couldn't tell fully what the assistant chef was doing. Though he did get a quick glimpse of stenciled letters, like those used by the armed forces on a package.

"Need some help?" the big man asked innocently.

The startled chef quickly slammed the cupboard shut. "What? No, no I don't need any help. Get back out there and pick up glasses or wipe Belmundo's ass, do whatever it is you do, African."

Clay was tempted to swat this chump but knew it wasn't the time to break his cover. "You looked like you needed help. You're so out of breath."

"Now you're a doctor," he groused. "Get the fuck out of my kitchen."

Clay held his hands aloft in a helpless gesture and sauntered out. As he'd suspected, that redneck officer didn't just happen to drop in to ask for directions. Whatever Claude and his accomplice had going, it involved a member of the U.S. military. But what could it be? And was it anything he should be concerned about anyway? The scam that Claude had going probably had nothing to do with the hidden radio and the Nazi agent-in-place.

Conversely, Clay considered as he crossed back into the study, if he didn't find out, sure as hell it might circle back on him. And frankly, he had to admit, getting the best of that imperious bastard Claude would give him a nice, warm feeling.

Ali was in the study, and doing his best to hover near Madam Scirola. Paula Funero, as usual, was having too much wine and went on how she'd be willing to trade the Nazis virginal blondes in exchange for the preservation of Renaissance-era paintings and sculpture. She was satisfied that enough recordings of opera existed that the sheet music could be sacrificed.

Scirola egged her on asking where these blondes might be obtained.

"I'll hire a goddamn retinue of black bucks like these two here," she averred in slurred Italian, "to take me on a expedition into Siberia." She cackled and eyed Ali lustfully. "Making frequent rest stops of course." She howled again, making a grab for the man that wasn't nearly as playful as she pretended.

Ali looked alarmed, and Clay had to work harder than he'd had to with the major not to show he understood. Though her intent was clear to everyone in the room. And so it went.

"I imagine the Crown and the Yanks aren't through with their excursions, are they, Captain Montclair?" It was 23:30 hours and the dinner was playing out. Funero had curled up on the couch and was snoring softly and steadily.

"How do you mean, Madam Scirola?" the captain responded, flint momentarily drifting behind his pale eyes.

"There's a reason you've moved efficiently and ruthlessly across three nations here in North Africa, Captain. We're all n the same side, my friends and I would like to think that your maps have Rome dotted in a red circle. That Operation Torch will burn its cleansing fire into my homeland and blind that self-important bastard, Mussolini." Her voice was a shaky whisper and the facade of indifference she normally maintained dissipated. "And with my own hands I'll climb that pole and remove the hated swastika flapping over the Acropolis and use it to wipe myself when my little friend visits."

Captain Montclair let a gap open between his upper and lower lip but couldn't for several moments produce anything resembling speech. He cleared his throat twice then finally croaked, "It's been quite an evening, madam."

Soon after the captain and his factotum said their good nights, Madam Scirola brooded and smoked, perched on the arm of an easy chair. Ali and Clay had to carry the sleeping faded beauty up the stairs and into the room that Shana Owens had prepared for the three guests. Actually it was a suite, and let into a smaller, comfortable wing. When the Nazis were in Tunis, it had been used as their quarters to deflower young, devout Muslim girls, who subsequently were then shunned by their families. As if the rapes at gunpoint were somehow their faults.

"What about her, Ali?" Clay asked as they set the woman on the bed. "She has eyes for you."

He snorted. "She has no money and I fear she is too dried up. She must be fifty-five."

Clay laughed harshly as the two walked toward the door. "How old do you think your madam is youngster?"

"That's different. She's still a good-looking woman."

"For a white woman," he granted.

"Like you'd take your nose out of it if you had the chance." Ali hurried back down the stairs.

The two servants finished cleaning up. Monsieur Belmundo went off to bed. Claude had vacated the kitchen and of course Clay found nothing incriminating in the cupboard. He wanted to search the place but that was awfully hard to do given the amount of noise involved in moving pots and pans around. And the great chance that somebody would no doubt come into the kitchen for a slice of ham or a sip of brandy.

Clay passed back by the study and saw Ali playing at being the bon vivant. Scirola and Leary were smoking and enjoying some apricot schnapps. Though he wouldn't go so far as to pour himself a helping of booze, Clay was tickled that Ali was also smoking and nodding his head to the conversation. He made sure he didn't look at Clay as the latter ascended the stairs.

He and Ali shared a room, the storage space, in the east wing of the second floor. Owens had quarters off the kitchen, but being indigenous, it was not unusual for her to be absent after hours. He'd knocked on her door when he was downstairs, and there had been no answer. Belmundo enjoyed a room with a window on the opposite end of this floor, and Claude and Druillet shared a room on the ground floor too. Somehow, he was going to have to stake out that radio on the third floor. And then he'd have to do what Snow had made exceptionally clear was his mission.

He stripped down to his athletic undershirt and was in his socks on his side of the room in his narrow steel bunk. It was one of two stacked bunks from a boat that had been torched in half for each man. Clay was too primed to read as he usually did at night and lay there, his hands behind his head. Quietly, someone knocked on the door.

"Shana?" he said hopefully in French.

"Not tonight," was the answer.

He got up and opened the door a crack on Annabella Scirola. "Does madam need me to make her a sandwich?"

She pushed on the panel and he let the door swing inward. "I am hungry for something, that's for sure, Monsieur Bahrim."

"I'm sure whatever it is, I can see to it in the morning."

"Too tired, Baku?" She boldly stepped into the room, easing the door closed but not letting the catch click. "You've struck me as a man who can go the distance."

"I'm not sure what Madam means."

"Is that so?" She stood close to him and he didn't back up.

"Where's your friend?"

"Where do you think?"

"It must be 'going native night,' eh, madam?"

"Funny man." She put her hand on his crotch. "Why don't you make me scream, Mister Comedian?" She rubbed him and withdrew her hand, smiling at his obvious arousal.

"Listen," she went on, "I know about Captain Chicago and his fight against the fasciste in Ethiopia."

Clay frowned, not sure of what to do.

"Captain Chicago," she repeated, walking around the stunned man. "They called you that, I understand, because one of the Amharic cavalry men assumed you were from the Windy City, land of gangsters and Paul Muni, like the movies he'd seen." She was behind him and put her hands on his upper arms, pressing herself close. "You're something, you know that?"

"How do you know this?" He asked in English.

"My brother, my good captain. He fancied himself something of a photographer, and he took pictures of the battles he and his troop were involved in against your doomed campaign on behalf of that egoist and thief, Emperor Selassie."

"It wasn't about him," Clay said, "it was about freedom. You see, madam, some of us weren't born to it. There are those who have to take what is due them, by wit and by verve."

"He included little notes with the pictures he sent home. Everybody knew about the tough American."

"And your brother?"

"Died, killed in a place called Keren."

"In Eritrea," Clay said, "an old town among high ridges and deep gorges." He turned around, grabbing the woman. "What do you want, Madam Scirola? Where would you like to put the knife?"

"I'm not my brother, Captain, I'll grant you that. But you heard me downstairs, I'm no follower of Il Duce. I want freedom too, Monsieur, I want an end to this madness of the Nazis and the Thousand Year Reich. I want to help you."

Clay choked, holding back his laughter. "Help me cut fish heads?"

She jerked free. "Don't be so Humphrey Bogart. I can be of assistance to you. You must be here for some reason, Captain Chicago."

"Stop calling me that for one."

"Of course, mon Cap-i-tan," she teased in central casting French. "But don't you think we should consummate our deal?" She walked backwards, undoing the buttons of her dress. She sat on the heavy cot, leisurely crossing her legs. "You're not scared of white women, are you?"

"I'm scared of all women," he admitted truthfully.

She patted the blanket next to her. "I won't bite, much."

He came forward. "This is not the beginning of anything."

"We'll see." She sat back and he joined her on the cot. It didn't take too long for nature to take over and he rationalized he wasn't giving in to her sexual blackmail and went with the mood. Though it seemed lately, he kept having to make love on a goddamn cot.

"So what are your secrets, madam?" he asked afterward, her head resting on his chest, clammy from their exertions.

138

"I don't tell all on the first date, darling."

Maybe he should simply throttle her and be done with the headache. "We don't exactly have time for a formal courtship, Annabella."

"You want to know which Nazi general's dick I sucked while he wore his jackboots, and sang uber ales as he climaxed in my mouth?"

"Something along those lines."

She kissed him on the cheek, scratching his whiskers with her painted nails. "Yes, I used sexual favors to stay alive, I'm not too proud or disillusioned to admit that."

"I don't condemn you for what you had to do."

"I believe you. Or at least I want to."

"There's no angels in war."

She gripped him and kissed him deeply, taking his face in her hands. "I know that Colonel Krieger, he was Prussian, got out a half day ahead of the allied forces. And I'm sure he wouldn't leave without a contingency plan in place."

He fondled her breast. "Yes?"

"I'm sure it's Claude. He was always going out of his way to please the Colonel, a large man with many appetites."

Clay sucked on her nipple and she moaned into his ear. "I see," he said between mouthfuls. "Does Claude speak German?"

"He does," and she slipped down his body, her tongue and teeth licking and chewing on him.

They made love again and it took more than his usual concentration to stay awake after she went to sleep. She might have almost two decades on Clay, but if she was any younger, he would have needed an oxygen tank. At 0:2:42, he sneaked out of bed and got back into his clothes. He had an idea to creep down to Claude's room when a creak on the carpeted stairs from above decided for him.

Prickly fingertips of worry coursed up and down his back as he waited, bifurcated by the doorway.

"Where are you, my Nubian nimrod?" Scirola gurgled, stretching in the cot.

"Shhhh," he hurried over to kiss her. The smell of sex and alcohol strong in this part of the small room. "You rest, we have more of each other to explore."

She made a sound and puckered her lips. "I can't wait." Then she rolled onto her side and was soon snoring again.

Clay withdrew and stood in the hallway, listening and deciding. He closed the door and went up the stairs, barefoot and on all fours he went up the carpeted steps to lessen the noise and weight on each level. At the top, he crouched on the landing, alert for anything. As far as he could tell, he hadn't tipped off the Nazi spy to his presence. He eased forward then halted at the sound of rummaging. It wasn't coming from inside the pile as he'd expected.

To his right was the hallway leading to the east wing. He went along, not sure of what he was searching for but no turning back now. There were too many questions to be answered. Particularly when he wanted to prove to Snow he wasn't just whistling Dixie.

Clay passed the door to the water closet mid-way along the hall. There was the sound of leather across tiles and he stopped and listened. Inside, someone was busy and he didn't think it was a early morning run to relieve oneself. He back-pedaled to the front of the hall, the way he'd come. He went low, peeking around the corner. Little light came in from the moon outside. He hoped to see better, but that wasn't going to be. When the door to the toilet opened, the best he could tell was a man stepped out. Quickly, Clay went as fast as possible without making noise toward the debris to hide in the opening to the hidden passageway.

From where he was hiding, Clay could see the bulky form as he paused at the head of the stairs. It was Claude that much he was sure of; there was no mistaking his gut, which sagged over his belt. Claude looked around, his facial expression unseen and unknown to Clay. But no doubt it was a look of concern. He went a few paces off the landing, looking this way and that. Satisfied that he was alone, he descended the stairs and faintly, Clay heard the kitchen door swing to-and-fro on its tight hinges.

He wormed his way out and went to the w.c. Inside he removed his lighter, which he'd had the foresight to bring with him, and flicked it on. He felt behind some towels on a shelf and even looked behind the overhead tank of the flush toilet but couldn't find anything. Maybe Claude had a real need to pee upstairs, but there were facilities on the ground floor. He felt through the dirty clothes bin but could find nothing. Ready to give up, he was walking out when his bare feet crunched on a smattering of granules.

He got on a knee and thumbed his lighter on again. He examined the particles on the floor then looked up. He then glared at the toilet, noting that the lid was down. Clay balanced himself on the commode's porcelain rim and reached up. The w.c. had a low ceiling and there was a panel above the toilet. He got the panel out of the way and poked through the squarish opening.

His lighter illuminated boxes, about the size of Red Cross care packages stacked around the spacious crawl space. he pulled one loose and stepped down to the tiles. By the flame of his lighter, he could see the box had German markings on it and he read what was contained within, but he still tore the tape off to make sure.

He withdrew a syrette of morphine, a small collapsible metal tube toped with a covered syringe. Syrettes were the field medics wonder, allowing the dispensation of the painkiller in instant doses. A very valuable commodity during the frenzy of combat and the need to keep moving to the next wounded soldier. But morphine had other uses too. Every serviceman knew of soldiers who would manufacture more pain than they were in for that extra shot of the euphoric-inducing wonder drug. And if you should happen to have a jeep full of the stuff lying around, well there was money to be made on the black market.

Clay worked out a scenario as he replaced the box. Claude and his accomplice had a deal with the redneck major. He could be selling the narcotic on the side to his own men, the British or even the Tunisians.

If Claude and his partner were found out, they might arrest him under the war powers act and given hard time. For Major Ross, he'd be court-martialed and imprisoned. But it wasn't espionage and it wasn't what he'd been sent to uncover. If he took a run at Claude, that might tip his hand and then where would he be? He didn't like it, didn't like the image of Claude getting fatter on profits from making hop heads of soldiers, but he couldn't do anything about it.

He replaced everything and walked out of the w.c., after first listening for anyone around. At the caved-in section, he looked around but didn't think the radio operator had been at his post tonight. Downstairs, the madam was awake.

"Where have you been?" she pouted, her head propped on her hand.

"Building a tank," he snapped. Claude lighting a cigar with a ration book, in a greasy loin cloth and his feet propped up on waifs shivering from withdrawal clouded his mind.

"Ha," she said too loud. "You're not much of a host." She pulled back the sheet, the outline of her ample body a distinct shadow against the gloom.

"Yes, well--" he began.

"Yes, well, get over here," she rubbed her hand between her legs, letting them part slightly. "I'm not such a prune, am I?"

"No, no you're not." He supposed, as they resumed their lovemaking, this was about her and not about him. She wanted to prove that she was still capable of being alluring to a man. Oh, he was sure the skin color had something to do with it, but he doubted he was her first taste of the "forbidden fruit."

She was on her back and he was laying partially on her, his hands caressing her breasts and moving over her rib cage. Gray light streaked the room, and they could see each other's eyes.

"I'll help you, Baku, or whatever your real name is. You can trust me."

He had her face between his hands and she turned slightly to kiss his palm. "You hate the Nazis that much or miss your afternoon teas and chauffeurs driving you to the museum more?"

Her look turned hard. "When I was younger, my good captain, one might suppose I did fuck my way into money. But I can assure you, I too know the pang of depravation, the desire to have a better life restored."

"That's not the same as never having it, madam."

"Nor does it mean I won't do what's necessary for freedom."

"Really."

"Yes."

Moments dragged and then they kissed like teenaged lovers, with passion and abandon.

CHAPTER 15

"Does she suck you deeply?"

"A gentleman doesn't say." Clay continued washing the glasses in the small tub behind the bar in the Tom-Tom Klub. It was mid-day and the old man, Lom, was already drinking and muttering to himself at a table.

"You plan to leave with her when the war's over?"

"You simply must get your jealousy under control, Ali."

"Do you?" he insisted.

"Keep drying." And Clay pushed several rinsed glasses and ashtrays toward the man.

"I have a right to know."

"Isn't Funero enough for you? Must you have every available woman?" Clay enjoyed the torment his companion was experiencing. "You black fellows are so insatiable."

"All right for you," he shook a glass at him as if it were the barrel of a pistol. "The hag is so drunk by sundown, she barely stays awake to get undressed. I might as well be making love with my grandmother."

Clay made a face. "I'm happy for you to continue your quest of winning the madam's hand. And of course keep your dream alive of the vast riches that await you once you return with her to the villa in Tuscany."

"I care for her deeply."

"Right you are." They went on working in silence, though Ali's consternation was thick. It had been four days since that day he'd discovered the radio, Claude's cache, and Scirola coming to their quarters that night. Even if he didn't have the mission foremost in his mind, he couldn't see being so beside himself as Ali was. It wasn't her whiteness that captivated the other man so, but that she symbolized to him. She stood for his escape from a world of servitude and a second-class station. For that, Clay couldn't fault him. He wanted the same, but was plowing a different field to get there. Who could say which way was better?

Later, he was out on the streets, infused by the vibrancy that was Tunis as he smoked. Women came from market, covered in masterfully embroidered cottons, gauzes and wools. Others were in black robes that went from their necks to their toes called abayas. And their heads were covered in scarves of matching pitch. For most, only their hands and veiled eyes were exposed as was the Muslim tradition. Some had headdresses with their dowry coins sewn into the patterns. As this was a port city, the sharp tang of the sea and fish on the docks was prevalent too. There were also numerous American and British soldiers about. Without fully articulating it, Clay knew there was something brewing. In the last two weeks, he'd noticed more personnel in the city. The madam was right, the allies were preparing another assault. And it wouldn't just be him that noticed it. His unknown radio operative would have made a report.

Clay yawned, flicking the cigarette away. He'd been doing triple duty and it was definitely wearing at him. Between his job, the madam and trying to keep watch on the stairwell for any early morning visitors, and Ali's haranguing, he was ready to shit or go blind as the old folks used to say.

"You never struck me as the day-dreaming type, Baku."

"Miss Shana." He bowed slightly. "Just counting myself fortunate to have so much to do so that my mind can't wander into any devilment." He smiled sardonically. One of the five times a day call to prayer started.

"Aren't we all?" She was dressed modestly but in a modern way. Her skirt showed her lower calves and ankles, and she wore no veil. She was carrying a mesh bag containing onions and figs, and on her head a crate of tomatoes.

"Let me help you with that. Especially since you've done all the work to get them almost to the embassy." He took the crate off her head as she chuckled. Doing so, the aroma of her hennaed hair, with hints of olive oil filled his nostrils. It was intoxicating.

"I wouldn't want you to strain yourself."

"I appreciate you looking out for me."

"Seeing as how you're so delicate."

"Exactly." As they crossed the street to the compound, a late model Citron sedan crept along the thoroughfare then sped up, causing the two of them to hurry along.

"Pig," Owens said in Arabic.

Vaslov was at the wheel and laughing at his juvenile antic.

"Come on," he said, getting the side gate open for them. In the kitchen, Druillet and Claude were busy. The chef, as was his custom, was scrubbing out his pots. Druillet firmly believed that only he could truly clean his cooking utensils correctly so that there was no residue of one meal onto another. One must enjoy the full and unadulterated flavor of the individual preparation Clay had heard him tell Claude.

"Over there," Claude directed, not bothering to look up from a sauce he was mixing.

The two put their produce down on the counter. Clay was making for the exit when Claude spoke, again not looking up from his task.

"Shana, be a dear and check on the towels in the third floor w.c. I believe they need replenishing. Belmundo had asked me earlier to remind you when you returned from shopping."

"Of course."

"Work, work," she said lightly as she crossed in front of Clay and toward the staircase as they both left the kitchen.

It made sense that she'd be Claude's accomplice in their morphine racket, Clay surmised. It might have been her who'd tumbled onto the syrettes in the first place. It wouldn't surprise Clay that Shana spoke German and had overheard a doctor or medic talking about the supplies. Or despite what she told him, she could have a cousin or brother who worked the docks, and was one of the laborers pressed into unloading Nazi supplies. Though why the hell she'd choose the loutish Claude as a partner strained his powers of speculation.

That evening, he and Wahid had duty in the Tom-Tom Klub while Ali was on call in the embassy. Owens was off-duty but was in the watering hole, sipping on a beer. Her mixed parentage allowed her certain leeways and certain restrictions, even more than other women, in Tunisia. But drinking alcohol in public anywhere but here would get her dragged by her hair through the streets by incensed men.

Lom was not around, no doubt sleeping off his afternoon drunk. Lenz was present but not Vaslov. There were also several American and British officers too, including Major Ross.

"What brings so many of them out tonight?" Wahid dumped some empties into the trash.

"Nerves," Clay hazarded.

Wahid twitched a look of incomprehension, and got back to serving drinks.

Clay put a gin and tonic down for Lenz who sat in a corner.

"Thank you," he said. He had a bound book, a leather covered journal and he was making notations in it. He didn't bother to hide it from Clay since he would naturally assume the supposed African waiter wasn't versed in German. Clay, who'd been watching Shana Owens and wondering when she and Ross would conveniently slip out of the club, casually flicked his eyes back at the salesman. Lenz was dutifully recording sales figures from scraps of paper next to illustrations of various gears and sprockets. Marked next to the gears were formulas and ratios explaining how each was employed in looms, clocks, turbines and so forth.

"Anything else," he said, trying to stay as long as he could to decipher more of Lenz's notations.

"Uhhh," he muttered, lost in his work. He went on writing.

Clay straightened up, feeling suddenly constrained by his tunic and the role he was playing. He knew about ratios and gear reductions. He could engage Lenz in several spirited discussions concerning machinery, engines and torque. He knew many stars by their location in the sky, and could recite how to make several complicated chemical compounds like other men could tell you a baseball score.

Not that, he reasoned glumly, even if he wasn't in the disguise of a servant, would Lenz be so eager to talk with a black man about anything involving analysis and the higher thought processes. Sure, Lenz had treated him decently, for one of his class and race. But try to step out of that role, well, then the man's true feelings would surely become apparent.

For an instant, he shook, ready to fling his tray across the room into their pale faces and lash out as at many of them as he could. Damn them, couldn't they see that he too was a man of letters and culture? That he could pontificate on Hegel or Satchmo with equal veracity? Rubbing a hand across his hot face, he knew the resolution of this worldwide conflict would not answer those longings in him or for the home folks.

"Hey, your pants are on fire," Owens kidded him.

"Which leg?" He smiled like a dead mackerel and went on past her. He was happy for her little scam. What the hell had trying to do right gotten him? He'd been pushed and prodded by his mother since he displayed precociousness at three and picked up the shard of newspaper wrapped around her collard greens and read the words about a church bake sale out loud. Education, his mother emphasized and reiterated, was the key to the kingdom.

His mother was a believer in Booker T. Washington's credo of pulling one's self up through fortitude and stick-to-it-iveness. He didn't disagree with that, but he'd be damned if he was going to go along with Washington's willingness to acquiesce on issues of Jim Crow and disenfranchisement in exchange for northern white philanthropists funding Tuskegee, the college he founded. An apologist, Washington assuaged white fears about blacks leaving the farm and moving to the city to make demands for decent housing and decent jobs. To be sure, Washington was for the creation of a black petit bourgeois. He did foster the goals of self-employment, landownership, and small business for black folk. He just didn't want to make waves, be the bad nigger. No, Washington was the good, exemplary Negro. The Negro you could depend on not to drink too much, not to step out of line or get in the white man's face. That by being industrious and keeping our heads low, we'd make steady gains in America.

"Shit," he blared, stepping into the makeshift pantry area.

"Be calm, my large friend," Wahid clapped him on the top of his shoulder. "Whatever it is that bothers you, remember these white men have guns at their sides." He gave him a toothy grin.

"You're a wise man."

"A realist, Baku."

Over his shoulder, Major Ross clanked a bottle down on the bar. "That's bullshit, Rodgers, and you know it."

Clay turned to glare at the scene Wahid was already looking at. Ross was addressing a stout man in a tight fitting seersucker suit. There was a dried sweat stain in the middle of the man's back in the shape of a giant doily.

Rodgers, who stuck a blunt cigar back in his mouth, garbled something but it was lost in the hum that had risen again in the stuffy space. Ross leaned toward the man, poking a finger in his chest. "You Secret Agent X-9 boys don't know what the fuck you're talking about." From his demeanor and volume, Clay assumed Ross was getting in his cups as the Brits say. He looked over at Owens, who watched this altercation but wasn't bent up about it. She seemed to be amused by it all.

The two were speaking in English. Ross, like a lot of his countrymen Clay had observed, acted like people in other countries hadn't learned second languages unlike Americans. It was a large part of the world that was more cosmopolitan, more varied due to richer histories and the influx of other races and ethnic groups. And if the bow-legged native didn't speakee the English, they were just plain ignorant. Or maybe Ross was being his blow hard self and wanted to show the Brits the Americans were lords of the manor.

"You need to keep it down." The one called Rodgers had his cigar between two fingers, and jabbed this in Ross' face. "You got a beef, major, take it up with Washington."

"I just don't like you sports going around with your orders wrapped in oil paper and your London Fogs, talking in code and moving fighting men around like they were pieces on a big game board." His twang had gotten thicker, yet his delivery was clear and articulate.

Rodgers' heavy shoulders lifted as he swelled air into his chest. He jammed the smoldering cheroot back between his lips and started to walk out. "You be clear on this," he snarled at the listing officer, "you have your orders just like I do."

"Only the guys I salute aren't creeping in the shadows."

"Colorful, major, very colorful." Rodgers made s sucking sound against his teeth and left. Lenz, who Clay was certain did speak English, pretended to be engrossed in his notebook.

"What was all that about?" Wahid asked no one in particular in French.

"Crazy Americans," Clay answered in the same language, catching himself from responding that he'd followed everything. As to the intent, that was a different matter. But it did occur to him this Rodgers could be here for advance work as the Allies prepared to stage an invasion into Greece or Italy. Or could be he was sent by Snow to check on him. Though if that were the case, he wouldn't have shown himself, as he'd know who Clay was.

A few minutes after 23:00 hundred hours, Lom began singing some ribald songs from obscure arias to the odd enjoyment of the few that were left. Shana Owens had departed some time ago and so had Ross. Lenz was dozing at his table, as Clay and Wahid cleaned up and left with the jubilant barkeep's blessings.

"Tomorrow and yet another tomorrow," Wahid waved goodnight and whistled into the dark.

"Indeed." Clay stretched, not from tiredness but from the tenseness invading his body. He smoked and gazed up at the night. Annabella Scirola came through the garden door. She'd dropped in at the Tom-Tom earlier. Ross and a British counterpart had vied for her attention, buying her a couple of drinks. But she wasn't too subtle in who she'd been paying attention to either.

"You should be careful, for my sake." He handed her his smoke.

As she took a drag, she engulfed him with her kola-rimmed eyes.

"You worry too much." She blew a whoosh of gray vapor.

"It helps me to sleep."

"Oh, that's the last thing I had in mind for us tonight, handsome."

"I'm not a machine you know." But he was feeling that familiar urge.

"Really, darling?" She touched his chest. And at that exact moment, Major Ross stepped around the corner of the embassy. Timing, Bojangles had once told Clay, was the second thing you needed to have to succeed; the first was a working pistol.

"What the fuck?" Gap-mouthed, Ross darted over. "What's this, you touching a white woman, boy?"

Clay went into his coon act. "No, bossman," he pealed in accented English, "no bossman." He backed up as he talked. Scirola's face was screwed into a disgusted scrunch.

"I knew you could do more than parley-vu, shine." Ross shoved Clay and he pretended to be more off-balance than he was. His reeled back as if reacting in terrific fear. "Ah, you scared, darkie, huh?" A big smile split Ross' lower face. "You ain't got to worry too much, burr head, I'm just gonna remind you about your manners, okay boy?" He hit Clay on the jaw and he slammed back against the gate. His eyes were bugged out and his mouth quivered.

"Oh stop, please," Scirola said in Italian. She'd asked the opposite last night in her native tongue as they damn near busted the slats on her bed.

Clay was tempted to let her in on the joke but he couldn't give it away, not yet. He clapped his hands together as if seeking forgiveness from the almighty. "No, no more bossman," he said in a blend of French and English.

"Oh sure," Ross said gleefully, closing in, his fist landing a good one in Clay's side.

The blow hurt him but he was hotter than Texas chili, and he was going to be satisfied. Fuck the assignment, so he wasn't nobody's Spy Smasher, too goddamn bad. He stumbled back to the gate leading to the compact garden of the embassy.

"You can't get away, boy." Ross came after Clay as he hoped.

"Stop this, you goddamn imitation Gary Cooper," Scirola said loudly in French to an uncomprehending Ross. She grabbed at his coat.

"Don't you worry, missy, I know you're scared of this darkie, but I got it under control." Ross waved her hands away and went in after his quarry. "Come on, you better take this like the yellow black ape you are." Ross stalked in on Clay who had stopped falling back once he was inside the high walls.

"I'll see what I can do, major."

His flawless English surprised Ross but he recovered and advanced. He also loosened the clasp over his service .45. "I'm gonna pistol whip the truth out of you, black boy." He swung and Clay easily blocked it, and countered with a punch of his own.

Ross put a hand to his gut, spittle wetting on his bottom lip. "What the fuck?" he whispered, unwilling to accept the last chain of events. "You, you hit me." He grabbed for the gun.

Clay leaped forward and took a hold of the man's wrist.

"I hope he beats your brains out." Scirola spat at the officer. And for the first time, Ross' brain reconciled itself with what he'd seen.

"You two--"

Clay walloped him with a solid right on the jaw and followed with a left to the breadbasket. He snatched the gun and tossed it in Scirola's direction.

"Black mojo bastard," Ross swore. He charged Clay and the two became a mass of arms and legs falling to the moist grass.

"I'll help you, Baku." Scirola kicked at Ross but he caught her ankle and upended her.

"Dry up, you lousy slut." The officer struggled to get to his feet but Clay latched onto the man's lapels and pulled him forward.

"This dance isn't over yet, Ross." Clay socked the officer again.

Now Ross plowed a fist into Clay's stomach making him wince. He was getting his second wind and was going to press with all he had. He got up and managed to drive a fist into the side of Clay's face.

Swirl patterns of stars collapsed behind his eyes but he stayed erect. Ross dove at Clay, seeking to get his arms around him.

Clay didn't resist. But he'd interlocked his fingers, and brought his combined hands down on the base of Ross' neck. This stunned him and his arms went slack. Clay kneed him and the other man got wobbly. An elbow to the back of the head dropped the major to the ground with a plop.

Ross breathed out invectives as he struggled to raise himself. "You're dead, you know that, spade, you're gonna be fuckin' dead, Sambo."

Clay kicked him in the side, sending the officer over. "You've done enough talking, boy." He bent down and roughly pulled the downed man's fastened coat apart. The brass buttons popped off like exploding kernels of corn.

"Get your monkey hands offa me." Ross groped at Clay.

The operative gave him a hard tap to the face to remind him who was in charge now. "Didn't I tell you to shush? You don't learn so good." He was having too much fun, but so what? He wanted to show off, he wanted to show Annabella what a man he was. He knew it would make her even more excited in bed.

Clay had reached in to the inner pocket of the officer's jacket and withdrew a bundle of folded money held together with a rubber band. He snapped the bills loose and counted the dollars, francs and pounds in the dwindling light. "You know why you ain't gonna be saying anything, cracker barrel?' he asked rhetorically. Like in a John Garfield movie, he slapped the notes across the shocked man's face. The eyes that took him in didn't blink, didn't look away. "Because I know what you've been selling on the black market, white boy, Mister Charlie Potatoes."

"Who are you?"

"Your mama's sweet thing, Ross." He replaced the rubber band on the money, and tossed the packet to Scirola. "Now me and my woman are going to drink and eat your money away, you cheating bastard."

"I'll —"

Clay tapped the man's cheek with the back of his hand. "Ah nothing. The only thing I need for you to do is tell me who else you've noticed playing hide and go seek up there on the third floor."

"What the fuck are you talking about, you black, I mean, you're not making sense." The sly expression he couldn't quite keep off the ends of his mouth wasn't lost on Clay.

"This is about you protecting your percentage, Ross. This is about your country needing you to do your duty when it counts most."

Ross chortled. "Well ain't you the coal bin Jack Armstrong." He started to get up and Clay hit him so quick, Scirola jumped. Ross rocked back on the earth.

"Look, son, I'm serious," Clay said gravely. "You better be forking over a name or sure as hell the beating I just gave you will seem like a rubdown in a steam bath." Not far away, the call to prayer melodically filled the air. "Come on, I bet a guy like you wouldn't completely trust some twist, especially one part rag head."

Ross was propped on an elbow. "You taking over from Shana?"

"Let's say yeah. But I have to know who else you've seen skulking up there around your stash of emsel," he said, using the slang for morphine.

Some of his usual craftiness came back into Ross' face. "Like you say, I can't trust anybody, no matter how much she gives me a hard-on." He chuckled conspiratorially, as if he suddenly saw he and Clay as part of the brotherhood of maleness.

Clay went along. "So you snuck by one night to check on things?" He stepped back as the crooked officer got to his feet, brushing himself off.

"Actually, it was last Saturday afternoon. Me and that broad got into this 'cause of her brother, or half-brother technically, see? He'd filched the shipment from a Nazi resupply boat about a year ago during the occupation."

"He works on the docks," Clay confirmed.

"Exactly. Some MPs put the pinch on him about a month ago when he tried to do the same thing with a British shipment. That's when he got smart and talked a deal with me." Another unpleasant smile.

Clay nodded and turned to Scirola. In an abbreviated fashion, explained to her what they were talking about in Italian. He also told her if Ross acted up again to use the pistol she'd picked up.

"I'll try," she said tremulously. She was holding it in both hands like it weighed fifty pounds.

"Just shoot," he encouraged. Then to Ross in English. "What'd you see?"

"How the hell is it you can palaver in those tongues?"

"Secret decoder ring. Come on, Ross, time's wasting."

"You on some kind of mission? For the State Department, that it?" Now he sounded worried. "You're not really interested in the morph deal, are you? You and that Rodgers are in on this together, aren't you?"

Clay was out of patience. Snow the Gray Man was looking over his shoulder and making a tsk-tsk sound. He grabbed Ross' shirtfront and shook him. "Look, you idiot, what did you see last Saturday? Give me something or I'm taking your gun and putting one between your lizard eyes."

Ross swallowed hard and whispered, "Good thing she don't understand us. It was your girlfriend, slick."

Clay frowned, not wanting to believe him. "Shana?"

"No, darling," she said in accented English. Annabella Scirola was holding the .45 just fine now. She had it leveled at Clay.

Chapter 16

"Shit," Ross eloquently summed up the situation.

Scirola came closer. "Looks like no one can be trusted in war, darling."

"You put on a good act," Clay said.

She batted her eyes coquettishly. "Did I mention I'd been in a few plays?"

"That hadn't come up," Clay responded bitterly.

"But something else always did, my black Apollo," she touched the muzzle of the automatic to his chest.

"So what about me?" Ross moved away from Clay. "You can have the dope, the money, everything. What ever it is you're involved with, doesn't concern me."

"Oh yes it does, Major Ross." Off-handedly, she waved the gun at him while still looking at Clay. "In May, there was a meeting code named Trident in your capital, Washington. That much our operatives know. What is unknown is it Greece and Crete the allies will advance to next or Italy?"

"How the fuck would I know, lady?"

"Oh, I'm sure the likes of you may not be in the actual meetings that followed, but you're high enough in rank to hear," she grimaced at Clay. "What's the word I'm looking for?"

Clay was on a slow boil.

"Rumors," she finished. "You must have heard those, eh, major?"

"Go to hell, you nigger loving wop bitch."

Scirola displayed theatrical shock. "Oh my." She hit him along the side of his head with the gun. "This is what you mean by pistol whipping, isn't it?"

Ross gritted his teeth, fingers to his temple. "Fuck you, I'm not telling you shit. All I gotta do is holler and that's the end of you, dago."

"Only if you holler." Quickly she stepped up to him and jammed the gun in his gut and popped off two.

Ross did a half-turn, horror and surprise on his face. He gasped like a suffocating fish and one of his hands clawed on Clay's tunic. Then he gave out and collapsed. Blood seeped from around the two hands he pressed to his fatal stomach wound.

"Are you crazy?" Clay bent down to Ross.

"I don't believe so, my bronze stallion."

"You have to let me get him help." Ross was curled up, red bubbles gurgling from his mouth.

"What a humanitarian you are, Captain Chicago." She put the gun under his chin. "But there is more pressing matters for you to deal with at the moment."

For the first time since they'd come into the garden, Clay was aware if how exposed he was. He looked around and was relieved to see that the curtains had been drawn across the French doors. He looked up at her. "You planned well."

She shrugged. "I spied on Ross and Shana conducting their business, and well, things fell into place I believe is how you Americans say it."

A feeling of impotence washed over Clay as he stared at the dying Ross. It was if the major were a pill bug and was drawing himself tighter and tighter into a ball to ward off an attack. But for this bug, it was too late. His hands dropped away from his hemorrhaging stomach. Ross' form became inert and he exhaled one final time.

".Now you hide the body."

"Where?"

"You're a clever fellow, I'm sure you'll come up with something."

He got up, trying to focus beyond the moment. Even given she could blame Ross' death on him, she knew he'd go on about the radio. Unless she was going to kill him, but she hadn't. Two bodies would be harder to explain at the same time. And she'd want to know where his radio was and what were his orders.

"The best thing would be if I could bury him."

"But that's impossible. Too much time and too much chance of being seen."

He glanced at the embassy.

"Yes, the basement it is."

"You'll have to help me."

"But of course, my sweet."

Inside the embassy they encountered Ali. "Well, the lovebirds out for a stroll?"

"Don't be jealous, Jean-Jacques," Scirola said. "But there's just something about Baku I can't resist." She looked at him longingly, her hand on the gun inside her stylish purse. "You'll have to excuse us."

She started to leave and Ali grabbed her arm. "I can do more for you than he can."

154

"Oh, I really don't think so." The hand started to come out of the bag.

"Get lost." Clay hit him hard on the point of his jaw and the other man staggered back. "She's my girl, understand?"

Ali started forward, ready to come to blows.

"Don't, Jean-Jacques," Scirola implored him in a soft, caring voice. "You'll only get hurt by Baku or by me."

"But," he began.

"No, no." She put two fingers to his lips. The other hand stayed in the purse strapped around her shoulder. "We're all adults. Let's have none of that now, all right?"

Ali looked like a kid whose wheel had suddenly fallen off his bicycle. "Yes, I suppose that's the best," he stammered.

"For all around," she added. A cruel glint settled in her dark eyes.

"Very well," an emotionally whipped Ali replied and sulked off.

"Come on, we have a lot to do this evening." Scirola jerked her purse toward the door to the basement. The two marched over to the side of the stairs where there was an alcove and the way down into the cellar. Clay creaked the door open and went down the wooden steps. Behind him, Scirola's heels clacked as she too descended.

At the bottom he tugged on the light cord and the bulb glowed weakly. He'd been down here before, and vaguely recalled the layout. There were the usual cobwebs and dusty wooden barrels, torn upholstered furniture, some garden tools and, incongruently, pipes from a standing organ.

"The tour is over, love," Scirola said in French, "time to get back to work."

"I'm glad you're enjoying this." He walked under a support beam toward the rectangular window at ground level. Fortunately, it was hinged and using a screwdriver he got it open. Clay crawled out into the gloom and unerringly went to the dead man's cooling body.

"How's our friend?" Scirola called out.

He hated the woman. He hated her for her caviler attitude toward murder and hated her for playing him like a ten-cent flute. Using a fireman's carry, Clay brought the body to the basement window.

"Let me move back for you." She smiled at the opening, the gun steady on Clay. "If you ruin things I'll not only tell them you killed Ross, but raped me too. I imagine Monsieur Ali would go along with that if I promised him my temporary gratitude. And the fine white gentlemen of the allied forces would be only too happy to bring to ground the ravenous black beast who overwhelmed me."

"Get out of the way."

She made a noisy smacking sound.

Clay shoved the corpse through the window opening. Ross was thicker than he was and given his lack of mobility, he had to push on the body. "Grab his arms," he told her tersely.

There was no response as Clay knelt beside the major's legs, his torso stuck in the opening. The gallows humor of the situation, a twisted version of Alphonse and Gaston, irking him even more.

"Very well," she finally said, exasperated. She pulled and he pushed and the body flopped into the basement with a decided wet sack thud against some of the barrels and then the floor.

"Come on inside," Scirola said.

Clay weighed his options and knew there was only one thing he could do. He looked from the gate back to the basement window and crawled inside himself. Ross' body was splayed across the floor, the legs resting against a ratty divan. He sighed and dragged the body to the furnace. There was space between it and the wall and he tucked the dead man into this space. He lingered for a moment looking at him, the shock of death emblazoned on the man's face. Clay then straightened up.

"Now what?"

"We have you make a call on your radio."

"What's going on down there?" Shana Owens called from the top of the stairs.

Neither said anything for a moment, then Scirola spoke up. "Ah, nothing, just that Baku was kind enough to accompany me down here so I could find an ottoman I was interested in."

"Really?" came the reply.

Scirola put the gun away and gestured for Clay to start up. As he did so, she grabbed him and planted a kiss on his cheek. Her red lipstick shone bright on his dark skin. His stomach retched.

"That's right," he said, "only we were mistaken, it's not down here." He turned off the light. Owens was silhouetted at the top. In a heartbeat he calculated his odds and didn't like the percentages. His neck burned from where he could feel the arrogant sneer he knew was on her face. He went on up, Scirola close behind.

At the top, Owens noted the lipstick on his face. "Too bad you couldn't find what you were looking for."

"Yes," he managed dryly.

"Silly me," Scirola chimed in lightly. Tenderly, she put an arm around Clay's waist.

The two trudged past and back out in front of the embassy. "What do you expect me to tell my superiors?" Clay looked around, trying to come up with a plan.

"That the spy has relayed to the axis that the allies are preparing an invasion of Greece."

"They're not big on my theories." He walked in a eastern direction, away from the embassy and his hidden radio.

"You can be very convincing when you want to be," she didn't finish her sentence. "What is your real name, my lover?"

"So you can put a marker on my grave?"

"Oh, sweetheart."

They were behind some of the stalls in the marketplace. It was closed up, everyone having left the mosques after the prayer at sundown and gone home to eat and rest. He told her.

"Wasn't that the name of one of your presidents?"

"Yeah, James Madison was the fourth."

"And the family name?"

"Why the hell do you care?"

"Don't be grumpy, Madison, its only business."

He stopped. "You're doing this for money?"

The gun was down at her side. It shook as a temblor went through her arm. "I don't have to explain myself to you. Where's that goddamn radio?"

He pointed a thumb behind him. "There."

She looked past him at the Aziz fish market. "You have a key?"

"There's a small shed on the side. For the right amount of francs, the owner lets me store the radio there."

"Then let's get to it."

"You think this will tip the allies hand?"

"If the guess is right, then I want to see if whoever's on the other end will confirm it. If the supposition is wrong, and you'll find this interesting, Madison, the Fuhrer thinks the allies will attack Sardinia or Peloponnese. He believes, Italy, specifically Sicily, to be too well fortified. Though Il Duce thinks that the allies may in fact come that way, he turned down Hitler's offer of an additionally five divisions."

She continued, "His self-esteem you know. Il Duce needs to prove to his German partners that the Italian Army is worthy."

They were at the front of the store. Two men were coming by along the walkway.

The automatic was pressed snugly in an upward angle into Clay's rib cage, right beneath his armpit. "Breathe easy," she whispered.

Clay merely nodded at the two. One of them was smoking and the other softly singing. The men passed on.

"Let's not dawdle, as the Brits say."

"By all means, let's not." He started down the passageway, like a condemned man on his walk to the guillotine. Here, after all he'd been through and all he hoped to do, he was going to die alone and unknown in an alleyway in a land not his own.

He glumly but resolutely accepted the inevitable outcome of this night. He got to the locked shed built into the side of the shop. It was wooden, about the size of an American icebox. The wood itself was rotting and there were planks missing from the sides.

"You keep your radio here?" She was ready to punctuate her dubiousness with a bullet.

"The best place." He took out a key from his pocket and fooled with the lock. "Hmm."

"Problem?" The gun was very big in her steady hand.

"No," he said. It didn't take much to wrench the hasp loose from the spindly wood. "I didn't pay my rent, he must have changed the lock."

"Right. You know I won't hesitate to kill you, Captain."

"Oh I know." He opened the door, and she cocked the hammer on the .45. Clay started to bend and reach into the box.

"Hold it." She stepped closer to get a view. But given the indistinct shapes and lack of overhead lighting, it was hard to tell what the forms were inside the cabinet. "Shit." She glared at him, bare malevolence contorting her face. "Get it before I decide to shoot you now."

As blasé as he could muster, he said, "I'm following your orders, madam."

"You better take me seriously." In her anger, she jammed the gun into his gut and Clay acted. He came forward rather than recoil. At the same time, he grabbed and twisted her arm with fevered might.

"You," she wheezed as she squeezed off two rounds. The gun flashed briefly, illuminating them. Their faces were something from a bas-relief depicting animal combatants.

Clay bore his weight on her and they crashed back, their feet scuffling in the dirt. Scirola was sturdy and propelled by her own fear, she didn't tip over as he'd hoped. She got one of her hands loose and came at Clay's face with her nails. He reared back and she jerked ferociously to get her gun loose.

"You bastard. You stupid American bastard."

"Shut up." He let her go so quick she sucked in air from surprise. She tired to get the automatic up but he belted her with a short jab before she could fire it.

"Wha," she gulped, blood flowing from her nose.

158

He hit her again and she wobbled. She was down for the count. He felt her pulse and it was regular as was her breathing. She made a noise and it startled him, as if he were somehow intruding on her privacy. He picked up the gun and tucked it in his belt in the small of his back beneath his tunic.

Standing over her, he wondered what the hell he should do next. There was no way he could carry her back to the embassy without being spotted. He had a half-formed plan to truss her up and force her to relay false information, but he knew that was insane. That wasn't going to happen. And even if he did, he knew what he had to do next. It was the same thing she was going to do to him once he'd made his report. She moaned. He felt queasy and knew from this day on, probably until he was too old and too feeble to remember, he was going to have a nightmare that repeated itself over and over.

Clay bent down. Even in the near dark he could tell that her face was lumpy from his fists. The flesh over one of her eyes was pulpy and swelling shut. He felt like a real big man.

Scirola's other eye fluttered open slightly "I want to live."

"You'd do anything, wouldn't you?"

"Anything." She held up a hand but didn't have the strength to reach the short distance to him. "I'll say whatever you want on that radio."

He knew she would. He bit his bottom lip to keep it from trembling. Clay tenderly put a hand under her shoulders, as if he were going to help her up.

"Thank you," she whispered.

He shook his head slowly from side-to-side, damning himself. Why couldn't it have been Claude? He would have felt bad for a while, but he would have gotten over it. Propping her up by the one hand, he pressed the .45 over her heart.

"Oh God, oh God," she blared, her eyes wide with the unknown and wonder.

Shutting down his emotions, Clay blew a bullet into her chest, the sound muffled somewhat by the flesh the muzzle was sunk into. She expired instantly. And now he had another body to dispose of tonight.

There were footfalls and none too distant voices. Clay pulled on the warm body and went deeper into the dark of the passageway. Two male voices could be heard and he was sure it was the two who'd been by earlier.

He waited, feeling much like Rashkanikoff must have felt in Dostoevsky's Crime and Punishment. His guilt was oozing out of every pore, the smell of death and corruption hovering around him. Stop it,

Clay, get a hold of yourself. This is war, and according to Hoyle don't cut it in these parts. Frantically, he imagined her unseeing eyes recording his very essence so she would know him when he got to hell and she'd come up to him and bite his face off. The men went on past, returning or going to whatever ordinary task awaited them. Surely, unlike him, it was not to commit cold-blooded murder.

He shook himself from his grim reverie and let his sense of survival take over. Not wanting to stain his tunic, he dragged Scirola's body to the end of the passageway. There he discovered a rickety fence against which leaned a rusted metal chair and some machine parts. But there wasn't enough of anything to hid the woman's body under.

"Shit," he cursed, feeling more and more like some pathetic fool trapped in a Poverty Row movie with only one kind of fate awaiting him. He dragged the body back to the cabinet and laid it near the busted door. His face drenched in sweat and air like rubber balls in his throat, he tried to move some of the stuff out of rectangular enclosure. As he did so, he latched onto a pickaxe, and he knew what he really had to do. He put the items back in and closed the small shed, taking a toolbox out to make it look like a robbery.

He first took the toolbox and scurried across the street. The he pitched it behind a café and started back toward the fish market. A jeep carrying British soldiers suddenly rounded the far corner and caused Clay to duck in the alcove of the shuttered brasserie. He crunched his tall frame down, praying their headlight wouldn't pinpoint him. That the invisible neon arrow over him wouldn't suddenly appear, blinking over and over again.

He let out his breath as the vehicle rumbled past. Clay then ran back to the side of the fish market and got busy. Where the errant machine parts were he moved those aside and dug out a long, shallow grave. He picked up Scirola's body. It was if he were holding a mannequin gone soft from the sun. An image of making love with her made him retch but he pressed on. The surprised look on her face highlighted her handsome features. Clay kneeled and placed the woman in the trench. Oddly, he'd misjudged the length, her high-heeled feet sticking over the lip of the depression. He put a hand to his hot forehead, forcing himself not to bray like a hyena at the absurdity of it all.

He slipped her shoes off and put one on each side of her as if it were ritual. Using the flattened end of the pickaxe and a piece of a broken fan blade as a scoop, he got the earth over Scirola. He then placed the useless chair and machine parts over the mound. It might give him a day. Ali had seen them together tonight but what would he say and who could he say it to?

Dusting off his clothes, he then remembered that the woman's corpse may be the least of his concerns. There was the matter of the dead officer in the basement, the hot sticky basement. Calculating the ambient temperature down there, he figured the smell say on day two would suggest a dead rat in the walls. By day three, someone would go down to investigate. He would have to be long gone by then.

Clay discarded another picture of Scirola, lying willing and open beneath him, breathing his name with fervor as he entered her. This time he threw up and had to steady himself against the edge of a building. Clay wiped a hand over his face, his knees made of rice pudding.

"In for a penny, in for the whole bloody pound," he reminded himself. He walked back to the embassy, purpose in every step. He went in through the side and immediately into an argument between Druillet and Claude. The two were sitting and smoking in the small garden.

"That's ridiculous," the head chef said, splaying his hands toward the sky.

"No, no," the assistant insisted. "Two milliliters is sufficient, I assure you." He crossed his leg and gave Clay the fish eye as the latter stepped through to the kitchen. Clay found the brandy used for recipes and poured himself a drink. He wanted another and another but knew that was foolish. He supposed he should report to Snow. Checking his watch, it was late morning in America so there'd be someone on the other end. But he didn't really feel like reporting in just now. He started to head toward the stairs and his room but that meant at some point he'd have to have a confrontation with Ali. The way he was wound up, he'd have a third death on his hands before the night was through.

He needed to pack. That way he'd sneak out later, destroying Scirola's radio before he left. And as he went on up, he knew he really had no choice but to contact Snow. He had to be told the escape route.

In the room he shared with Ali he gathered his belongings into his duffle. There was some stuff he would leave behind as he wanted to travel as light as possible, so the Gladstone would remain. Just as he was cinching it tight he heard footsteps and shoved the bulk under his bunk to beat the opening of the door.

"Alone?" a mildly surprised Ali said. He stepped into the room.

"Women," he huffed. "Listen, sorry about earlier. Really, she's not worth all that business, okay?" He stuck out his hand.

Ali arched an eyebrow but decided to accept the offer. "So she dumped you, huh?" He couldn't hide his hopefulness as they shook.

"Yeah, you know how it goes. A big, and younger dock roustabout.

You know that demitasse place that stays open late on the pier?"

Ali nodded.

"We were walking by there and it seems she'd already made the acquaintance of this chap."

"That's too bad."

"Isn't it?" He sat heavily on the cot.

"I know. I got tired of that hag Funero myself."

Sure you did, pal. "What can you do, right?"

"Right."

"Smoke?"

"Sure."

Clay shook one loose for him and another for himself. In silence, they enjoyed their harsh Murads, occasionally picking flecks of tobacco off their tongues. The meditative mood was interrupted when a drunken voice filtered from the street below. They looked out and could see Lom weaving about in wide circles. He was singing and slurring in German. Ali shook his head, smiling. Clay didn't know the tune but could make out a few words, seems the diddy had something to do with a soldier's life and the hell it was.

The two leaned on the sill, their backs to the excruciatingly bad wobbler. The duo finished their cigarettes, tossing the butts out the window. Lom was further along, humming and belching.

"I'm going to get some sleep." Clay began to unbutton his tunic.

"Me too."

There was a knock and Clay hoped he didn't show his panic.

"Ali," a female voice demanded.

"Miss Bridget?" Ali answered, opening the door a crack.

"Have either of you seen Annabella?" She peered past him.

"I couldn't right say where she is now mademoiselle."

"We were supposed to meet for coffee after she," Leary let it trail off but didn't bother to conceal her furtive glance toward Clay. "Maybe, maybe I'll wait for her downstairs."

"Oh course, mademoiselle," he said. He assumed she was going to wake up Belmundo. He would come back here and grill him in the lady's whereabouts. Thereafter, he might call in the allied occupiers and he'd be in the shit. He weighed doing something to her as the door slowly closed but better sense returned to him quickly.

"I'm all in," Clay managed to quip casually. He stretched and yawned.

Ali frowned but refrained from commenting. The men stripped down for bed and doused the light.

Gary Phillips

"Don't forget to say your prayers," Ali only half-joked.

"Heathen," Clay replied. Pinpricks of anxiety jabbed his skin as he lay fully and nervously awake. Any minute Belmundo would be back, Leary regaling him of how the big black buck was schtupping the good lady against the better advice of her friend and confidant. And wouldn't this be Ali's chance too? He was twisted up about Clay's relationship with Scirola and now he was going to get what he deserved. It wouldn't take much to find her body if the MPs came and put him in cuffs and retrace his steps. And he wasn't forgetting that greedy bastard Ross was cooling down in the basement. The hands on his phosphorescent Elgin showed oh-one-seventeen hours.

He reached below his cot and pulled his duffle closer. He had Ross'.45 set near the drawstring opening. He felt inside and the gun's casing, grimy with sweat, was more reassuring to him at this moment than mother's milk. Its three remaining shots the possible difference between imprisonment and flight.

"What are you going to do, Baku?" Ali said quietly.

"Nothing to do," he maintained. The Elgin ticked away in his ears. In between his heartbeat, there came a soft knock at the door. Surprised he croaked, "Yes?"

"Baku?" It wasn't a voice he expected.

Ali was at the door and opened it quickly on the worried face of Shana Owens.

"You've got to get going, Baku. They're on to you," she said in French.

He let the artifice drop and said in English, "How do you know?" He also removed his hand from underneath the cot.

"Of course you'd know how to speak English," she replied in that language. She took a step back, giving him an appreciative up and down as he stood there in his boxers. "You might want to put on something a bit more warm, handsome. We don't have much time. Scirola's friends are talking with Belmundo now."

In French, Ali asked, "What are you two saying?"

"Why are you helping me?" he asked Owens. In the dark, he got dressed again. The gun at the ready.

"You took care of Ross." Shana was at the doorway, looking back at the stairwell.

"You didn't go for the lovers needing a hideaway routine." He said calmly as he moved toward the door.

"What is it, what's happening?" Ali barked in French. He too was up and had clamped a hand onto Clay's arm.

163

"Sorry, mate." Clay whipped around and viciously clubbed the man twice with he flat of the sidearm. Ali keeled over onto the cot. He paused and felt reassured by his steady pulse. Then Clay went into the hall with Owens.

She looked past him at the unconscious man and shut the door. "Come on."

"I can explain, Shana," he said in English.

"You're American," she concluded.

They were on the stairs, the sound of a door opening and closing very audible. It would be Belmundo, and Clay wouldn't doubt he might not have a old "Ruby" pistol from World War I with him as well.

"I've got a place for us to hide," he hastened. They went up as quietly as possible. On the third floor they got on all fours and crawled into the space beneath the rubble. Belmundo's voice carried up to them as he attempted to rouse Ali.

"Hurry," Clay warned, as they crowded into the confines of the man-made tunnel. "This way." Clay crawled past the dug out opening in the wall and indicated for Owens to get inside.

She bumped against the radio set. "What is this?"

"What the madam was up to, Shana."

"This was your mission in Tunis? To find this radio and silence the operator?"

"Yes."

"So you're a regular Bulldog Drummond, eh?" She giggled, touching his arm.

He told her his name.

"They didn't give you a code name?"

"Operator Spook, baby." He laughed bitterly.

Owens frowned, not understanding the word's colloquial use. "So was Ross involved with her? He was a thief, but it's hard to believe he was a traitor?"

"That's right. He just happened to get in the way, Shana. A not so-innocent casualty of this death business we're calling a war."

They were face to face, their bodies stretched at angles to one another. "You sound like a cynic, Mr. Clay."

"I'm a realist. It's not exactly a bowl of cherries that waits for me back home."

"Then maybe you should think about a new home."

That shut him up for a few moments. "So did Ross threaten to throw your brother in the hoosegow if you didn't go along?"

"Let's just say he demanded a lot, okay?"

"What about Claude? He's going to be upset that his side action has been cut off."

She cursed in Arabic. And in French she said, "He's a greasy pig who will someday get exactly what he deserves."

"That's fine by me."

They waited another two hours while voices and flashlights swept about the embassy. At one point, there were footsteps near them in the carpeted hall. Clay had been dismantling the radio using the tip of his folding knife and he stopped, waiting for whoever it was to move on. Finally things settled down again and the two chanced to re-emerge from their warren.

"I can get you on a ship, Madison."

"Like it or not, I'm a soldier, Shana. I have to report in. Look you've done enough to help me, once we get out of the building; I want you to go on your way. And you didn't give me much of an answer. Won't Claude be a problem for you?"

"He'll be mad, so what? He's nothing to me."

"I mean if he should try to--"

She touched the side of his face. "He'll make a lot of noise but not too much. With his connection dead, what can he do?"

The pair were heading outside, their destination his radio set buried beyond the rear wall.

"You're not talking about framing him are you?"

"Should I tell the Army otherwise?" The two were at the kitchen's swing door. It would seem obvious that Leary, Belmundo and Funero would had gone to the command post after finding Ali knocked out."

"I'm not a fan of Claude's either," he replied, pushing into the darkened kitchen. "But hanging him up for a killing he didn't commit, that's plain wrong."

"You'll be long gone, big boy," she slapped him on the back. "And I don't think they'll have much problem blaming you for the deed, eventually. A little diversion but not saying this or hinting at that won't be too harmful."

That was logic he wasn't going to argue with. Out in the garden, he tossed his duffle over the wall and gave her a boost. She was strong and once she got a hold of the top, hauled herself over. He clambered up and soon they were at his hidden radio. Clay powered it up with its dry cell and got an operator. There was some waiting then Colonel Snow came on the line.

Clay made his report efficiently and tersely. The less that devious bastard knew, the better for him. He finished with, "What's my escape route?"

"See a man called Rodgers. I can have him meet you behind the Tom-Tom Klub at oh-six-thirty hours your time. He'll know you."

That meant that Rodgers, who he'd seen Ross talking to earlier, had his own transmitter. That might also mean that Snow already knew he was a wanted man. "I need to have minimum exposure, Colonel."

"I understand, my boy. You've done a great service for your country, Madison, and I'm going to see to it that you're justly compensated."

"Very good, sir. Over and out."

"Over and out."

Clay clicked the unit off and looked to the sky for inspiration.

"Well?" Owens asked. She was sitting next to him on the moist ground, the pre-dawn air around them was heady with the smell of mint leaves from sprigs of the stuff nearby. The two rose.

"He was too goddamn friendly," Clay concluded grimly.

"You don't trust your chief?" Shana had her hands on her hips and her mouth puckered. "And you're on the run from your own Army?"

"Buzzard's luck, baby." He was giddy with nihilism.

"So now what?"

"You go home. I thank you again so much, Shana. More than I can express."

"What if I don't want to?"

"Why are you so eager to help me?"

"Somebody should."

He was standing closer to her, breathing her in, lost in her liquid brown eyes. "This is nuts."

"Yes, war is, Mr. Clay." She kissed him.

Reluctantly, he pulled away. "Are you trying to kill me, woman?"

"Maybe I'm a back-up Nazi spy and I've been sent to destroy you with love. Or I work for the Soviets."

A delicate worry crept behind his eyes and she laughed.

"Relax, soldier, I was just having fun."

His heart started pumping again. "I have to go back, Shana. What else can I do?"

"Oh, a mama's boy, huh?"

"I can't stay in Tunis. The Army will nab me for sure. And I can't depend on Snow to bail me out."

"It's a big world, Mr. Clay."

"So it is."

They waited in the dingy light before dawn, not saying much to each other. They were hiding in one of the stalls looking out onto the rear of the Tom-Tom Klub. The vigorous smell of figs and fish embraced them, but it was soothing, reminding them that the Earth held many small wonders. In the semi-dark, the adherents started toward the mosques. Clay rose from his crouching position, his ears pricked and his body primed. Shana had been napping, her head had been on his knee.

"What do you want me to do?"

"Cover me."

She frowned again and he explained what that meant while handing her the gun. "I've never shot one of these."

"Just wave it around."

"Yes, sir." She saluted, grinning sickly.

A jeep's motor was heard and the two ducked back into hiding as a group of Mps rolled past. "Don't fire that thing unless you absolutely have to," Clay said. "Bastards are on the hunt for me bad." He snuck out the back of the stall and went in a loop to come around the other side of the watering hole. He hadn't seen Rodgers, but he certainly remembered him from the Klub earlier. And he had to assume that he'd been given a full description of Clay, no doubt before he left for Tunis.

How interesting it was when Lenz was the one to casually walk into view. "Clay," he called out quietly, peering into the dawning light. "Clay," he repeated.

"What are you doing here?" The gun was down at his side, his body pulled back into the recess of gloom still available to him.

"Always the cautious man, eh?"

"Where's Rodgers?"

"I'm he."

"Bullshit."

"Shall I tell you who won the World Series? Or better yet, I know that Sugar Ray Robinson's real name is Walker Smith."

"And I know what Rodgers looks like, Lenz. You were there when Ross was talking to him."

He smiled serenely. "Why I do believe you're right, old son. But things are not always what they seem in this game of ours."

"I'm not amused, Lenz, I'm too tired for silly riddles."

"I'm here to get you safely home, Clay. Isn't that enough?" He took a step forward but stopped as Clay stepped forward, his body tensed for a fight.

"Is that necessary?"

"When it's my life, anything is necessary. Now speak clearly and slowly, old son."

"The man at the bar tonight was pretending to be me, that is Rodgers.

He was sent back in by the Germans to take care of their agent, Madam Scirola."

"He pretended to be you, with you in the room?"

"The Wehrmacht believes I was elsewhere as we wanted them too. Part of my mission was to flush this fellow out then take care of him."

"Ah," Clay said, stepping further toward the man. "Well, you've certainly lost your accent, you're English sounds right."

"You see," he said expansively, throwing open his hands as if welcoming a comrade returned from a long journey. "Let's get you fed, some coffee in you, a change of clothes," he flicked at Clay's exposed shirt tail with his hand, "and then you can be on your way out of Tunis."

It was just too good he reflected as he and the man he'd known as Lenz started across the dirt street. They were heading in the direction of the stall but Shana had ducked back down. The plan was that if he didn't say her name, she was to remain hiding. The sun began to rise and the melodic call to prayer wafted from up on high. Three men rushed by offering apologies as the two tall men headed in the general direction of the docks.

For whatever reason, Clay didn't call out her name. He was conflicted. America for goddamn sure was not the land of liberty and nickel cigars for the Negro. Conversely, it was all he had. He'd been to the homeland of Africa on an academic exchange, but he was no African, not in that sense. Hell, wasn't it his duty to fight for something better, something if not to call his own at least for the ones after him on his native soil?

Lost in his daydreaming, Clay had been unaware of the blade in Lenz's hand. Evidently, because he was on his left, the man had let him get ahead by a step and was crossing behind him, the weapon in his right. That's how Owens has seen the brief glint in the rising light of the sun.

"Madison," she yelled, running up, the .45 loose in her hand.

Instinctively Clay brought up his arm and the blade sliced into the meat of his forearm.

"Sorry, orders," Lenz proffered as he made a swipe at Clay's side, up toward his ribs to pierce his heart. Lenz must have assumed shock would immobilize the other man. He was certainly feeling those emotions, only they galvanized him.

Clay grabbed the taller man's wrist and rather than try to stop his thrust, let him complete it. Simultaneously, he shifted his body, twisting on his feet. In this way, Lenz was propelled across Clay's hips. The attacker's momentum had him bending over and Clay wrenched the arm holding onto the cutter.

"Slippery cuss," Lenz said. They were now in the narrow passageway between stalls.

Owens was behind Clay and he signaled for her to stay back. "I've got this," he said.

Lenz punched Clay in the stomach with his free hand. It was a strong blow and made him cough for air. They separated briefly and Lenz was at him, hacking and jabbing with his blade. Clay was cut again along his upper arms as he threw them up to defend himself, while also backing up.

"Madison." Owens leveled the gun, but didn't shoot.

"Like I said, Clay, I like you personally." Lenz made an underhand jab aimed at the big man's gut. Clay knocked against a stall and stumbled, going down hard on his backside.

Owens' gun hand was shaking and she squeezed off a round that went wide. She wiped at her tearing eyes as Lenz bounded for her. Clay wrapped his arms around the man's ankles, upsetting him.

Lenz grinned wantonly. Like a vampire in some old fashioned penny dreadful he arched the knife down to finish his prey off. But Clay had produced his own knife, the folding one he kept strapped above his ankle. He sank the knife into Lenz's chest, where the heart was.

Lenz dropped the dagger. It was three sided, bronze it looked with a dark handle. It reminded him of drawings he'd seen in textbooks about ancient fighting weapons. The tall men didn't bother to grab his chest that leaked red, staining his pressed shirt. He sank to his knees, a resolved cast to his features.

"Very good, brother Clay, very good indeed." His face was drenched in sweat. His hands were at his sides.

The streets were reassuringly vacant due to the early hour and the faithful inside the mosques praying. Clay put a hand on the dying man's shoulder. His blood trickled from his wounds and stained the fine material of Lenz's pinstripe suit. "You are Rodgers? Snow wanted me dead?"

Lenz's eyes glazed over. He laughed hoarsely.

"Goddammit, Lenz," he shook him, "you're on you're way out, man. Come clean."

Lenz gurgled bubbles of red colored saliva. He threw his head back. It seemed he was trying to laugh but there was no life left in him to accomplish the task. He then pitched forward. He was still alive but Owens was already tugging on Clay.

"We've got to go."

"But," he protested.

"Now," she emphasized.

He was starting to run then turned.

"Clay, for all that Allah holds holy..."

He took his knife out of the dying man. It took effort to withdraw it through the muscle and tissue. Lenz gasped, wide-eyed in fatal wonderment. His hands flayed at Clay's face as he let him go and caught up with Shana Owens. And soon the two were running like scared children through the peaceful Tunis morning.

Chapter Seventeen

It wasn't as hard getting used to as he'd imagined. Truth to tell, he liked being alone most of the time. Giabretto was stationed in what was left of the upper tier of a statue factory in the line of sight to what was left of a destroyed church and its small graveyard.

From a corner where the light rarely touched, three angels, blistered and pockmarked from shell explosions, glared at him hour after hour, day after day. He supposed he should have given them names but he hadn't. Giabretto found it more comforting to consider them a set, inseparable in this hellish quietude that his war had become.

He shifted from sitting scissor-legged to his knee, his rifle leaning near him. It was a modified M-1D, a Garand with a range up to five yards, when the wind was right. But there was little wind. There was a match barrel and flash suppressor, a set action for the trigger so the squeeze was smoother, and a leather cheek piece to rest that part of the sniper's face against. For reasons that hadn't been explained to him, the rifle had been fitted with a Russian scope, the fittings having been bored out to accommodate standard-sized screws. The scope had 12X power and crosshairs on its lens. In the three weeks that he'd been in the building, he'd had occasion to use the thing twice.

The first time it had been a patrol of Germans. There were four men checking out this pocket of a town that had become a kind of European Dodge City between the enemy lines and his. He was bored, and had cranked off a round at the kraut sergeant. The high velocity round got him in the toe of his boot and Giabretto had gone flat as the troopers shot all over the place. He had enough sense to know if he tried another shot, he'd be cut down or blown up by a potato masher for sure. Eventually, the squad withdrew.

The second opportunity had presented itself as a halftrack churned through the day before yesterday. The machine had stopped and a soldier popped out like a camouflaged Jack-in-the-box. He was turning, surveying the scene with his binoculars and Giabretto's shot had penetrated his helmet toward the top. The body had flopped back like he'd been sucker-punched. The binoculars went sailing and the halftrack's driver slammed into reverse and left the area.

Giabretto had scurried out of his aerie and hid in a different location but the krauts hadn't sent in a cleanup crew. The defeat of their vaunted 6th Army at Stalingrad had taken a lot out of the axis, and they weren't about to waste personnel on what may or may not be one lone sniper. But really, his job was to watch and listen, and watch some more. He had a radio, a telescope, a steno pad, pencils, and made periodic reports back to base. And that suited him just fine.

Oiling the gun's chambers with his soaked rag, he couldn't help but reflect on what Silas Mayhew and the rest of the Red Ballers were up to now. There was another push coming up and that meant those guys were going to be in the thick of it. Even though he'd taken drastic measures to avoid confronting the man, he surely wished him no ill. He finished rubbing down his rifle and carefully placed the rag back in the canvas bag with the red cross stenciled on its flap. Originally the small knap sack had been used to carry gauze and what not for bandaging the wounded. Now Giabretto used it for his gun's oil can, rags, extra springs and other field equipment. He laughed knowingly. If he got out this mess half way alive, maybe he could sell that idea to one of those radio shows his granddad used to listen to faithfully. One of his favorites was the Shadow, sponsored by Blue Coal, when he was a kid. Sure, each episode would begin with him doing a spirited number, Dorsey or Ellington...no, no, he'd write a signature song, something that the listener would readily identify as his program.

Yeah, the Adventures of the Singing Sniper staring Gil Giabretto. These are the stories of the man with secrets who faced down the ratzis with his wits and his special rifle that fired golden bullets of freedom. Giabretto laughed some more.

Giabretto snatched the telescope up and took a look around. Nothing, not even a goddamn bird. Contemptuously, he tossed it aside and leaned out the opening, his window from which to deliver death. Yet no matter what he did, what new skin he slipped into, he was always going to be Horace Lee Scott, that boy who was so scared that night those pale faces hung Jonsey, he made a silent promise to himself. They were never going to get him. The white man would never catch him because he'd be right there beside them, nodding their nods, and combing his straight hair.

He could feel the hollow stares of the statues on his back. Most of the time he found comfort in their presence, but now, he knew they were really mocking him. If their arms could move they'd be pointing at him and if their lips were capable of life they'd be whispering to each other.

"Stop it, stop it." In his mind, he'd rushed the tallest one, his rifle ready to smash its mortuary glare. But he lost the will and sunk to his knees, gulping in ragged chunks of air. He grabbed his head and rocked slowly, wishing it would all go away. Why did they have to do that to Jonsey, he'd asked his grandfather later. The old man could only shake his head and admonish his grandson to keep his head down and his tongue still. He mustn't tell anyone what he and those other boys saw. Burn the faces of those white men out of your memory forever, he'd warned the youngster.

His grandfather had been a spare figure of a man, his back still erect despite decades of field labor to bring him low and feeble. But that day he looked as if another century of sin had been heaped upon him as he cried in front of his nephew, begging him to promise that he would never again say anything about what he saw. His tears ran into his whiskers and he had a hold of the young man by his shoulders, holding him so his tobacco-seared breath assaulted him.

"If I'd a-seen it, I wouldn't care," Grandpa Clarence said. "I'd go tell it on top of the bank in town 'cause that's the highest building we got. But you jus' startin' on this road of ours, Horace. God may judge me different, but I won't have you in danger, no sir. Your dead mama would never forgive me, no she wouldn't."

Horace Lee knew what his granddaddy was saying, but he'd wanted him to tell him to get the shells for his rifle. He wanted him to tell him to get the kerosene so he could fill up a couple of canning jars, and then they would go and burn those cowardly killers out, and cut them down one by one as he drew down on them with his Sharps.

Instead he could only mutely agree with the pragmatism of the old man. But he couldn't stand to look at him. Standing there, a boy-man who should have been on the verge of discovery of self and the world, a terrible truth descended upon him. There was no good to come of being black, he concluded clearly and decisively. His salty tears welled on his tremulous lip, and like the melting petals of a flower of ice, fell to the bare floor of their sharecropper's shack.

No, goddammit, the fuckin' program wasn't going to be called the Crying Sniper. He wiped at his eyes with the back of his hand. Come on, he cajoled the universe, make some jerry come riding along in a sidecar or on a recon through the town. Okay, he won't kill him, just graze him, all right? Anything to force his mind off a past he can't go back to, couldn't acknowledge unless he wanted to crack up.

He rested the rifle on the ledge, as if it were a juju that he could invoke the presence of a German soldier. But none waltzed into view and Giabretto had to relive the night he ran away from home, a few years after Jonsey's lynching. His grandfather had sent him to the store that evening and he returned with the fat back and turnips. He'd made some extra money at one of his odd jobs, sweeping up at this juke, the only social place for coloreds in his little hometown. He'd been paid off with a bonus by the tough broad who ran the joint, Zenovia. She'd gotten a hold of some smoked hams and given one to Grandpa Clarence.

They had a feast that night. His grandpa had poured him a taste of the Old Overholt, and he pretended he'd never drank rye before. Horace Lee was already six feet and his olive complexion and unruly hair had gotten him in the back door of a few older housewives on their side of the tracks. Even a foray with the white wife of a mill hand. She'd been curious, she said, for a long time about darkie love and wanted to see for herself if there was anything to those rumors. And he being so light-skinned, it wasn't like she was getting it from, well, say, a blue-black nigra she'd giggled. Though afterward, she said she might have to try one of those next.

Horace Lee cleaned up the table and washed the dishes. His grandpa had fallen asleep listening to Lum and Abner on the radio. He stood looking at him, wishing he could remake the world and that it would treat a good man like him fair. But that was not the world they had been born into. So if Horace Lee Scott couldn't escape reality, then there were ways to make a new one. Like a writer who puts a fresh sheet of paper into his typewriter, ready to write a new scene for the Green Hornet or Sergeant Preston of the Yukon, then he too would weave a new existence into being.

He kissed the old man on the forehead and with what few clothes he had, left Malvers, Arkansas. Hot Springs wasn't too far away and the town was wilder than a dog snorting black pepper. There was gambling and hustlers, jackleg preachers and cops so crooked they peed backwards. There he passed himself off as a mulatto and was an errand boy for a madam at one of the brothels, the Lucky Penny. He would sing and play piano for tip money on the weekend when the soldiers and businessmen came down from Little Rock to let their hair down.

He was calling himself Lee Scott then to make it sound whiter, as if one of his had been such. One warm evening, he'd been sent over to the Brickyard Casino, so called because it was on the second floor of a brick factory. His job was to collect some winnings owed to the Madam. He made the pick-up but stopped to shoot some craps. The kid was on a roll when a man came in that he mistook for someone just like him. This man was dark, but not overly so, his black hair combed back and he dressed well. Clearly he was from out of town.

The stranger drank and laughed and was evidently known to the proprietor. Not wishing to risk the madam coming after him with her pistol, he returned to the Lucky Penny with her money. Later, he snuck back to the gambling emporium, fascinated by tthe man. He was still there and Horace managed to edge up to him when he went out back to pee.

"Say, cousin," he'd begun conversationally, "what parts you from?" The country in his voice thick.

The other man gazed at him, and then pissed on Lee Scott's shoes. "Get away from me, you high yellow coon. We ain't related. You ain't no piasan." And he laughed and laughed. "Just 'cause some bitch in your family got poked by massa, that ain't got nothing to do with me, you simple idiot." He shook himself, zipped up and calmly walked away.

Horace Lee wasn't mad, just mystified. From one of the girls at the Lucky Penny he learned something about the Eye-Talians, as she called them. She'd been to Chicago once and told him about the gangsters Al Capone and Frank Nitti. He was fascinated and finally, when Scarface and Little Caesar played on a double bill at the second-run Sedona, he sat in the colored section four nights running to see those pictures over and over.

He got the patter down and the mannerisms and tried them out over and over in his room at the Lucky Penny. Soon he was slipping slang words and the inflections of Paul Muni into his speech. He sounded so ridiculous with his Hollywood gangster Italian that the girls would giggle and tell him to stop fooling around. Nobody realized that Horace Lee was trying on a new skin. But he was no Victor Frankenstein, no mad scientist who had some rudimentary understanding of biology and genetics. His was an experiment from scratch, so there was bound to be excess.

But when he saw another moving picture, one of those musicals, Belles Over Broadway or some such claptrap with Dick Powell, the epiphany struck him. Due to robust hormones and the whiskey he got to sip since childhood, his voice had settled comfortably into a baritone register. More than one girl employed at the Lucky Penny would ask him to sing a specific song on Saturday night.

He adapted the smoothness of Dick Powell with the tough guy act of the movie's interpretation of the Sicilian. Those exotics who were white, but only barely so. For were they not hot-blooded, given to vendettas, and threatening and beating on their women like animals? And as he'd come to learn, there were dark-hued Europeans, the Mediterranean types, enough so that the new phase of his life might work to his advantage. For a while the notion merely festered in his brain, swirled around like the last remains of Ovaltine at the bottom of a glass of milk.

Though it did burn in his stomach as if that milk was sour. He just had to make a new way for himself. He just had to have a chance at life that his granddad never had. It wasn't his fault, goddammit. He didn't make the world be wrong, he didn't set the rules. And one sweet night at the Lucky Penny, he got a chance to cheat in the white man's fixed game.

It was a Saturday, and he was playing "Black Bottom Stomp", a Jelly Roll Morton number when some gents stepped in to get their wicks wet. One of them reminded Horace Lee of the previous Italian fella. But this man was plumper, reddish in the face and, it quickly became apparent, more gregarious.

"Play a'nuther one, son," the tipsy man said, laying a dollar across the top of the upright. "You got fingers that sparkle, boy, yes you do." The man let the bill casually slip from his grasp as he spied the girl he wanted to spend some time and money with.

"Good to see ya, Gil," Zenovia clapped the man warmly on the back. "Been too long, hasn't it?"

"Yeah," he'd answered, getting his arm around the madam, his hand massaging one side of her ample buttocks. "Got in today to see a couple of accounts and got to kick some dust up by noon tomorrow."

"But in between time you'd like to get a little wet." She let loose with that belly buster of hers that wrapped its way around the rafters and back down again.

The one she called Gil gave her another squeeze and leveled a finger at Polly, the girl he'd been ogling. "Gimme that one," he breathed like an indulgent child given his pleasure in the chocolate store. "I loves dark meat." He produced a cigar and licked its end lasciviously.

"Hope you been takin' your vitamins, shugah," Polly said. She was a copper-colored mulatto with straight brown hair that shone like polished metal. She was very popular among a certain persuasion of the Lucky Penny's customers. She took his hand and led him upstairs to the "screw factory," as some of the women referred to the second floor.

Horace Lee resumed playing tunes and singing a few Cole Porter songs that Minister Frederic, a Lutheran, particularly enjoyed. He found it to be too syrupy, but it always got the good reverend looking hound dog blue, remembering something long ago and far away. But then he'd be ready to make a trip to the assembly line and give it the ol' college try. Which in his case included him mumbling from Ecclesiastes while Dora

Mae nibbled on his knob.

"Oh shit, oh shit," Polly spat urgently as she clumped down the stairs. "Where's Zenovia? Where's Zenovia?" she blared.

Horace Lee and Macy, the bouncer the madam brought on for the weekend rowdies, were heading up the stairs as Polly ran to find Zenovia. This wasn't the first time an emergency had happened at the brothel. In the room they found Gil naked as a jaybird except for a pristine white and starched athletic T-shirt. The only thing that marred the look of the shirt was the splotch of a brown, viscous liquid upon its surface.

Macy, a stout individual who'd served with Black Jack Pershing's outfit in World War I, felt for a pulse in the man's neck. He slashed a finger across the middle of his Adam's apple to indicate the ample man's demise.

Horace Lee shook his head in wonderment. "Got hisself fucked to death." The two men snickered. This hadn't occurred to anybody else since Horace Lee had been there, but he'd heard from the other girls about men croaking in the sack now and then. Rather than drive potentials away, such a reputation increased business. The rumor being along the lines that the women at the Lucky Penny had red-hot pussies. That only a real man could buck the bronc there.

"Shit," Zenovia exclaimed behind the two. "Come on, we got to get this mark out of here." She shoved Macy as she spoke.

"What's the rush? Just call Ranny and he'll come collect the stiff."

Ransome Wardlow was the county sheriff and was on the pad to a dozen houses of pleasure in and around Hot Springs. Out of his kickback money he kept the coroner and one of his assistants happy too.

"Can't," Zenovia remarked tersely.

"Can't what?" Macy demanded. There was another rumor that the two were secretly married and that he was a silent partner in the business. But then, there were a lot of stories concerning Zenovia.

"He's got friends."

"So do all of us."

"Friends we don't want comin' around here. There can't be nothing tying us to him, Mace, nothing." She had a hand on his upper arm and dug nails into his muscle.

"He's not some kind of salesman?"

Zenovia made a sound. "When he said accounts, he meant the ones they force to carry their cigarette machine, juke boxes and their booze."

"Oh," he said, his eyebrows twitching. He looked at Horace Lee. "Well, looks like we got some spade work ahead of us." And he snickered at his little joke.

They buried the man outside of town on a sloping area among some maples and cottonwoods. To ensure making identification difficult, they cut the labels and tags out of the man's clothing as they'd buried him in his goods. Macy had taken the bills out of the man's wallet and handed it to the young piano player, like it was an overcoat to the hatcheck in a nightclub. He wasn't sure what he was supposed to do with the wallet so he stuffed it in his pocket. They rode back, each to his own council in Macy's Hudson.

Back in his room, Horace Lee examined the contents of the dead man's wallet. His name was Gilbert Gianni and his driver's license had been issued in Cicero, Illinois. But there was another license stating his name as Franconi Giabretto from Steubenville, Ohio. There was also a business card with the name Tony Papendraos on it and was from a bowling supply and trophy company in Trenton, New Jersey.

Lying in his bed, he was unable to sleep. He was excited about the mystery man who'd died getting serviced by Polly. She'd been upset by it all and had to be given a sleeping powder. Funny, he would reflect later, burying a man without telling the law was committing an illegal act, but that didn't faze him. That was simply part of his job. What really had Horace Lee going was possibility.

Such was the name of the thing heretofore he couldn't identify, but it coursed in his blood like a fever. He got off the bed again and looked through the cards and identification, his fingers touching them as if each one offered directions to somewhere else. And of course they did, for their words had given form to the desire cocooning inside him.

The next month, supplied with more than four hundred dollars in tip money that he'd amassed plus a bonus from Zenovia for helping Macy with the body, he said his goodbyes. He told them he was going to Memphis and see if he could make it as a blues man. For a going away present, Polly gave him her triple-decker and tongue kissing. Even Zenovia gave him a hug at the train station. Horace Lee enthusiastically waved goodbye to the Lucky Penny employees and waited until they were out of sight and then walked to the other side of the tracks to catch the train back to his home.

"You know I heard about you." His grandfather said upon first seeing his grown form walking up his rickety steps. "Callin' yourself another name and what not."

"So I figured." He set down his cardboard suitcase and they stared at one another, each seeing what four years had done to the other.

"You got taller. Know'd you would. How long you gonna stay?"

"Night or two." His voice was his natural one, not the white one he'd learned to do. He'd practiced in the white section of the passenger car. There was a couple of looks but that passed as he crossed one leg over the other and casually read the paper like he wasn't nervous as a long-tailed cat on a porch of busy rocking chairs.

He chopped some firewood for the old man and cleaned out the flue over the cast iron stove. There were some loose boards in the tiny bedroom and he replaced them and fit in new pieces of sticky pine. He trimmed back a sagging limb the size of an elephant's trunk that drooped from the maple tree onto the shack's tar and paper roof. There was a gopher hole beside the house hidden by some stinkweed. Horace Lee poured some lye down the hole and capped it with fresh dirt.

Sitting on the porch that evening, lightning bugs buzzed and circled in an aerial ballet about them. The old man was like that painting he'd seen once in a magazine. It was called the Banjo Lesson by a man named Henry O. Tanner and depicted a young black boy on his dignified grandfather's knee as he leaned to play the banjo. And the fact that Tanner was a Negro and had gone to live in Paris made a powerful impression on him. Even then, he was contemplating a way out, a way to throw off the trappings of blackness.

Yet all the while he also loved that old man and what he stood for sitting in his rocking chair, slowly creaking to-and-fro. Horace Lee sat on the steps, sipping from a coffee cup of whiskey.

"Smells like rain coming," Grandpa Clarence drawled.

"Yep." He took another swallow.

The old man continued creaking and the lightning bugs continued flashing and flying. "You go to your mama's grave?"

"I hadn't."

"You should." Creak, creak.

The boy lit a cigarette and tapped ash onto the porch. His grandfather looked over at him then went back to staring into middle space. Finally he said, "You goin' north, ain't you?"

"Yes, sir."

"New York?"

"I expect."

More creaking and more contemplating. One of the bugs dashed its brittle body against the house. Horace Lee wondered what could have so bothered his little life that would make him do that. But he supposed despair was a relative experience.

"What you gonna call yourself?"

The old man could see right through him. "I haven't settled on that

179

yet," he fibbed.

"Uh-huh," came the doubtful reply.

They let some more space drag out then grandpa Clarence said, "You ain't the first one to do this. And I can't rightly say I agree with you, but shit, it's a different world you're going to be stepping into."

He wanted to answer him, but he couldn't manage the words.

"But there's gonna come a time, when who you are is going to matter. When, well," he paused, "you cain't be anything but what you are."

"I never knew my daddy, mama never would say much about him. So maybe it ain't like I'm running from something, but to it, grandpa."

The older man stopped rocking and drank from his coffee cup of whiskey. "Yes, that could be. I have considered such now and then, yes, surely I have. But we both know that in this world, you is one or the other, Horace Lee. The people you have to deal with or even pass in the street will make that decision for you."

"That's just it, I want to make the choice. What's wrong with that?"

"Nothing, son, it's the way it should be, only it's not the way things is."

"And I should accept that?"

"Many do. Though some try to buck it."

"Like Jonsey?"

It was Grandpa Clarence's turn not to have an answer.

CHAPTER EIGHTEEN

As Gil Giabretto looked out on the town square, he remembered leaving his grandpa's place a day and a half later, the sun high and bright in a clear lake blue sky. From time to time he'd send money to him, maybe even putting in a coaster or matchbook from one of the clubs he'd sang at. But never one of the playbills or anything indicating his new name. As if absolutely admitting his transformation to the only person he loved would break the spell. For, like the Shadow, he had the ability to cloud men's minds.

Restless, he shifted his binoculars, scanning the surrounding countryside. By rote he started on the left and slowly cranked his vision to the right. At a position of about two o'clock a tank was coming up then proceeding down a rise studded with dry grass. He tensed with anticipation as he kept looking. He expected several tanks to follow this one, yet it seemed this was a solo effort. That was certainly not the way that panzers traveled. Maybe this one had been cut off from its steel-clad brethren. And now it was going to stop in the town and disgorge its crew, who would search for food or maybe even tools to fix a part. If he took out a tank's crew, they might give him a medal. He got more excited and slunk back so as not to expose himself. Giabretto readied his weapon and waited.

The tank continued onward, ascending another small hill and disappearing momentarily from his line of sight. The grinding of its synchronized gears was the only sound in the dead air. He calculated how many soldiers could be inside one of those things. Four tops. He would have to be patient. It would do no good to cut down one or two of them, and still have that cannon swing around and blow his perch out from under him. Conversely, if only two of them got out, then what? It was his job to take out krauts and sow fear. Therefore he'd have to take the shots and be prepared to leave his position should the tank's turret start to move. Giabretto slowly rubbed his cupped palm back and forth along the underside of the rifle.

The tank was now at the top of the small rise, rumbling quietly. To its left the road was the road leading into town. Giabretto sighted through his scope, trying to get a bead into one of the two observation slits on either side of the front of the tank. He had an impression of a pair of eyes behind one of those slits. The range was still too far anyway. The tank's turret swung on oiled bearings back and forth, the driver inside taking a look around. For a moment, he wondered if the machine would park there and let its occupants out to scrounge for supplies. If that happened, he'd go downstairs and hunt them down one by one as they fanned out. The krauts would want to cover as much ground as possible, and that would make picking them off easier to do.

The tank belched smoke from its exhaust and began its descent. Every revolution of its treads brought its human cargo that much closer to the delivery of his rounds. Giabretto didn't consider himself particularly bloodthirsty, but he wasn't bothered by the demands of his job. There had been this story, one of those first hand accounts, by an army sniper in the Pacific Theater in a recent Yank magazine. This guy used a 1903 Springfield, a .30 with a lot of kick and velocity. He talked about sniping from the brush and from wooden platforms he'd rigged in trees and what not. This man, who wrote the article under the pretend name of Jack Armstrong, the radio hero, said he'd put down something like 20 Japs over the course of 10 months of being a sniper.

The point wasn't about him bragging about how many kills he had. What Jack Armstrong now had was sleepless nights where all those nameless Japs he'd croaked had come back to torment him in his sleep. They had faces and wore shoes and spoke English or came to him with parts of their faces or heads missing. And these mugs would just stand there and point at the messy wounds he'd inflicted on them. He'd seen a head shrinker and chaplain, but he couldn't shake the nightmares. He was glad, Jack Armstrong wrote at the end of his article, to be going home. He was through with "killing through glass," as he'd called it.

Giabretto had no such qualms. Every dead kraut was one less obstacle to the war being over and him resuming his career as a singer. He was figuring to also do some acting and if he racked up some dead Germans to build up his reputation, so much the better. This world had taught him that sacrifice and a good heart only made your disappointments that much sharper. If things was on the fair and square, then his Grandpa should have been able to realize his desire of owning a feed store. But this was about survival, about being the toughest or most cunning dog in the pack. Fuck the generals and fuck the poor bastards who got in your way.

The panzer was slowly treading down the last hillock that would let them out onto flat ground. Could be the report about the sniper in the town had been spread around and the jerry's in the tank had received the news. Giabretto turned on his radio but got static.

The tank seemed to be going too slow, too stealthily. The iron beast got halfway down the hill, more smoke issuing from the exhaust pipe. The back of Giabretto's neck was clammy as he sighted down the scope, forgetting about his radio. He twisted the alignment screw, matching up the crosshairs perfectly. Something was up.

The tank shuddered and its engine quit. Involuntarily, Giabretto held his breath. The turret turned and the machine's barrel rose as it did so. Through his scope, it was as if the unblinking black eye of that barrel was boring in on him. And just maybe it was. The swiveling quit and the faint sound of voices came to him. He exhaled evenly as the tank's hatch flipped back and the helmeted head of a soldier popped up. Giabretto stayed poised and ready. Times was on his side for killing.

The first man dropped off the tank, quickly followed by the second one. This man was gesturing with his hands and from the striping he saw on his sleeve, Giabretto could tell this one was a sergeant. He pointed at the tank and then arched back, opening his hands and arms as if asking for supplication from above. The first one shook his head and lit a cigarette. Could these be the only ones? The sniper concluded to take out the lead man first, as that was the standing order in any situation. But he held, and was rewarded less than a half a minute later.

A third man, with goggles and a headpiece, also came up through the hatch. Only this one didn't get out and he was talking to the other two. He was resting at the top of the turret, not moving out of the tank. The scope shifted to this man, as he was potentially the most dangerous as he could quickly be back inside and shot the cannon. The two outside the tank walked back and forth while the corporal smoked. Evidently, something was wrong with the tank and now they had to make a decision. Either abandon the vehicle then walk to rejoin their lines, or search in the town for a possible part they could jury-rig?

There were a few trucks around, and certainly the crew had spotted one or two when they were on the rise. Giabretto smiled as he felt his sweat cool on the leather piece rubbing on his cheekbone. There was a Mercedes Benz delivery truck, listing where one its rear wheels had been blown off, alongside a building right off the plaza. They would proceed there first. It was the most logical place.

The German corporal flicked the remains of his cigarette away. The sergeant was handed his MG-34 machine gun with the basket magazine from the driver, and the two started down the rest of the hill. But the third man, he wasn't moving, only telling them something as they went. Why the hell didn't he get out of that tin can? Wasn't he the driver and therefore the one most likely to have mechanical ability? And the other two, now laughing as they descended, why didn't they have tools with them if they were going to take a part? Or, Giabretto reasoned, they were simply going to scout out what they could find and return to the tank to make a decision. He shifted his weapon between the man still sticking half way out of the turret and the two now at the bottom of the hill.

His radio crackled and Giabretto fooled with the dial. He could make out a few words but was more concerned with his present situation. He left the instrument alone.

Those two he could pick off like ducks, one right after the other as they were grouped together, loose and casual. But they were less of a threat than the one still in the tank. Giabretto lifted the scope off those two just as the third man was going back inside his vehicle. Hastily, Giabretto got off a shot that zinged off the plating directly in front of the disappearing figure. The bullet may or may not have ricocheted and struck its intended target. Giabretto had already swung the scope from the driver and fired two more leading shots at the sergeant and corporeal.

Stupid, he should have waited.

Giabretto blasted away the corporal's face, an eerie reminder of how his own Corporal Schiller had fallen. His body spun and stumbled and dropped like wet rags into the grass of the plaza. The sergeant had flung himself to the side and now had crawled behind the delivery truck. He was smart, he hadn't returned fire. He did call out his pal's name but there was no response. Then he called out again and Giabretto knew what that meant.

The tank turret started to turn again, the driver obviously not wounded enough. Giabretto remained crouched. He knew they couldn't be sure where he was and he didn't count on them wasting shells. But then again, the two left of the crew might do their own math and figure it was worth the expenditure.

Giabretto didn't dare peek out any more than he could see from where he had his body bunched down. The sergeant's machine gun might not have the range of his rifle, but that goddamn tank more than made up the difference.

The turret stopped, and the barrel was cranked downward. He followed the line of sight and it led to a three-story building of wood and stone. Part of its structure was eaten away as if by giant termites. A puff, then a swoosh of flame, followed by a crack as the tank let a round loose. The shell's distinctive whine filled his ears then the face of the building exploded. There was enough of a concussive blowback to knock him down.

The driver yelled at the sergeant, who yelled back. The noncom stuck his head from around the corner of the truck and Giabretto weighed taking a shot. If he missed, he'd be one rotten egg. But he had to do something. They might decide to work their way around, and then what? Once they zeroed in on his building, he'd have to move fast. He glanced up at his grave marker angels, but there was nothing in the way of inspiration coming from them.

The soldiers were talking and that dark eye of the tank was turning to do more business. This time it was a flat, low building between where he was and the one they'd just shot at. They might imagine he was camped on the roof, but he doubted it. They had to assume he'd been here for days and would not stay out in the elements that long. The driver said something again and the sergeant answered him in a curt manner.

What the hell? Giabretto gripped his rifle tightly. The choice might have been made for him as the turret swung away from the low building and onto where he was. He could swear the interlocking of the gears was now the only sound in the universe as that black hole inched upward, about to bore through him. The sergeant, down on his belly, poked his upper body from around the truck's tire. It was a dare, to see if the sniper would try a shot, and thus confirm his hiding place. Giabretto knew better than to bite. The barrel of that big gun was pointed at the opening on the other end of the building. A shot boomed and Giabretto was again wrenched from his feet by the force of the shockwave. A ceiling joist shook loose amid the rain of plaster and dust, and he balled himself up to escape injury.

His ears rang. Giabretto clamped the flats of his hands against the side of his face but the noise inside his head persisted. It was if he were back in that Douglas Skymaster they came over on with his ears plugged up during the descent. Only this time a fire alarm accompanied the annoyance. He strained but could discern nothing audibly, beyond the goddamn bells. He moved and got his hand around the rifle, shaking his head trying to clear his ears.

Momentarily he could hear snatches of his radio squawking.

"The Red Ballers have to--"

Then his hearing went out again.

To his left, in the range of his peripheral vision, he detected movement. The rifle was aiming and the trigger almost pulled in the milliseconds it took for him to pivot into firing position. Two field mice had scurried atop a small pile of rubble, scared, their little furry bodies trembling.

Their wet bright eyes fixed on Giabretto, their whiskers silvery threads of condensed light. They hurried down the other side of the hill, going wherever it was mice went when they ran for shelter.

He rose slowly, his back pressed to the wall next to the trio of angels. The blast had rocked the statues but they remained upright and intact. From the corner of the truck he could see part of the sergeant's face, his mouth working. They had to be discussion whether it was worth taking another shot. Giabretto tasted the salt and dirt. It made everything real again, if only for a moment.

Giabretto went low again and duck-walked around the statue, cradling the M-1. The light behind his radio's dial fluttered, indicating command was calling but he couldn't hear nor had the time to reply. He cleared the statue, then belly crawled toward what was left of the doorway. This led to a bombed out hallway and the once solid stairs to the second floor. He was at the landing, and paused. The ringing had subsided to some degree and he hoped that meant his hearing was coming back. But no, he confirmed after stamping his feet, he was still deaf. Shit. He started down and this time the panzer's shell must have tore into just where he'd been. He was jerked back and forth, then his footing gave way and he fell forward.

Defensively, Giabretto tried to use one elbow like he'd seen on those newsreels of football players running a block. With the other, he held onto that rifle like a baby to its mother's breast. In his eerie silence, Giabretto tumbled as portions of the roof came away. Portions of the stairs buckled up like the ridged back of some behemoth. He came to rest, having fallen against broken pieces of wood and plaster. He was like a turtle that'd been flipped over onto its back. There was pulsating pain throughout his body but it didn't seem as if anything were broken. Laying there, blinking back sweat and blood, he wondered if this was what it felt like to make that jump to the other side. His grandpa hadn't been much of a church goin' man, so Giabretto didn't have much in the way of reference.

He craned his neck as he wiggled his fingers. The rifle, he had to find that damned thing fast. He tried to get up and it was if he'd been sucker punched by the invisible man. Giabretto fell back on his pile, and momentarily he wanted to let it all overcome him, lift him up and take him way from all this madness. But that was only a passing weakness. Death was too distasteful to consider today. He struggled up, fighting the creeping panic mewing in his guts. He spotted the stock of the rifle. Like a giant pack rat, he plowed on all fours over and through the mess. Just then, a dull thud of machine gun fire sizzled the air in front of him.

His only warning was the puffs of detritus as the bullets sank into the building material around him.

Giabretto rolled and fell back on the opposite side of the demolished stairs and building. His hearing hadn't returned. There was only a kind of hint inside his eardrums, like the nerves were regenerating at a snail's pace to be of any use to him. There was more machine-gunning from the German's schnauzers and he had an impression that the sergeant was shouting. There was dirt in the barrel of his gun, though he didn't think that would be a problem. He kept his weapon so well oiled he was sure it wouldn't gum up the firing mechanisms. That was the least of his worries as he got moving again.

He went to the left, trying to keep his footing while also looking all around him. Certainly his body was causing stuff to creak and groan, but there was nothing he could do about that. It was just too bad he couldn't hear. Giabretto threw a piece of concrete over the top of his pile. Nothing happened, or at least he assumed as much, as he detected no evidence of rounds being let lose. If that kraut knew he couldn't hear, he was meat on the hook.

He'd reached the far end of what remained of the building. Amazingly, part of a window sash and its glass were intact in a section of wall. Outside, the peaceful countryside looked ideal for a picnic and a game of baseball. But the birds, he couldn't hear them chirping. Giabretto got angry all over again. It made him reckless, he crept toward the top and his foot gave way. There must have been a sound because suddenly the top of the German's sergeant's helmet was in his line of sight as he raced toward the building. Giabretto fired. His enemy sought cover.

Giabretto went as flat as he could on the mound. He was aware he was bleeding all over and probably would be going into shock if he weren't so wound up. He could only stay this way for so long. The sergeant would start pumping his rounds into the mass, as it was not packed tight at all. And he only had the one magazine. Though having the tank's 88s as back up was a big plus in the German's favor. Though the sergeant being so near now would have his buddy hold off firing on the building. And the sergeant charging forward probably meant the tank was low on shells.

There was a disturbance of the debris he was balanced on and suddenly it gave way again. Giabretto went plunging into the maw exposed underneath. He collided with something hard and this jarred the rifle from his hand. It was lost again and it might as well be have been in orbit around the moon. The schnauzer was firing from below. Pieces of wood and plaster kicked up, and a dull thud, like faraway thunder, resonated deep inside his skull.

He twisted and gyrated and clawed at the junk around him while he kicked like a man tying to get out of a whirlpool. A series of gunfire erupted again and Giabretto screamed, "You fuckin' kraut motherfucker!" Some of the bullets seared across the flesh of his back. He plowed forward, not sure of what he was doing. Now he was back in the light, coughing and blinking. His hearing was still shit but he was aware of movement near his right leg. He sat up.

There was the sergeant's arm and hand sticking out of part of the now collapsed pile. His radio smashed and useless. He got into gear just as the German came out of the pieces of the shop. The non-com had been looking around for his weapon and saw it nearby, leaning against some concrete fragments. But Giabretto was on the man's back even as the latter scrambled for the machine gun. He planted a blow at the base of the man's head and this stopped him from trying to reach his MG-34. The sergeant, a wiry man with large hands, turned and managed to grab Giabretto by the material of his shirt. Both men rolled, their bodies coming off the shards of lumber and slammed into what was left of a front wall.

The sergeant was mouthing words at Giabretto but it was like the humming of a basket of snakes. Each man sought purchase on the other. The German had a hand around Giabretto's neck and the recently promoted corporeal was pushing a hand against the other man's face. The strangle hold was effective but Giabretto managed to get to a knee while the sergeant was still partly leaned against the wall.

Giabretto winced, his eyes tearing as the sergeant's fingers dug into his neck. Giabretto got more weight behind his hand on the side of the man's face. The German was using his other hand to beat at the American's shoulders. Giabretto countered with blows of his own to the enemy. His opposing hand slipped and part of his thumb went into the man's mouth and he bit down.

Giabretto gritted his teeth and leveled a punch in the German's solar plexus that jarred him enough so that his hand shook lose. The sergeant stomped a foot down on Giabretto's. The two went into a clench and, like prizefighters, boxed out of it. Giabretto threw a left that went wide. The other man went low and came up, clipping him again.

The German's big fists zeroed in on Giabretto, snapping his head back. He got a forearm up, warding off a blow aimed at his heart. He delivered two himself.

He snarled something and Giabretto could hear about every second word. "Right back at you, Frtizy," he said and jabbed the man's ribs.

The sergeant said something else. And like a record that was missing some of its groove, snatches of the words were evident to him. Then the sergeant lunged, trying to get both his hands this time around Giabretto's neck, but the American reared back. As he did so, he took a hold of the upper arm of the German and he was now on top of Giabretto.

The German smiled, his blood and salvia dripping down on the corporeal. But this had been his plan and he allowed their momentum to keep them going while he leveraged a knee into the German's chest. He then turned and this freed him from the man's grip. The two got to their feet. Trying to move fast, Giabretto found himself hacking and gasping for air. This gave the other man an opening and he clobbered Giabretto with a sock to the jaw. He staggered back. The sergeant momentarily turned, yelling toward the tank then pressed forward. Driven by everything that had gotten him to this point, Giabretto was on his feet, colliding with the other one. They went down again, this time tripping across the rubble. As he got his footing, he half-turned and could see the hatch on the tank opening.

There was no time for more worry because he had enough to occupy him. The sergeant lashed out, rising up and swinging. Giabretto head-butted him. It was the sergeant's head this time that whipped back in recoil; Giabretto followed that move with two quick jabs to the man's stomach. The German sagged and Giabretto buried a shoulder in his sternum. They passed right in front of the opening, and for a hot second he figured the driver might open up with one of the two eight millimeters machine guns mounted on the tank. The two hit the wall hard, the air gushing out of the wobbly sergeant like an open wound.

The German was tough and took a swing that glanced off of the GI. The sergeant's teeth were red from blood. Giabretto grabbed the man by the back of his neck and bore down. As he did this he rammed his knee up and the point of it impacted the bridge of the non-com's nose. He felt the bone give way, and Giabretto finished the man off with a straight left to his temple. The enemy soldier withered to the floor as if he were a marionette whose strings had been cut.

Giabretto gulped and looked around. The hatch of the tank had remained open. He went down in a crouch and peered into the rubble, searching for either his rifle or the sergeant's machine gun. Oddly, the non-com had no side arm. And his hearing wasn't quite right yet. It was like he had a gallon of water in his ears. Everything was indistinct and lacking clarity. Giabretto looked behind him but of course there was just that damned tank stalled halfway down the damned hill. Was that a truck coming up the road from the direction of base? That must have been what they were trying to tell him on the squawk box.

He went back into the rubble and dug around. He cursed after a jagged splinter tore the flesh over his thumb. He pushed more into he pile and was rewarded with a piece of cold metal that felt very familiar. He laughed and he was pleasantly surprised to find he could hear himself. Giabretto wrenched it loose and he came away with his rifle. Wood and pieces of wall fell all over him, cutting into his back and upper shoulders. But he was too overjoyed to feel any pain.

He spun and came out of his crouching position. The rifle's weight was a comfort to him, his wounded hand pulsing with the excitement coursing through him. He started forward, the sounds of the birds chirping sharp and clear in his ears. The first shot from the driver's Lugar tore into the bone of his chest and buried itself in his lung. But the Singing Sniper couldn't be stopped. There was a radio show to do after winning the war, wasn't there?

The driver had been hiding beside the bombed out entrance, and had ducked back from view. It didn't seem he was used to doing his killing up close Giabretto reflecting that it must have made him skittish. A foreign taste flecked across his lips. He was down, in a firing stance beside the pile of debris. Wait, just wait he told himself. The driver's head popped into view, just like those not-so-long-ago times when the curious turkeys would bob up. The rifle cracked once and true and the bullet entered the driver's eye socket and exited the back of his head amid a red mist. There was an exhale of a sigh, and the expired body fell sideways,

Giabretto struggled to his feet, the rubber floor undulating under his feet. The rifle was now too heavy to hold onto and he let it clatter onto the cement. He wiped sweat away from his forehead, a chill working its way through him. The hole in his chest reminded him he should do something about it. He bent down to the sergeant and ripped away part of the man's shirt for a rag. This he placed inside his own shirt, pressing it against the tender wound. The cabaret crooner walked crookedly outside, the trilling of the birds calling to him.

Up the road the trucks grew closer. He could see there were two. Unsteady, he walked toward them. Come on Giabretto, they're waiting for you at the station, man. First they want you to do a Gershwin number, something light but with that biting undertone of his. Then maybe something by Goodwin or Fletcher Henderson, or better yet, "It Had to be You." That always got the dames going. Yes, sir, he was going to make Manhattan his again.

He slipped on a loose rock and landed on his back, like a tortoise left too long out on the water in the sun. His lips puckered but no words were forthcoming. He could hear voices as brakes squealed to a stop.

"Giabretto," Silas Mayhew yelled, running toward him. Giabretto smiled at him. Mayhew kneeled beside him.

"Oh, man," the Red Baller said.

"Hand me my rifle, would you, Silas?"

"Sure, Gil." It was lying across Giabretto's legs and Mayhew put it in the dying man's hands.

"It's Horace, my name is Horace Lee Scott," he told Mayhew. He held tightly onto his rifle. He would need it to go hunting with his granddad.

CHAPTER NINETEEN

August 1943, Greenwich Village

Birch stood on one side of Perry Street as the brightly painted cab rolled past him near the curb. On the other side of the street he could see that nosey broad sitting in the window at a booth. He had to admit, she was pretty sharp for a woman and a darkie to boot. He lit a Chesterfield and let the sharp tang of smoke drift leisurely into his nostrils. Too bad he was going to have to give her the rough treatment. He wouldn't mind having those ankles of hers clamped around his hips. No, not at all.

Snow's man checked his watch and played out in his mind the scene Palmer must be having right about now with that bent kraut Alnon Krupp. The Colonel wanted to swat this guy down but had to be careful, had to handle him with the kid gloves. He was a pill, had a real hatred for "ze Schwartzes" he'd say. Every day he'd get up worried what scheme A. Philip Randolph or Walter White or some other head Negro was up to. Krupp's stomach gurgled constantly and the bags under his eyes got heavier with the more sleep he lost.

Krupp was some kind of relation to the munitions family in Germany. And even separated by the Atlantic, money knew no such borders or conflict. This Krupp made sure some of his money went to the right senator's campaign or the sympathetic government bureaucrat. And to doubly prove his loyalty to his adopted country, Krupp sent regular memos to J. Edgar Hoover reporting on any activity or anti-white rumblings he counted as subversive inside the Pullman Company. To Krupp, three Negroes getting together to play cards was suspicious. So when he got word of the planned rally advocating for colored soldiers being activated, he no doubt envisioned revolution.

To Krupp, and to Hoover to no small degree, Snow had chuckled, the blacks were getting way too demanding way too fast. It was enough he'd had to swallow the recognition of the porter's union. That was not his decision, the record was clear as to how he voted. But now these monkeys might be in the homeland, and that was too much. The world was tilting too far out of kilter if that was to be the way things were to be. That was why, according to Snow, he'd hired a couple of strikebreakers he'd used in the past to educate Crimpshaw.

Birch snorted, letting the inhaled smoke squirt from a side of his mouth. So Palmer had been sent to be the peacemaker. Palmer was the one with education, the college man and all that rah-rah. Snow had intercepted that last memo to Hoover where Krupp bragged about snatching Crimpshaw. About how his goons had worked him over and had the yellow nigger whimpering until he pulled a straight razor from his sock and got away.

Birch ground out his cigarette. A brunette in a crisp silk outfit strolled along with her poodle. He tipped his hat and got a half-smile for his effort. Snow certainly didn't give a rusty fuck what happened to Crimpshaw or his pal Randolph. The rally wasn't the point as far as he was concerned. The coons could jabber all they want about this, that or how many holes in a slice of Swiss cheese as far as the Colonel and X-2 was concerned. But when Snow ran an operation, he ran it airtight. And he couldn't have a free-lancer like Krupp making all sorts of moves that might call too much attention to important business. Like this trimming Birch had to dispense on the reporter.

If Crimpshaw had been busted up, the Yids, Birch theorized, at the New York Times would be all over that and make the goddamn union into a bunch of martyrs. And that meant more flashbulbs popping and more eyes and ears on them leading into the rally tomorrow. And that meant there could be too many somebodies around who might ask the right question of the right source when Yates got her talking-to.

The operative watched Yates nod and make a notation on her pad. The guy she was talking to looked around then sipped his coffee. He was smallish man you would ordinarily call a nobody, a chump in a corduroy car coat and glasses, someone you wouldn't waste a hello on. Only Birch knew this from days of tailing her, he was a file clerk at the Municipal Hall of Records. And the day before yesterday she'd been to see him in his section on Chambers Street. Turns out, Birch found out later, that this guy, Mort Slezak, was one of the people in charge of keeping the City's death certificates in order. Birch wasn't sure what it all added up to, but the usually unflappable Snow's voice had climbed a notch when he'd made his daily report to the Colonel over the phone.

"Have a spirited discussion with our dusky Brenda Starr," he'd ordered. "Make it very clear to her she needs to drop this nonsense." And so that's what he planned to do once she got through with this clerk. He didn't know what, if anything, the Colonel wanted done about Slezak. By the time Yates had stepped out of the deli, Birch had finished three more cigarettes. The clerk had already left and she'd been re-reading her notes. Now, as she walked up Seventh Avenue, he crossed the street and closed on her. He figured he'd keep shadowing her and an opportunity would present itself. Maybe he'd brace her on the steps of the subway, come up to her like they were old pals so he could get a hand on her upper arm. Then whisper in her ear that "this case was closed to her, a dead end, see?" Yeah, just like Bogart in one of his movies. She'd know how easy it would be for him to shove her down the steps, and nobody would think anything of it. Just some poor lady who tripped and fell on her way to catching the A train.

Birch hung back, his eyes on the fine backside of the colored dame. Crimpshaw was a lucky bastard, he told himself lustfully. Maybe he'd give her something to write about all right. They got to the corner and she turned on Fourth Street that turned into Seventh Avenue. At the juncture was the subway. There weren't a lot of people around at this time of day, this would be perfect.

He passed in front of a green grocer and a cab pulled to the curb just ahead of him. Birch tensed. The car was a Hudson, just like the one that had driven past him earlier. The passenger door opened and a large colored man stepped out, gun at his side. The car's springs groaned with relief.

Birch let his hand dip inside his coat but the ruse worked. The other guy, the one he hadn't seen was already behind him. He must have been inside the store.

"You robbing the wrong white man, fellas," he snarled.

"This ain't about that," the one behind him intoned.

The large man in front of him folded his arms, his legs spread apart. The cab idled smoothly in contrast to the hammering Birch could feel against the inside his chest cavity. But he damned sure wasn't going to let these sambos see him nervous.

"You better let me get about my business, boys." Yates was getting further down the street.

"Here's how it is, okay." The one behind him stood close, but there was nothing poking in his back. "We know about you, you got that? We know about you and your friend. We got you spotted while you been busy on Miss Yates."

"What the hell –"

"Shut up," the other one said. "You two leave off Miss Yates, you got that?"

"You niggers know better than to stick your burr heads in white folks concerns."

"And you better learn to take your nose out of black folks'

194

business."

The sap cracked viciously against the back of Birch's head and his knees became unhinged. The man replaced his revolver. Then he got into the back seat of the cab along with the large man.

A bleary-brained Birch held onto a lamppost. "You spook bastards," he spat. "You Pullman porch monkeys are going to pay for this." He then slid down to the pavement. A small crowd had gathered and watched intrigued as the cab drove away, leaving him bleeding and mumbling on the sidewalk. He saw Alma Yates standing at the edge of the crowd, frowning.

CHAPTER TWENTY

August 1943, Washington D.C.

Colonel Snow reread the field report about Birch's misadventure in Harlem. The undercurrent of Palmer's glee, as he was the one to file it, was all too evident in the phrases he'd chosen in composing the missive. He put the paperwork aside and sighed heavily. Bad enough that the coons had gotten the best of one of his men, but the incident exacerbated the growing competition between the two. He would have to reel that in. Snow believed in teamwork and sacrifice. For not only did he have the nuisance of Alma Yates to handle there was the business of Madison Clay plaguing him. Given the lack of reliable sources in North Africa, the first two weeks or so after his escape, Clay's sightings had been sporadic.

Snow picked up the phone handset. "Bring my car around," he ordered and hung up.

Transport by sea was sure to be Clay's method out of there and Snow's hastily acquired mercenary had drawn a bead on the big buck when he finally showed on the docks. But the white woman Clay was traveling with was as tough as a man, and had snuck around and gutted his hireling before he could put one through Clay's head.

Thereafter, the clever black bastard and that Owens woman had been like smoke. A mixed couple in the States was rare enough to be spotted, but it was tougher in certain parts of the world where some kind of goddamn racial flummery contrary to the laws of God and man had seemingly been practiced since before the invention of the light bulb, Snow reflected.

Shrugging into his winter topcoat, Snow considered his options with Yates and decided that for now he best leave her be. She had yet to write anything in her paper about the microwave experiments until she had something definitive. He wasn't a hundred percent sure how'd she tumbled onto even a hint about what had been conducted in Arizona, but the cake was far from all dough yet. Let her run around like a chicken with its head cut off and if she dared to put word one on paper, he'd find some jackleg coon preacher or colored mis-leader to denounce her.

Yes, that was the way to deal with that reporter. No strong arm tactics, but spread stories about her being a loose woman, she was shacking up with that Crimpshaw after all, writing sympathetic articles about Communist leaning unionists. Yes, that was the way to do it. The subtle way, the indirect way that would have more lasting effects that merely dragging her into an alley and breaking her teeth.

"Colonel," The night watchman said as Snow stepped across the empty lobby of the office building with no address off H Street.

The head of the agency under no specific line item in no specific Congressional budget touched an index finger to his brow and stepped into the street as his Packard pulled around. He got in, a wind starting up foretelling a cold night.

"Straight home, sir?" his driver, Jarvis, asked.

"I think to the club. I could use a drink or two."

"Yes sir." Jarvis engaged the new fangled Electromatic clutch and they drove away. "Radio?"

"Sure, why not?"

On came some speech that President Roosevelt was giving. "Want me to change it, Colonel?" He negotiated a left onto Connecticut.

"No, let's see what amusing things our grand patrician has to say." He was in the process of lighting a cigar when he put his attention toward the front and went wide-eyed as Jarvis reared back, the Packard speeding forward and banging against a parked car.

"Jarvis," Snow yelled and at the same moment was reaching across his driver who'd fallen against the car's door, letting go of the wheel. Snow had a hold of it and was righting the car when he realized they'd skidded across the trolley tracks and there was an oncoming train whose conductor was applying the brakes. Sparks spewed from underneath the trolley's metal wheel and people shouted as the two vehicles collided, the Packard getting broad-sided. The trolley shoved the car along until it came to a halt in an intersection, causing a cross-town bus to swerve and smash into a market. Other cars and trucks were knotted this way and that in the intersection as people gathered around the Packard.

"Hey, buddy, you been tying one on?" Somebody shouted.

"There are two in here. They look hurt," someone else said.

"Let's get them out of there," yet another said as a cop ran over blowing his whistle.

As the crowd shifted and gawked, Madison Clay made himself part of the throng. A bleeding Colonel Snow was lifted out along with his unconscious driver, Jarvis, who Clay had drugged his thermos of. Clay was positioned behind a newsie craning his neck to see what was going on. Being taller, Clay reached his arm around the kid and quickly plunged a hypodermic into Snow's arm through the material of his coat and just as quick withdrew it.

"Clay," Snow rasped, his icy blues flamed with recognition.

Over the babble the cop ordered people to step back and give him some room.

"Clay, get him," Snow repeated, blood running down his face from his head wound.

"Don't worry mister; we got your chauffer safe alright,"

"No, no," Snow began weakly but couldn't finish.

By now a second officer had come to the scene and as they barked commands, Clay had stepped back with the others and soon was lost as he receded. The poison he'd injected Snow with was not an exotic, the doctors would be able to identify it easily. It was fast acting and Snow would be dead before he reached the hospital. The colonel might even be able to provide a description of his executioner to the ambulance crew before he expired. But so what? Clay reflected grimly, he wasn't planning on ever returning to America anyway.

CHAPTER TWENTY-ONE

"I hate this," Silas Mayhew complained yet again as he continued patching cracks in the airstrip. The hot tar he was swabbing sloshed and gurgled as he worked his mop under the unforgiving sun.

"And we hate hearing you bellyache about how much you hate doin' this," Henry Jackson cracked. A few others of the 24th Infantry unit also laughed.

Mayhew swallowed a comeback, sucked down more grimy fumes and continued swabbing. Though the brass said something about need and numbers, he knew he and some of the other Red Ballers had been shipped off to the Pacific for punishment after the gray boys got their clocks cleaned in the mess hall dust up. And even though he'd been drafted, was the last man in Harlem who would want to enlist, it nonetheless galled him that he wasn't seeing any action, despite the heavy casualty count.

And it galled him that the officers they got were southern peckerwoods who'd just as soon use black troops for barracuda bait as anything else. And it really galled him that the so-called great General MacArthur, had never once come to review the black soldiers under his overall command. He was too busy shooting newsreels of him puffing on his corncob pipe marching to shore out of an L.C.T. Because building and repairing an airstrip for the white flyboys to get part of the glory was not what he wanted to be telling his grandkids.

"Look here," Stallings said in his baritone, "I ain't all that eager to go and kill them nips anyways. Seems to me they ain't got nothin' against us."

"They bombed our country, niggah," Louis Lamar bellowed indignantly. He was a boxer and made occasional forays to other bases in the Solomon Islands for exhibition bouts. "How come you so goddamn thrilled about them yella runts?"

"Aw," Jackson began, "he's just that way 'cause he had him some slanted pussy once." That brought on another chorus of laughter, including Stallings who made a wry face.

"But I know what you mean, Stall." Jackson continued. "Here me and you enlist, begging the Army to send us into the jaws of Nipponese death, and what do they do? Got us working harder than Georgia mules in this hellish heat and humidity, unloading ships, hustling freight, digging latrines and this shit," he swung a hand backward, taking in the air strip the men were working on, "all day so's they can go and send Tojo packin' out of Guadalcanal, Mindanao, all over. They get the headlines and we, as usual, get the real shit-stained short end."

"To top it off," Mayhew contributed, resting his mop against his tar bucket. "The officers go around saying we're lazy and scared, but since we ain't seen no combat, what gives them the right to even suggest that?"

"It's what they believe, 'cause they pappys told 'em. And it's probably what they seen from them backward cracker towns they come from where some beat down old Negro got to tip his hat and get off the sidewalk and generally bow and scrape." Stallings, up the strip from the other three, resumed using his pickaxe to cleave loose chunks from the pothole on one side of the runway at the periphery of the jungle. Carved into his muscular bicep were twin "Vs" slightly offset one to the another. Several men in the 24th as well as other all-black regiments were very serious about the Double V Campaign. He'd already done brig time for slugging a black MP when in basics at Fort Huachuca.

Jackson and Lamar were mixing cement in a wheelbarrow. The strip was used constantly and the frustrated men of the 24th rotated the maintenance duties.

"Some of 'em know different," Jackson observed. "But really, what the fuck has that president of ours done? And he and his missus supposed to be the Negroes friend. Randolph and Walter White and Mrs. Bethune have tea and cookies with them up there at the White House, right? So how come that ain't made no difference?" He used the blade end of the shovel to break up some lumps in his mixture.

Jackson allowed, "Maybe Eleanor is doing us a favor and don't want us to get hurt."

"Sure, that's it," Mayhew added, then tapped his bare chest with a finger. "Let me tell you something. Those Black Rattlers from WWI used to come to the place where I tended bar. You should hear some of what they went through. And my Grandma on my mother's side remembers stories about her uncle when she was little had been with this same damn infantry division as ours in the Civil War and afterward."

"What're you sayin', Mayhew?" Jackson asked.

"You think the Army put us together by accident?" Mayhew answered rhetorically. "This unit, and the 28th and the 10 Calvary, fought with honors against the rebs and in the Indian Wars that followed."

"No shit?" A surprised Jackson uttered.

"No shit. Buffalo Soldiers the Indians called us because of our color and kinky hair." Mayhew wiped his forehead with his sweaty forearm. Overhead, two P-51 Mustangs slung by.

"At least the Tuskegee boys are in it," Jackson commented, watching the trailing exhaust in the sky.

Stallings said, "Yeah, but I read in the Crisis those fellas ain't seen no dog fighting since they sailed out for North Africa in April. Here they are in part of the motherland, and they're not even allowed to fight for the darker race's freedom."

"You better be careful, son, you sounding like one of them Negro intellectual soapbox agitators," Lamar remarked. "You know the Army don't cotton to that kind'a talk, soldier. You better not let one of these pale faces find you reading that NAACP magazine or the Courier for that matter. I heard they threw some boots in the brig over on Morotai for reading what they call subversive material."

"I got rights," Stallings exclaimed.

"Not in this war, and not afterward either," Jackson intoned solemnly.

"That's what I'm talking about," the deep voiced man answered.

"Cool it," Mayhew warned as Captain Markeson approached.

"You soldiers seem to be jawin' more than repairing my air strip."

"We on it, Cap'n," Jackson mixed steadily.

Markeson stared into the mid distance as he spoke. "I need to go fetch something in the jungle." He dug in his shirt pocket, and subsequently bit off a piece of chewing tobacco.

The four exchanged looks, but no one spoke.

"A goddamn set of maps some fool Seabee managed to loose."

Still the men said nothing.

"This engineer has already been sent on to another assignment." He shook his head and spat. "He comes back to base with the patrol and don't bother to take a count till the next goddamn day, can you beat that?" Markeson spat again. "And he don't say nothin' about it 'cause he don't want to look like the sap he is. The sap." He chewed and continued staring, his hands balled and thrust against his sides.

Stallings broke the spell. "These maps important, Captain?" Markeson slowly turned his head to glare at the man who dared to disrupt his musings. The shovels stopped scrapping, the mop stopped mopping, and the pickaxe hung at the questioner's side. Eventually the officer declared, "All you have to know is the generals want the egghead's drawings back, okay?"

"Yes, sir." Stallings gave a half-salute.

"So you and me and one of you others are going out with a driver to get those maps back, okay?"

"Very good, sir." Stallings stood straight.

"Now who else is going?" Markeson kept his gaze on Stallings.

"I'll go," Mayhew said.

"Then you two be ready at oh-fourteen-thirty with light packs and your carbines. Am I clear?"

In unison the four answered, "Yes, sir."

They waited until the captain was out of sight then gave each other some skin.

"Let's not get too excited, it's just a damn errand."

Mayhew said, "But those maps are important, and the Army's entrusting that duty to us."

"Two-thirds of the goddamn white regiment is monkey food or laid up in the hospital." Lamar pushed a thumb in the direction of a row of tents with red crosses on them. "It's probably because they don't think it's important that they're willing to send two spooks to go fetch them maps."

"It's better than doing this all day." Mayhew dipped his mop in the tar bucket and went back to work. The next three hours dragged more than usual for him but for once since being in the service, he had something to look forward too. Ten minutes before the appointed time, the light patrol were on the road. It was a rough, rutted path hacked and burned into part of the jungle.

The American and indigenous left-leaning guerrillas, the Hukbabalhup, the Huks, had pounded back much of the primary Japanese forces on the island. It was estimated that by year's end, this largest landmass among the Solomons would be in allied hands. But that didn't mean the soldiers of the Rising Sun subscribed to that timetable and had simply gone off to drink sake.

"This going to take long, sir?" The driver was maybe all of twenty and still had peach fuzz on his cheeks.

"You got a date with Betty Grable?" Markeson looked from left to right as they went along.

"No, sir, it's not that, exactly." Quickly he looked back at Mayhew and Stallings. "It's just that I've don't trust them darkies with guns, sir," he whispered.

Gary Phillips

"And why's that?" Markeson asked in a too loud voice.

The private swallowed hard, catching a glimpse of the two impassive Negro faces in his rearview mirror. "I did basic at Camp Benning, Captain," he said as they bounced over ruts. "And there was a shooting match went down betwixt these coloreds and whites. Yes, sir."

"We ain't in Georgia, private."

"I know, captain, but you can't trust these black devils." He was no longer making an effort to be quiet.

"I don't necessarily disagree with you, private. But the fact remains, we're desperately short handed. And that crippled do-gooder FDR promised during his re-election campaign to activate the Negro, and is throwing a bone out for getting their vote." He jerked a head at the two men behind him. Neither acknowledged the gesture. "So, we got to grin and bear it. I've got my orders and you've got yours."

"That don't mean I won't be keeping on my toes."

"Me too." And the front end of the jeep wrenched savagely but the private got it back on track.

"Not much road left," Stallings observed dryly.

Mayhew stifled a smile and gripped his rifle tighter. Goddamn crackers.

The quartet's jeep limped along at five miles and hour over the diminishing path and came to the end less than a minute later. The captain consulted a map and a compass. "All right, we've got to hot foot it in about a mile and half in a northwesterly direction." He pointed as he got out of the jeep. The others followed.

Mayhew purposely got close to the nervous driver. "How about us buddying up, pal?"

The private blanched, looking at Markeson to save him. The officer had a sour set to his mouth. "Stallings, take the point."

"You the one that knows where we headin', cap'n." But he was already moving into position. He'd slung his rifle on his shoulder and used his machete to chop at a bunching of thick foliage. The captain fell in, then Mayhew and then the private. The procession hit patches that were clear and other times stretches choked with growth. There were tall shrub-like plants with yellow-orange florets and orchids of various types sprouting up from the ground and blanketing hillsides.

"You could open a hell of a flower store around here," Stallings quipped as he slung his blade. A knot of birds with plumed tails sprung into the air, screeching. "We must be getting close," he hoped aloud.

"Hold up a second," Markeson ordered. The four came to a halt, keeping at least an arm's length between them, each one slightly

203

crouched. Their heads moved around as if on ball bearings, every sound soaking into their skin as they strained their eyes to scan the landscape. A Japanese soldier's dark tan uniform blended only too well with the surroundings.

"Okay, I see the tubes on the other side of that coconut grove. Stallings, get it, we'll cover you." Markeson took his binoculars away, staring straight ahead. He wouldn't look directly at the soldier.

"Sure," Stallings answered.

"I got you, man," Mayhew said, stepping up. "I'll shadow him Cap'n."

"No, you stay put like I ordered."

The two friends grinned glumly at each other and Stallings started off. His boots crunching across the brambles sharp in each man's ears. White butterflies dashed with gold fluttered around the soldier's heads.

Despite what his C.O. had told him, Mayhew inched forward, turning in half-circles, back-and-forth as he did so. The private and the captain were also antsy. Sweat stood on all their strained faces.

Stallings had his rifle in one hand, the stock braced against his leg, his finger on the trigger. He was standing near the two cardboard tubes lying partially in the brush. He squatted to take the maps in his free hand and momentarily looked down to make sure he did so. He exhaled, a quick gleam of something catching his attention. Mayhew reached out and pushed aside the greenery and glared at the elliptical shape. It looked just like the picture he's seen of one in a Stars and Stripes. Calmly, he picked up the tubes and stood. He forced himself to walk back out of the clearing the way he'd come in.

"We might have company," Stallings said, standing next to Mayhew.

"You sure?"

"There's a Japanese canteen with a shrapnel hole in it near where the maps were."

"That don't mean they're still around."

"And it don't mean they went on a hike either."

"What are you two goin' on about?" Markeson demanded. Behind him, the private turned and took a step. The first round of the .25 cracked and Markeson went prone as the rest dove into the colorful Bougainville flora. No one spoke, waiting for the next bullet. There was only the excited cacophony of the birds.

"Where is that bastard?" Mayhew mumbled.

"Might be more than one," Stallings added.

"Shut up, shut up," the driver clamored. "We've got to get out of here."

204

"We will," Stallings responded evenly. He detected no movement from Markeson.

Listen, I'm in charge, the driver said. "I've been in the field."

"You're still just another buck private." Mayhew crawled forward; he couldn't stand to be still in this kind of situation. The spindly spider-like leaves of exploding red orchids brushed his cheek. His breath was cold on his lips. The scared soldier deepened his brow, a sound drifted to him. "They ain't far," he warned.

"But where?" Stallings came up quick and fired off two in rapid succession then ducked down again.

"Hey," the driver barked. "No shooting until I say so."

No one fired back and none of the Americans moved. "We gotta do something" Mayhew advised. "We gotta draw them out."

"No, this ain't no time for nigger shit, Mayhew. This is time for thinking," the driver said.

"Then what's your plan, man?" Stallings asked.

"I'm working on that."

"That right?" Stallings quipped.

"You can be court-martialed for disobeying, soldier."

Stallings cracked, "Don't you worry, it's just some nigger shit." The two black men chuckled.

It got quiet again. Mayhew crawled forward several feet and this time was sure there was other movement. He couldn't hear voices or footsteps but sensed it. "They're near," he said, gritting his teeth.

Mayhew got up on a knee, chancing a look around. His foot squished a ripe guava. He breathed shallowly, the jungle noises receding to him as he tried to slow everything down so as not to miss anything. To his right, at two o'clock there was a disturbance, the colorful florets swaying slightly. Maybe it was a monkey or a sloth, but so be it. He let loose with a burst of blasts and was answered in return.

"Open up," the driver yelled,

The men did so, yelling and shooting. But there was no return fire.

"Maybe we got them," the driver hoped.

"Maybe." Mayhew glared at those florets but he knew if one or more of the Emperor's boys was still kicking, they'd be lying in wait.

"What do you think?" Stallings said.

"Man, I don't know. But we've got to check. Otherwise we'll get picked off like the captain."

"What about it, head private?" Stallings called out. There was no response.

"Where'd that son of a bitch go?" Mayhew worried. "I'm guessing it's only one man. If it was more they would have opened up on us."

"So what do we do while he makes like Tarzan? And I'm still not convinced it's only one. They could come out of there at any moment."

"You worry too much, Stall."

"My problem is I don't worry enough," he countered. He adjusted his helmet, sweat cascading from his forehead. "I say we circle each way and see if we flush him or them out of the bush."

"That may not be what the captain wanted us to do," the driver said, coming back into view. "We did our job and got the maps back." He paused, then, "I checked Markeson. He's gone."

"Yeah, well, he won't be giving any more orders," Mayhew said. "And if we walk away, our backs might be getting lined up in the enemy's crosshairs. We have to take care of this."

"We do what I say we do," the driver said.

Mayhew regarded him while weighing his words. "Here's what's going to happen, me and Stall go in this way and you go the other way 'round. That way we're coming at him from two sides."

"Now you talkin', baby," Stallings seconded.

The driver didn't appreciate a Negro coming up with the plan so he had to do something. He had to show that he was in control. "Stallings is on me, you go through the front door."

"Fine." Mayhew started off.

The driver said, "We better have some kind of password in case we can't see each other and spot some bushes moving."

"Like what?" Stallings asked.

"Satchmo," Mayhew said.

"Solid." Stallings said as he and the driver went low and began circling around.

Mayhew belly crawled through the thick ground covering. Flies and ants and fear crawling all over him. He kept sharp, searching and listening.

Mayhew halted, he was sure there'd been a disturbance not far from him, to his left, closer to the inner diameter of the grove. Just like if it was a Japanese who'd heard him and was now trying to bushwhack him from that angle.

Keeping his eyes on the area to his left, Mayhew blindly felt along the ground. He patted something oblong and with a slick skin, a mango. He lifted it and bowled it underhanded through the interior of the grove. He then looked for something else to throw in a similar fashion. He found part of a coconut and repeated the action, making sure to place it just ahead of where he'd pitched the mango.

There was the light crunch on the dry grass and Mayhew banked on his idea working. If the man or men gunning for them concluded he was moving ahead of where they were, he'd have to scout forward to check. He did his best to sink down and make himself invisible in his surroundings. Come on, you slippery bastard, come on, he willed. Birds cawed and the heat roasted Mayhew. Suddenly as if the man had materialized from another dimension there was a leg discernable to him not five yards ahead. There was only one leg, therefore one man he hoped and prayed. The rest of the body was lost in the still wall of greens and browns.

Mayhew fired from his prone position and charged. The Japanese soldier returned fire from his 25-caliber weapon, remaining crouched in the grass. As all sound flooded from him as Mayhew locked his sights on the enemy soldier. A bullet sizzled past Mayhew's arm taking flesh with it and still he poured it on, fanning his carbine back and forth like a scythe.

He stumbled and collided with the enemy who'd risen up, swinging the butt of his rifle like Josh Gibson going for a homer. Mayhew's M-1 came loose from his hands as he sought his balance and part of the other rifle's stock caught him alongside his jaw. His opponent had run out of ammo, but not fight.

Down on a knee Mayhew lashed out and buried a fist in the lower abdomen of the enemy as he tried to club him with the rifle. The Japanese soldier stumbled back and Mayhew leaped. Too late he realized the other man had loosened his bayonet from a scabbard and was jabbing it at Mayhew's heart.

Mayhew screamed as the blade pierced his upper chest into the muscle. He grabbed the other man's wrist and together the two tumbled to the earth. The long knife was pulled free and it flashed against the sun. Mayhew jerked his head aside and the blade sunk into the dirt, nicking his ear. The Japanese put two hands on the hilt of his bayonet to pull it out and Mayhew took his cue. He got a hand around that neck and squeezed like when he was a teenager on his grandma's farm and had to pull the head off a chicken for Sunday supper or get a whupping if he didn't.

The other man gurgled and drove fists at Mayhew's face but he could barely feel the blows and now had the enemy soldier in an awkward position, Mayhew's weight bending him back.

Face to face, each breathing in the other's air the men struggled. The Japanese used the edge of his hand to strike at Mayhew's rib cage and for a moment, black stars went off behind his eyeballs. But he wasn't going to give up, he wasn't going to die in this lousy jungle for some lousy war he wanted no part of.

"Mayhew," Stallings called out, but his friend couldn't answer.

Another chop and this time Mayhew knew a bone in his side was busted, but still he continued, both hands clamped onto that neck. The other man was gagging, his teeth rattling in his mouth. But the wounded man wasn't done and with a fury that surprised Mayhew, he put a punch into his stomach, upsetting his grip. Mayhew fell back and the man fell on him.

They wrestled but the other man was weakened, trying to suck in air, get his throat open and deal with his enemy. They thrashed about and rolled near the bayonet stuck in the ground. Each noticed it but Mayhew's panic made him faster and he grabbed it and wrenched it loose. A moment of regret flicked in the other man's eyes as he sought to get his hands around the GI's neck. And the light went out of those eyes as Mayhew stuck the bayonet in his back. He scrambled to his feet as the Japanese soldier rose, trying to reach around to free the blade but pirouetting slowly. He went to both knees, gasping, his hands on his thighs.

"Stachmo," Mayhew yelled several times, wincing and pressing a hand to his side. He felt hollow and used up. Behind him the Japanese soldier was immobile but alive, breathing shallowly.

Stallings and the driver appeared. "Should I?" Stallings raised his gun to squeeze off a shot at the dying man.

"No, forget that," Mayhew said.

"But," the driver began.

"Let it go." Mayhew and the other man stared at one another then broke contact.

The Japanese soldier, he was a corporeal, watched the GIs leave and he put his head down, his chin on his chest. The American soldiers transported the captain's body on a makeshift litter. Later Mayhew was congratulated by the other colored enlisted men.

"Way to go, brother."

"That's showing those gray boys we in this to win just like they are."

"You might get a medal, man. Get it pinned on by MacArthur himself."

That night, Mayhew tried mightily to sleep but it wouldn't overtake him. Indeed sleep, real sleep, wouldn't overtake him for many more nights.

CHAPTER TWENTY-TWO

Alma Yates finished retyping pages of the edits on the latest installment of her series. This piece contained interviews with colored sailors who talked candidly about the lack of opportunity for Negroes in the Navy as they were mostly relegated to mess duty or if they were lucky, they might be oilers in the engine room. Tomorrow morning she'd phone in to rewrite to file her story. She stretched and worked a cramp out of her neck when there was a knock at her hotel room door.

"Telegram," the voice said on the other side of the door.

"Coming," the reporter said and got up from the desk and crossed the room. "Yes," she said, opening the door to the pleasant-faced bellhop who handed her the Western Union envelope.

"Here you go, ma'am," he said, handing the telegram over.

"Thank you." Yates tipped him a quarter

"Thank you," he responded and departed.

Yates stood and read the telegram. She crinkled her brow and re-read the message from her editor at the Pittsburgh Courier. There were reports out of North Africa and into the Middle East that a black man thought to be American, and known only by his nom de guerre, was leading a kind of guerrilla band of Senegalese, Arabs, Algerians and some French whites going after enemy underground agents still performing sabotage and the like post the Axis surrender in that theater of operations. Former Afrika Korps Field Marshal Rommel was quoted as saying this "Captain Chicago was an opponent of the highest caliber."

Her editor finished the two-page telegram telling her he knew she was still trying to ascertain the particulars of the microwave experiment, but this too could be a very interesting story. If it were true. He gave her a time when he'd call her to talk more about this as he already had ideas to raise the money to send her overseas.

Yates placed the telegram next to her typewriter and sat and stared out the window, wondering what sort of boots she'd have to buy for travel in Africa.

Corporeal Silas Mayhew lit a Lucky Strike and slowly took a drag. He blew smoke and looked down at the plain wooden cross topped with the helmet belonging to Horace Lee Scott. The grave the cross cast a shadow across was marked Gil Giabretto. As there was no next of kin listed with HQ, the decision was made to bury the singing private here in the small graveyard of Trois- Points near the bombed out church. Mayhew and the other Red Ballers were pulling out at 0300 hours, but he wanted to stop by before leaving. When the gray boys had planted him they hadn't told any of the colored troops since they still believed he was one of them.

Mayhew smiled thinly. Weren't they all in this together for the duration, he ironically reflected. "Yeah," he said to himself, "victory at home and abroad." He finished his cigarette and tossed it away. "Rest easy, Gate." He saluted the dead man and walked off, hands in pockets, whistling, the air still, the sun bright and high in the sky. He shipped out for the Pacific later that day.

- END -

Gary Phillips grew up in South Central Los Angeles. Because his Uncle Norman, his father's brother, was among the black ex-pats who settled in Paris after World War II, young Phillips spent more than one summer overseas with his relatives exploring French arrondissements.

On this side of the pond, Phillips came of age hearing from his dad Dikes and his friends, tales of the days of Central Avenue, the Stem, when segregation was in full effect in L.A. and the Avenue was the center of black life – folks transported from Texas and the Deep South. Back when the thoroughfare and beyond was bustling with businesses, hotels, and jazz joints like the Club Alabam and Jack's Basket.

These stories and experiences have fueled Phillips' writing in and out of the crime and mystery genre. He's edited anthologies, written novels, short stories, comic books and film scripts. Please visit his website at: www.gdphillips.com/.

Photo Credit: Ibarionex R. Perello

Freedom's Fight